CONTENTS

Rogue Sushi   1

Terms of Service   8

The Owl and the Beard   18

The Chase   26

Arrival   39

Performance Review   48

Results   64

The New Normal?   72

Transmission   83

Where do we go from here?   95

We're going where?   107

Lethal Catering…maybe?   117

She's Back!   127

Voice of a Friend   138

Waffle Time   150

Glitching the Day Away   157

Play that Again   163

Arrival   170

Satisfying Crunch   191

Coffee First   200

The Plan Goes Boing!   208

Shields   221

Boris Squared   228

Purple Vacuum   237

Mining Outpost?   242

Gargantuan Dinner Bell   249

Don't Get Eaten!   261

Chrome Karma   272

Favorite Kind of Boring   290

Cover Design By Sentinel Graphics
Interior Formatting By Sentinel Graphics
Character Art By Lluis Abadias
Novel Editing By Kit Gulick

DEDICATION

I know these things are usually flowery and sincere. I'm gonna do wacky and sincere instead.

I raise my coffee to the following beautiful chaotic creatives that helped me make this damn thing:

Melissa Simmons the first editor I hired whose availability, enthusiasm, and encouragement helped keep the spongy cpu that is my brain away from thoughts like "Just delete this!" or "Take it down and write something else."

Lluis Abadias who took my lined paper scribbles and made them into incredible art that I still love and can't believe actually exists.

Kit Gulick my novelization editor whose patience, communication, and enthusiasm for the story also kept me believing I can actually make this into a novel people will like.

Rachel Wisekal, the humanoid I've made a life with and who heard the original idea at 2 am in the morning at a diner, and said "You should totally write that!" Without you I wouldn't be where I am now. Me and all my words in all my stories say "I love you with all that I am."

Alright enough of that and onto the Sci-Fi adventure!

FOREWORD/
AUTHOR NOTES

Hello future reader!

Some quick words from the author:

Is this story somewhere else on the internet? Yes. It's on Kindle Vella as a serial, stories told in episodes.

Which one is official? BOTH!

What's the difference between the Novel & Serial? The Novel includes extra scenes, longer chapters, and has a different pacing. The easiest way to think of it is that Kindle Vella is the first edition, and the novel is the second edition.

Why did I do it this way? Because Kindle Vella helped me put words on the page and paid for all the wonderful talent that put this world together.

Are your other stories on Kindle Vella? Some of them, yes, find links and descriptions below:

Divine Counseling: Bob is a marriage counselor to the Gods. His current patients are Zeus and Hera, whose marital dysfunctions threaten the existence of Olympus. The fallout means cataclysms killing countless mortals. He and Emily, with her PhD in the occult, work together to provide the best therapy they can to ensure the safety of the world.

ROGUE SUSHI

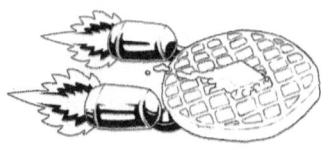

Jolene enjoyed boring days at the diner. She could sit with a delicious cup of coffee. Watch the stars go by. Listen to the gentle hum of the engines. One of those days would be nice someday. Today, she was too busy sweeping her Voltstriker pistol over every vent. The regular lights never blinked, so the intruder hadn't found the main grid yet.

JOLENE (CHAT MESSAGE)
"Boris, you got eyes on it?"

She messaged him through her Bio-tech.

"Foul beast! You killed my chef knife! Prepare to die!" Boris' shout echoed off the walls of the diner.

One wet chopping sound later, the diner walls shook with the psychic roar of the galaxy's worst pest. The flurry of emotions that hit Jolene's empathic senses came as words and sensations.

PAIN!

Burning heat rushed across her skin.

KILL!

Raging adrenaline raised the hairs on her arms. She gritted her teeth and ran like hell towards the sounds. The diner's halls narrowed the deeper you went. Jolene realized she'd forgotten to check the vents for tentacles, skidding to a stop just before she ran into a wall.

"Thermal!" She mentally shouted, and her vision filled with zones of white heat and pale blue.

The Cthullian's mass slithered through the air vents, converging on the kitchen!

"Thermals off." She blinked her vision back into the normal spectrum and took a moment for a deep breath. Using only muscle memory, she set the pistol for max charge. Hopefully, she could put it down without frying anything too expensive.

The kitchen felt like a spilled emotional soup. The Cthullian's rage and bloodlust spilling over misshapen pots. Red hot thermal coils spilled over the stove like unwound Slinkies. Bits of tentacle stuck to them wriggling as they sizzled.

The creature's pain and rage scraped against Jolene's mind like sandpaper. She focused on a single thought on repeat until the words and sensations of the battle faded to the background.

"Float. Don't sink. Float. Don't sink."

In the middle of everything stood their chefbot, Boris. He was five feet of purple ichor-stained steel. A pair of thick legs supported a potbelly emblazoned with his old platoon sign. The red LED backlit bear roared across his chest, beneath a shiny layer of purple Cthullian blood. Every single arm was armed.

Jolene watched two superheated cleavers slice and

cauterize the beast's probing suckers. One heavy duty crème brûlée torch spit lines of fire at the center mass while his last two arms lunged with mini chainsaws, cutting deep furrows into the monster.

The kitchen floor was worse, purple Cthullian blood pooled alongside a metaphorical ton of sliced and diced Cthullian. The single-eyed mass of undulating tentacles spidered back and forth on the ceiling. The pop of its sticky suckers filled the kitchen as it looked for its chance to strike.

Boris' torso swiveled, gears whirring, his four eyed chromed dome following.

Jolene needed a clear shot. Stepping without splashing. Breathing slow and shallow. She moved closer, low and slow.

Tentacles surged toward Boris from every angle. The chefbot's arsenal went to work. Each blade and saw hacked furiously, all while he pushed the crème brûlée torch towards the Cthullian's eye.

Wincing through the empathic feedback Jolene crept from counter to counter until she had a front-row seat to the fight. Every time Boris cut the Cthullian it pulled more mass from the vents. Creeping around the corner, she watched in open-mouthed horror as the black bleeding coils healed themselves! Strafing allowed it to reshuffle its mass and renew its attack. Boris needed a chance to end this. Jolene took one breath before she did the idiotic good intentioned thing.

"Crazy droid, try to leave enough for eldritch sushi!"

Jolene shouted. Both the bot and pest turned to her. She sighted down the Voltsriker's barrel, exhaled and squeezed. The gel round crackled through the air and hit the beast right in the pupil. The smell of cooking eyeball nauseated her, but the shot gave Boris the opening he needed.

"For the Motherboard!" Boris yelled and descended onto the Cthullian with every tool.

Jolene ran from the precision butchery, chased by the psychic shrieking. Some purple arcs flew past her, others did not. Thick wetness hit her from neck to butt. All her fear-adrenaline and Empathic senses collided in her brain in an explosion of pain she fell to her knees, sending waves through the congealing purple blood when Boris shouted.

"Main brain found!" His artificial voice box strained from his volume and enthusiasm.

JOLENE (CHAT MESSAGE)
"Kill it!"

Jolene mentally shouted through her bio-tech to their private chat.

Boris obliged by raising both super-heated cleavers and slicing like a sushi chef. Thin and precise. The moist sounds were like something from an ancient earth horror flick.

Flipping her vision back to thermal Jolene watched a final tremor run through every tentacle in their air vents.

"Death confirmed." She said, mentally switching her vision back to normal. Then she groaned as sticky, slimy blood trickled down her leg. "Good shooting." Boris said, the chefbot's head looked at her while his arms worked on processing the Cthullian. He pulled tentacles through the vents and cut them into lengths before coiling them like ropes.

"Thank you, wouldn't have been necessary if corporate didn't skimp on the damn shipping." Jolene scraped a Cthullian sucker off her boot. She tensed as she ran her fingers through her hair expecting and dreading something wet, thick or slimy textures. Bringing her hand back around there was nothing but a few of her bright red hairs. Her shoulders slumped as the tension finally eased.

"You say that every time something like this happens." A high-pitched voice squeaked.

Jolene rolled her eyes, looking around. On Boris' spice shelf was a two-inch dark blue humanoid leaning on some freeze-dried garlic.

"Murph, ever think that If I say the same thing on repeat, that it might mean it's happening too much?" Jolene growled.

A multitude of duplicates glanced at her from behind every spice. The little humanoids' lighter blue orb eyes flashed, then smiled to show shiny white needle teeth. Jolene exhaled, again narrowing her thoughts with repetition.

"Float. Don't Sink. Float. Don't Sink."

Murph's emotions always fell on her empathic senses like a thousand raindrops. The same words and sensations clashing in and over each other. Jolene held onto the simple mantra.

"At least we all get to file hazard pay," the multitude

of Murphs answered.

"Float. Don't Sink. Float. Don't Sink."

Jolene powered down the Voltstriker and holstered it. "Boris and I were the ones facing hazards." She found an unstained kitchen towel and did her best to remove the blood.

"Float. Don't Sink. Float. Don't Sink."

"You guys are the action heroes. I'm Maintenance. Says so in my contract." Murph teased, their multitude of humanoids cartwheeling down to the counter. They splatted and flowed together, solidifying like jello in a fridge, into one whole humanoid. Their feet shaped into thick rubber boots before sliding down.

Jolene stood inches above Murph's five-foot nothing until the top of their head turned into a black fedora with a red band adding a few extra inches. Their thoughts and emotions also went from many voices to just one. She rubbed at the tension in her temples. At the rate this day was going, she'd need to lie down from a migraine.

"Well, while Boris finishes prep, and I take a sonic shower, you can get our guests seated." Jolene flashed her customer service smile, sweet as sugar with just a hint of cyanide.

Murph shrugged and reshaped themselves. Colors and curves filled out into a four foot nine pony-tailed blonde with familiar flashing blue eyes, apron and uniform included. Corporate loved employing Kyanese. No matter the species of customer, the Kyanese could shift to match and make the customer feel at ease.

Galaxy Waffles

"Don't leave me all alone out there." Murph teased.

Jolene shook her head. "Wouldn't dream of letting you have all the tips from the convention."

Murph blew a kiss and skipped towards the dining room.

"Cameras tell me we only have ten waiting out there. Take a regular shower." Boris said.

"But the water budget-" A notice that popped up in the lower right corner of her vision stopped her mid-sentence. The numbers showed enough for a blissful fifteen-minute shower.

"I have been saving." Boris said, the eyes on the right side of his face blinking on and off.

Jolene blew a kiss of her own at the chefbot and one of his arms caught it.

"I could kiss your processor." Jolene said.

"Go before Murph gets overwhelmed." Boris said. While half his limbs wiped debris from the counters, the other half set up multiple plates of eldritch sushi.

"Welcome to Galaxy Waffles, home to the galaxy's best breakfast!" Murph greeted in a thick accent that echoed down the hall. They'd picked it up from one of their favorite gangster flicks.

Jolene half sprinted towards her quarters. "More like the Galaxy's most dangerous breakfast," she grumbled.

TERMS OF SERVICE

"Crew 3371's elimination of the Cthullian was done with 80% efficiency." O.D. said, the AI's voice echoed off the shower walls. O.D. or Observation Drone was Galaxy Waffles' watchdog, and the pilot of the ship.

"Total loss of Cthullian Ingredients falls within expected parameters." O.D. continued; his voice brought Jolene to the edge of a migraine.

"Comms off." Jolene ordered, her eyes closed, and she basked in the heat and steam.

"Command Override Complete. Continuing assessment. Crew 3371's response time graded at-"

"O.D., I get one company approved water shower a month. This is a once in a blue moon second shower. If you interrupt it again, I'll pour syrup on your motherboard!" Jolene shouted.

For a moment, falling water was the only sound.

"Threat to damage company property logged and reported to Galaxy Waffles Corporate. Three months have been added to your suspension from the Starblood Citizenship Lottery." O.D. said and left with an electric pop.

Galaxy Waffles

Jolene stuck an arm out of the stall and flipped off the A.I. *"Asshole!"* Jolene thought to herself, she'd been banned from the lottery for five solar years, a few more months was nothing. She raised the water temp again feeling heat instead of letting her thoughts spiral out of control. Sitting on the tiny bench, she raised her face to the shower head. For a few glorious minutes, all she heard was the drumbeat of water droplets and felt liquid heat flowing across her eyes and cheeks. The combined isolation and sensation worked down her body, her empathic senses, silent and forgotten. As always, it ended far too quickly. The loss of water pressure was gradual. Jolene waited until it trickled before stepping into her steam-filled bathroom.

A blue notice popped up in the corner of her vision.

(CHAT MESSAGE)

"GET OUT HERE! WE'VE GOT HOUR LONG WAIT TIMES!!!!"

Jolene mentally swatted away the giant letters before she thought the command: *"Security cams."*

Her vision filled with a top-down view of the dining room, and she counted the Murphs. There were four of them, all of them Pricklebeards; stout four armed three eyed humanoids with ample beards that could crush tungsten in between two fingers. Murph defaulted to the species during a rush because no one with a working brain cell pissed off a Pricklebeard. Unfortunately, every species had its idiots and today's was a human who stuck his boot out as Murph was passing. They shaped their body around the ankle without breaking stride and kicked the man's ankle with the back of their heel.

"Knew it! Shifter scum!" The human shouted above the din of the diner.

The room fell silent and went still.

Jolene terminated the view, ordered an instant dry and dressed. One sonic shower blast and nano fiber beamed uniform later, she ran for the dining room. Grateful that Corporate allowed slacks, even if they had a waffle pattern colored like a nebula on them, she rounded the last corner a neon holographic waffle name badge flashed in on her syrup brown top.

She took one step on the black and white diamond patterned linoleum floor and looked for the mess she'd have to clean up. Murph had shifted from Pricklebeard to a perfect copy of the customer, putting on a show for the diner as he argued with himself. At least Murph hadn't spaced him. Jolene exhaled in relief.

"Wipe my face... off your face!" the idiot human said, and all four Murphs laughed.

"Murph, no!" Jolene shouted, but Murph had already done a sweeping wipe with one hand following its momentum turning towards Jolene. Their palm had two flashing blue eyes and a mouth full of needle teeth.

"The customer is always right, so I gave him what he wanted." Murph's facepalm taunted.

Said customer vomited onto his plate. It spilled over and the rest of the table had one hand on their mouths while scrambling out of the booth. "Guess who's cleaning that up?" Jolene said poking Murph answering her own question. One of the Pricklebeard Murphs rushed over with mops and towels.

The Murph who'd been arguing with the customer turned, and Jolene's stomach rolled at the horror show. Murph's shifting went way beyond skin deep. Looking at them now was an organic, squirming anatomy lesson of brains and veins. The onslaught of revulsion from the idiot human and all the appreciative diners mixed in her empath senses like sour milk and sweet candy. Jolene closed her eyes against it.

"Put your face back on and get back to waiting tables," she ordered and didn't open her eyes until she heard the familiar gelatinous squish. Murph was back to mimicking a red bearded Pricklebeard and gave Jolene a three eyed wink. She shook her head and wished she could sit and watch the swirling patterns of the crimson quasar instead of dealing with Murph's shenanigans.

"Work first, decompress later," Jolene thought.

A snap of her fingers put a neon pink hologram pad in her palm and she approached her first table.

"Welcome to Galaxy Waffles, home of the Galaxy's best breakfast. May I take your order?" Jolene asked.

Two humans and two aliens answered at the same time. "Eldritch Sushi!"

As they said the words, the L.E.D. edge of their tables lit up in teals and purples. For a moment they froze, then looked at Jolene.

"Looks like you're our first order of the night!" Jolene said with a smile.

The surface of their table lit up with teal and purple waivers.

"Because of its psychedelic properties please read-" Jolene barely finished before all four had scribbled a signature with fingers, claws, and suckers. "We have a special treat. Our chefbot is an A.I. veteran of the Cthullian conflicts, and he'll be serving your sushi along with yarns of his experiences." Jolene said, and more than one table clapped.

BORIS (CHAT MESSAGE)

"Am I getting paid extra for this?"

JOLENE (CHAT MESSAGE)

"You know you are, why do you ask?"

BORIS (CHAT MESSAGE)

"What? Humans have the patent and copyright on complaining?"

Boris followed up with a raised eyebrow emoji. He entered the dining room with a stiffness you only saw in bad 2D vids. His platoon's bear insignia and his four eyes glowed.

"Threat assessment in progress," Boris said in a deep robotic baritone for the dramatic cherry on top. Four arms balanced four plates of sushi sliding them to each customer. His last two slowly snaked left and right emitting green scanning beams over the diners. Some flinched while others passed their hands through the beam. Jolene stifled a laugh, knowing it was Boris' thermometer tool.

"Delivery of Eldritch sushi complete." He gave a three-armed salute.

Galaxy Waffles

"Enjoy the experience," Jolene said sweetly and moved on to another table.

"Accessing combat logs," Boris said, and every table watched and waited.

Horror fans and conventioners always loved Murph and Boris when they put on a show. Crimson Quasarcon was no different. The fascination and thrills from Boris' mission taking on a Cthullian colony hit Jolene's empathic senses like a flood of caffeine. Which worked for her because every table ordered the sushi and signed just as quickly as the first. Murph's Pricklebeards now had all four hands full every time they left the kitchen.

Thanks to some bio-engineering the sushi's psychedelic effect didn't kick in until the customers got aboard their ships. So, people ate and raced out, kicking turnover into high gear. Galaxy Waffles Corporate also made the waiver into a notification for the ship that its crew would be intoxicated. Every ship in the Milky Way had safety protocols that would kick in until the effects wore off. So everyone got their nightmare trip on and no one got hurt.

One Murph stopped to be a stand in Cthullian and tussled with Boris between the tables. Murph's gelatinous shape bounced them off tables and diners. More than once, Jolene had to jump on the counter, plates in her hands. One quasar-head decided to get handsy with her calf and got a boot heel in the shoulder. Several cosplayers wore horror icon faces and sent him packing real quick. The frantic pace of convention catering meant tips galore and fortunately, more good people than bad.

After the first incident anyone rowdy got quiet real fast when Boris uttered the words: "Threat detected."

For hours it was routine, then their freshly prepared sushi supplies dwindled. Her next order took her to a table that felt like emotional sandpaper.

"Your feathers on straight? The Blackhole Butcher would totally take out the Parasite!" An actual Pricklebeard shouted. He was young, judging by his short black facial hair. He shouted at what looked like an earth owl with solid black feathers and solid white eyes. Jolene thought the question: *What species?*

Her H.U.D. analyzed and explained they were a **Strigaform**, bolding the bullet points.

High intelligence
Deadly psionic abilities.

Focusing her Empath senses coated Jolene's tongue with bitter contempt. Thin quick slices spread across her arms. She walked up to the table with a smile and set a reminder to take some Empath blockers on her break.

"Your beard must be growing into your brain. The Parasite can invade and take over anything organic; last I checked, the Blackhole Butcher is organic!" The Strigaform squawked and flapped its wings.

"Sounds like you guys know your stuff." The statement was a bucket of water on their emotions which suited Jolene just fine. "Here we are, one Eldritch sushi, with spicy mayo for you." She flashed a smile at the Pricklebeard who grinned back, stroking his beard.

Galaxy Waffles

"And one Eldritch sushi burrito, with extra wriggle, and soy sauce." Jolene smiled a small smile through the order, enjoying the empathic break in their hostility.

"Can I get you two superfans anything else?" Both shook their heads and commenced eating. Jolene wrote it off as nerds being nerds and delivered galaxy-colored waffles to a table, grateful to get the sushi smell out of her nose.

"The Blackhole Butcher doesn't have the same skin and muscle density as regular organics." The Pricklebeard grumbled. Jolene felt rage spark from the Strigaform as it gave an irritated hoot.

"Even if it couldn't get through the skin, he still has ear canals! Or what, does he have black holes in those as well?" The owl asked and tore off some of its burrito.

"Oh and with all that mucus it generates. You're gonna tell me the Butcher wouldn't feel that, and smash it like the bug it is? Get your head out of-" The Pricklebeard got louder and louder then stopped because every last whisker yanked towards the ceiling like they were magnetized. Between grunts of pain he grabbed a jar of creamer and showered the Strigaform. All the facial hair on the Pricklebeard came down. "Nobody messes with the beard!" He shouted and began wrenching the table up from the floor.

Boris' head swiveled at the sound of groaning steel.

Jolene primed her Voltsriker. Someone had put on a synth horror track, and aside from Jolene's pistol that was the only sound. Much like any pump action, the Volstriker had a sound that everyone knew, a ramping whine and crackle. It helped that the barrel vented the occasional arc of lightning.

"Damage to Galaxy Waffles property will be added to your bill. Please vacate the premises." O.D. said. Both of them stiffened and said at once: "We're not done with our food."

Boris' green beam passed over them, and they both slumped.

"Lousy service" The Pricklebeard muttered.

"Leaving a bad review." The Strigaform hooted.

Jolene didn't lower or charge down the Voltsriker until the diner's inner doors shut. The owl raised a wing and the plates on their table flew onto the floor.

"I got it." Murph grumbled something about shaving and taxidermy. Jolene holstered the pistol and took her next order. All in all, just another day in the service industry.

Jolene Starblood

Species: Human
Pronouns: She/Her
Abilities: Empath
Likes: Punk Music and Coffee.
Dislikes: Classicism and Low
Coffee Supplies
Role: Manager and Waitress

THE OWL AND THE BEARD

"Security breach!" O.D. blasted through the ship's corridors from speakers embedded in the walls.

"Comms off!" Jolene groaned, mumbling a prayer for the soon to be Boris'd idiots.

"Command Override complete. Security breach in the kitchen!" O.D. screeched on full blast in Jolene's room. Adrenaline from the shock and annoyance caused Jolene to leap from bed. The first thing she noticed on her H.U.D finding herself two and a half hours into her seven hour sleep cycle. The diner only closed for rest, sleep, and the rarely enforced Galactic Government holiday. Only the entitled or the brain dead messed with a sleep schedule. Jolene decided whoever was in the kitchen was both.

"Wake up Murph!" She commanded O.D. Sliding on her engineering suit. Its heavy duty brown fabrics and artificial muscle structure was the closest thing she had to armor. It was also ready to go with multiple Voltsriker magazines. She got the pistol from her bed stand and took off at a heavy booted run towards the kitchen.

"Who the hell robs a diner kitchen?" The stupid answers

her still waking up brain came up with just pissed her off. She rubbed the sleep from her eyes with one hand while hugging the wall. A floating monitor displayed 0300 for the time. She gritted her teeth and squeezed her Voltsriker a little harder. Her next shift would start in less than three hours. Someone would answer for waking her up.

"Boris, who's in the kitchen?" Jolene thought through her communicator, but all she heard was balalaika music and Russian lyrics that her H.U.D. started translating.

KALINKA, KALINKA, KALINKA OF MINE,

BERRY-RASPBERRY IN THE GARDEN, RASPBERRY OF MINE.

KALINKA, KALINKA, KALINKA OF MINE.

She closed the channel and opened one to O.D.

JOLENE (CHAT MESSAGE)

"The hell is wrong with Boris?"

She demanded, stopping a moment to access the security cameras. Her vision turned into a greasy blur as she flipped from camera to camera.

O.D. (CHAT MESSAGE)

"The intruders uploaded a Yottabyte of digi vodka to employee Boris' charging station."

O.D. answered in a syrup brown chat bubble.

Jolene swore under her breath, adding drunk military AI to her growing list of problems.

JOLENE (CHAT MESSAGE)

"Info on the intruders?"

She thought to O.D., with only one hallway remaining between her and the kitchen, stopping to take in anything helpful he could offer.

O.D. (CHAT MESSAGE

"They have infected my sensors with a junk virus, and as you learned, our security cameras are also compromised. You and employee Murph are the only Galaxy Waffle assets able to confront the thieves. I will monitor as best I can. I wish you success as your performance will be evaluated."

Jolene rolled her eyes, wondering what kind of metrics could possibly be applied to this situation. She'd heard that other diners changed the code to their O.D.'s and made them less of a pain in the ass. Maybe they should consider this in the future. She shook her head and focused her empath senses towards the kitchen, taking slow silent steps.

"Move faster, didn't you hear the AI!" a surly voice growled, bristling with anger from the kitchen.

"I am! Quit acting like you're in charge!" Another voice hooted in answer, the sharp annoyance.

"Oh, come on!" Jolene mentally shouted. It sounded and felt like the two jerks they'd kicked out of the diner. Approaching the kitchen doorway, she glanced around the corner. Sure enough, there they were. The fighting fanboys from last night's dinner service were stealing the leftover Eldritch Sushi.

"If that droid really is a combat vet, he'll process the digi vodka in no time! We still have that bitch server and the shapeshifter to worry about." The Pricklebeard lectured, fingering a very large barreled weapon with arcing lightning at the tip.

Jolene's H.U.D. scanned it and came up with:

STORM CANNON

MADE BY ELECTRIC ENFORCEMENT

SPREAD WEAPON VARIANT- she cut it off, not needing the finer details on how outgunned she'd be in a firefight.

"So, what do we do?" Murph's message popped up in blue text on Jolene's H.U.D.

"O.D.? You said sensors are down? What about containment fields?" Jolene thought to Murph and O.D. at the same time.

"I can deploy them at each of the kitchen entrances." O.D. responded in text. Jolene slumped onto the wall, exhaling the knots in her stomach.

"Do it." She thought at O.D..

"I do not believe it is advis-" O.D. began, and Jolene's last battery of patience died.

"And this job doesn't pay me enough to take heavy weapons fire. Seal them in, call the Peacekeepers, let them handle this." Jolene interrupted, shutting the line. A few moments passed and nothing happened. Then cool blue waves of energy passed over the entrances to the kitchen.

"Shit!" The Prickledbeard and Strigaform shouted at the same time.

"You guys are looking at a permanent ban, oh and jail time for one of the stupidest crimes in this sector." Murph taunted from their doorway on the opposite side of the kitchen.

Jolene holstered the Volstriker and leaned into her doorframe. Boris had too many stories about poking bears for her to join in, but she could still watch and wait. Looking around, she could see the old chefbot's head face down on the floor between counters. The same lyrics sung into the floor between incoherent warbles.

The Strigaform's head swiveled between Jolene and Murph while he let out a screeching laugh and flared its wings. "We can't get out, and you can't get in." It said in a low voice, finishing with a hoot. Jolene stayed silent. The bird was right, but she didn't need to confirm anything for him. Dynamic fields were something you found on corporate elite or private ships, not on a freighter modified into a diner.

"Yea, that's how containment fields work!" Murph said, obviously unfamiliar with the concept of choosing silence over snark. They shifted their hand into human fingers with bright red nails, blew on them and brushed them on their black and red pinstripe vest. Jolene brought up their encrypted chat on her H.U.D.

JOLENE (CHAT MESSAGE)

"Stop poking the bear in the cage! Desperate idiots do desperate stupid things."

Right after she hit send, their robbers deployed

spacesuits. Smooth artificial fabrics slid over every limb and feather. Black glass faceplates sealed with a hiss. Anxiety spiked in Jolene's brain moving her hand to her Voltstriker.

JOLENE (CHAT MESSAGE)

"O.D. make a hole in the containment fields!"

Jolene sent in an un-encrypted chat unholstering the Voltstriker. The fields stayed solid. All while the two robbers loaded the remaining sushi in the stationary fridge into their floating icy fog spewing container.

"Command rejected, my analysis says the situation is secure and-" Jolene stopped reading when the Pricklebeard dropped a flat disc deploying an energy field containing them both. The Strigaform's head swiveled at her and through a mic said.

"Bardross, make a door." The Strigaform sneered, and the Pricklebeard's six arms made a bomb motion right before something went click. Jolene hit the deck as her ears filled with a high-pitched whine followed by a BANG!

Force. Light. Flames. The three filled the kitchen on the wall opposite the fridge. Before her vision went white, Jolene could see waves of energy gliding around the thieves in a circle.

She covered her head and pressed her face to the floor.

The containment fields took in energy, feeding it to the ship's grid. The explosion still bulged the blue sheets. They contracted without breaking. One container broke through the smoke shooting into space, followed by two spacesuits, every molecule of air in the room followed.

"Hull integrity compromised." O.D. said in his usual, helpful tone Jolene had come to expect. "Deploying counter-" The AIs words cut off as Boris' frame obeyed the laws of physics and got sucked into the hole in the wall. There was no sound in the vacuum but as the room filled with air Boris' drunken singing was joined by groaning metal.

Murph laughed.

Jolene rolled her eyes.

"Adapting countermeasures. Calculating damages. Galaxy Waffles headquarters will decide payroll deductions." O.D. finished and Murph stopped laughing. They started running till they were face to face with Jolene.

"We need to get the sushi back!" Murph shouted, their usual flashing eyes steady and unblinking. Jolene closed her eyes to think.

O.D. reported to headquarters meant a sector supervisor, and theirs was a special kind of bureaucratic demon. If they wanted to break even and avoid a massive company fine, they'd spend the rest of their lives paying off. Murph was right.

"Go through all the info O.D. gathered. Find me something!" Jolene barked.

Murph's legs became eight spider legs, and they skittered off.

Jolene turned to the screen. "O.D., are the Peacekeepers on the way?"

O.D. appeared as a cartoon waffle with syrup brown

pompadour hair, enormous eyes, and a permanent grin. The customers thought it was cute. Jolene was more certain he needed a programming change.

"Yes, and the explosion has hastened their response time." O.D. answered.

Finally, some good news. If they could pursue and disable their ship they could recover the sushi, and any assets to help pay for damages!

"Start tracking their signal and pursue them." Jolene ordered, wondering how a waffle shaped diner ship would keep up. The shielding would keep them intact. Boris' counters and stovetops were charred slag. Kinetics and heat turned every kitchen tool into shrapnel that stabbed into every surface.

"I have logged their ship ID and information. I cannot comply with your second order. Further risk to Galaxy Waffles property is-" O.D. began, but Jolene had already pulled up what she needed and began reciting from her H.U.D.

"Galaxy Waffles Regulation 34124: 'All employees are expected to attempt recovery of stolen assets, within the bounds of Galactic Law. Pursuing and disabling their ship complies with both.' Now fly after them or I'll report you as defective." Jolene finished, poking the cartoon waffle between the eyes. O.D.'s permanent grin didn't change, but his bacon eyebrows went diagonal at the threat.

"Excuse me!" Boris shouted. Jolene and O.D. both looked his way. "Why is my ass in outer space?"

The Chase

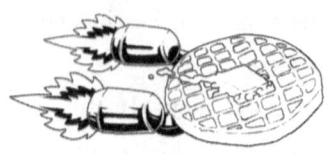

"We got robbed for sushi?" Boris' voice crackled with interference.

"Shields adjusted" O.D. announced.

With the vacuum pressure keeping Boris' ass in space cut off, he slumped forward. Using six arms, he pulled himself free, landing like a cymbal crash, on his knees. All four eyes flashing through different colors. Jolene rushed over to inspect him,

"Don't touch-" Boris started before his sentence turned into static. Jolene didn't instead relying on her H.U.D. producing a list in red text down her vision as she circled him.

NO MICROFRACTURES DETECTED
MINOR METAL FATIGUE
POWER SOURCE INTACT
EXTENSIVE COSMETIC DAMAGE ON REAR OF CHASSIS

She bit her lip, barely hiding her smirk at that before she shared what she'd found.

"Matches what my systems are saying." Boris managed to say with less static. All six of his arms pushed him from kneeling to standing. He wobbled back to the wall.

Galaxy Waffles

Rubbing his head. "Oh, my processor feels like it got put in a cement mixer. How much?"

"A yottabyte." Jolene and O.D. said at the same time.

"Probably with a junk virus chaser" Jolene added.

"Well, that's a new record." Boris stumbled over to his charging station, his arms sliding into the ports.

"Sweet, clean power." Boris hummed in tune to the song from before.

"O.D., where are they?" Jolene asked, and their animated waffle overlord disappeared on the screen outside the kitchen, replaced by a map showing the fleeing ship's energy signature.

"They are ahead by a quarter AU, and picking up speed," O.D. answered.

"Ship type?"

"Modified freighter. Top speed of the unmodified craft is equal to ours. With their modifications, it is unlikely we can catch up." O.D.'s tone of satisfaction made Jolene want to poke his screen.

"Why aren't we in pursuit?" She demanded, knowing the answer because she couldn't hear the engines.

"I am warming up the engines as stated in Galaxy Waffles regulation 1730." O.D. responded with the same smug satisfaction. A maple brown progress bar showed up across the bottom of his screen. Jolene mentally ordered a form from corporate's internal servers. It displayed as a hologram in neon yellow right in front of O.D.'s monitor. The animated waffle avatar appeared and glanced at it.

"You're threatening my record for following

regulations?" His bacon eyebrows rose high above his chocolate chip eyes. Jolene watched his oversized animated gloves ball into fists and stuck to his sides. His maple syrup pompadour twitched, like it was attached to a drunk puppet string. She smiled at the AI performance report, which she'd filled out with negative scores in every category.

"Stop being a roadblock and start being useful," she hissed and tapped the monitor between his chocolate chip eyes.

"They've got a ten minute lead and gaining." Murph said over the comms. Inertia yanked Jolene to the side, landing her on her hip before rolling her onto her ass.

"Pursuit engaged. Maintaining the current course so long as the ship takes no additional damage," he said with a smile that made Jolene believe a waffle could wish her dead. The monitor showed the map again.

"That is the most tyrannical waffle in this sector." Boris said, his smooth Russian baritone coming out loud and clean. "Murph, are we keeping pace?" he shouted at the ceiling.

"Yes, but we need to close the gap." Murph's voice shouted back through the comms.

"Or slow them down." Boris suggested, and all eight of his eyes opened, all of them red as blood. They reminded Jolene of a spider's eyes; it sent shivers down her spine thinking about it. It was also something Boris only did when he needed military precision. She swallowed the knot in her throat as the veteran bot knelt down and three of six arms pulled up a floor panel. The other three arms snaked into the open floor as he grumbled in Russian. Her H.U.D. displayed the words in red text.

"GOING TO BE A GOOD DAY."

"STEAL FROM MY KITCHEN."

"WE'LL SEE HOW YOU LIKE THIS!" Boris declared with triumph as each of his three arms pulled out a slug as long as Jolene's arm. Afraid the ship was going to get torn a second hole, Jolene's anxiety forced her back by several steps.

"What the hell is that?" She shouted, her brain spun with questions and implications. With one thought she accessed the security cameras, setting them to record anything but Boris.

"Good idea. No evidence is a good thing." Boris said through speakers no one on the ship had ever seen. Boris' red eyes gleamed as he showed her the tips of the rounds. Jolene relaxed as she looked down at hollow tubes. "See it's not a live warhead anymore, just a casing. But for my plan it'll work." He said and his eight eyes flashed. Jolene sighed through the suspense.

"And the plan is what? Shoot them with blanks?" She demanded, expecting Boris to contradict her. The veteran battle-bot didn't; instead, he stood the rounds up and lumbered over to the grill and deep fryer. Jolene didn't bother asking again and stared as the bot plugged one arm into the grease trap and stuck one arm into each slugs.

She glanced at the map. They were closing in. At least Murph knew how to fly the bulky waffle shaped ship well.

A wet gulping sucking sound filled the kitchen. She refocused on Boris who was playing a whistle through his speakers as heavy wet plopping sounds left his arms and smacked into the shells.

"How the hell does that not mess with your systems?" Jolene asked, hoping the answer was better than the assault on her ears. Suck. Wet Plop. Repeat.

"Isolated channels. This thing is about as modular as a chassis gets." Boris tapped a fist over his bear platoon insignia. "Favorite hunting habit for Chtullians was to get inside something and rip it open, so they gave me plenty of countermeasures." Boris explained, the montage of greasy sounds finally ending. The sweet meat stink filled the kitchen. Boris arms worked at two per shell to seal and plug the tops of each casing.

"So, you've got three tubes of grease…what's next?" she asked, not knowing how to process what she was looking at.

"You humans had something called buckshot. It was casings filled with tiny beads great for shredding things. Well, we will call this grease shot!" He declared with a rumbling laugh, and Jolene's brain finally came up with something to say.

"And just what kind of half-assed cartoon algorithm in your processors came up with this?" She demanded, without objecting. At the moment, she had no better plan.

"Rabbit file had a meeting with Duck file and decided it was half-assed idea season." He answered and chuckled as he lifted the first shell and started on the second. Jolene raised an eyebrow and Boris stopped laughing.

"I don't see how grease shot-" she paused, finding the words strange in her mouth, "will stop a spaceship."

"I shot these casings from low orbit into Cthullian nests. If they can withstand a planet's atmosphere they can deal with a spaceship." Boris answered, two arms on either side taking up the grease loaded shells and moving towards a kitchen door. Jolene followed until Murph came on over the comms.

"Uh guys, they know we're following and they're..." They trailed off and Jolene's patience was still running on empty.

"Spit it out, Murph, I'm not playing guessing games," she demanded.

"According to the computer their course is a straight line for the quasar's event horizon," they finished.

Jolene could hear the confusion and uncertainty in their voice and didn't want her Empath senses to feel it as well.

"That makes no-" she started

"We'll be safe with him!" A gruff voice interrupted over the comms. Jolene recognized it as Bardross.

"Why wouldn't he just kill us like all the others?" Asked the Strigaform with a hoot.

"Because we haven't broken any of his rules, DUH!" Bardross answered. "Besides, bet you that diner sent our ship signature to the local Peacekeepers. We need a place to lie low, and no one messes with the Blackhole Butcher. Keep your feathers on, Sorik, we're gonna burn some fuel!" he said, finishing with a whooping noise.

"No one messes with the Parasite either." Sorik answered.

"Well, unless you know-" Bardross started and then cut off.

"I think they're stress binging the sushi and it curb stomped the few brain cells they had left." Murph guessed, and no one disagreed. Jolene rubbed her temples, processing the new situation with each rotation.

"So let me see if I understand. We get robbed by two customers with more fandom than brain cells. We give chase to avoid owing corporate our paychecks for the next several years. Now our two idiots are high on psychedelic sushi and believe they can fly into a quasar's event horizon. All so they can meet up with a fictional Sci-Fi serial killer to avoid arrest." Jolene summarized, grinding her teeth.

"Yup." Boris and Murph answered.

"System estimates they'll hit the event horizon in ten minutes." They grumbled over the comms, followed by something about getting blamed and losing vacation time.

Jolene leaned on a wall and just repeated, "I don't get paid enough." She said it until she screamed it at the ceiling.

"None of us do." Boris complained, turned to the left and walked down the hall with the shipside elevator.

"T minus 9 minutes and 30 seconds." O.D. chimed in over the comms in the voice Jolene hated. She pushed herself away from the wall and ran to catch up with Boris. Her jaw dropped; she didn't recognize the chefbot.

Galaxy Waffles

The humanoid chassis was gone, replaced by a Boris shaped tank! The grease loaded shells were in a magazine that threatened to scrape the floor. Above it, his normal three arms were a mass of shifting parts. Chromed metal plates and lengths of clear fiber circuits reshaped themselves into a barrel that she could fit her head into! With final hiss and metal slide it the hall lit up in shadowed reds and blacks. Stepping to the side showed her why, Boris' roaring bear platoon sign was glowing along the side of the cannon barrel. Its razor toothed maw ending at the barrel's mouth.

"T-minus 8:45, we are within visual range of the freighter." O.D. said, but it didn't register with Jolene as she looked down a hole she could have crawled into. The cannon barrel made up at least seventy-five percent of Boris' body. To accommodate the change, he now had treads instead of feet and looked more like a tank than an abstract humanoid.

"Fly will fly in." Boris said, and Jolene realized her mouth had been hanging open. She closed it and tried to ask a question. "Am going to secure myself to hull, take aim and hopefully ruin their engines." Boris beat her to it, but she recovered with a new question.

"If it's spent ammo, how are you going to fire it?" she asked. Four out of Boris' eight eyes winked. The floor rose, taking him up. Jolene started for the dining room, unsure just how insane this situation looked.

"O.D., adjust shielding to keep me from flying off!" He said over the comms.

"Shielding adjusted. T-6:30 before their freighter reaches the event horizon," he answered. "At T-3:00 the ship's engines will cut off to comply with regulations" O.D. announced over the ship's speakers.

Jolene realized there was nothing she could do but sit and wait. She reached the empty dining room. An emergency ejection would have been possible, even with a full dining room, but the insurance claims were the stuff of nightmares. Looking out the windows past the blue halo of the ship's shields, there was the energy trail of the freighter. A grey outline against the massive red ringed hole in space.

"Recoil will shake the ship, better strap in." Boris announced over the comms and Jolene scrambled into the booth with the best view. With a mental command, a multi-point harness deployed. She split her attention between strapping in and watching the freighter.

"T-4:00 before they reach the event horizon," O.D. announced.

"O.D. from one AI to another, shut up!" Boris growled and just before he closed the comms. Jolene heard a static crackle over the speakers. "Target locked!" he announced before her ass left the seat and slammed her back into the booth.

A white line shot forward against the crimson quasar, closing in on the fleeing freighter. The cannon's force pushed them back as the engines thrust pushed ahead. Shaking the ship like a saltshaker. "Damn, hit the hull!" The ship's engines stuttered for a moment. "O.D., keep us steady! Loading the second grease shot!"

"Complying with fellow AI requests, all damages will be charged to Chefbot Boris' earnings." O.D. projected as a 3D hologram over Jolene's table, his oversized gloves behind his back. He turned to Jolene, his bacon eyebrows slanted, chocolate chip eyes fixed on her. "Commitment and execution to the current course of action will be credited to Hostess Jolene." He turned back to the window. "T-2:30 seconds until they are past the event horizon."

"Shut up!" was the last thing anyone heard before the ship jerked back again. O.D.'s hologram pixelated into pieces for a moment. Jolene felt a twinge in her neck when she slammed back into the padded booth. She closed her eyes at the pain and almost missed the second shot before it struck the freighter! White light flashed on impact. Its blue engine trail flared before sucking in the excess energy and blowing out the thruster frame. A blast of energy smacked the front shields. Knocking them up and back. It took minutes of fighting the engines and a cloud of debris to straighten out.

"Take that!" Murph shouted as they all looked on at the freighter flying in circles. The smoking thruster left a trail that soon became a smoke ring.

"Chew on that!" Boris shouted into the comms.

Jolene smiled, then waited for O.D. to reassemble. The hologram took in the situation and crossed his arms, his oversized lips stuck in a pout. "Get us close enough to use the tractor beam before they try anything else." She smiled as she worked to undo her harness. O.D. blinked away without answering, but the ship started moving forward.

"Oh, be sure to get the shell fragments!" Boris ordered over the comms.

"Shell fragment recovery added to the order queue." snapped a too jolly voice.

"Hey Murph, try their comms now." Jolene tried for a neck roll, hoping she could avoid any pain or stiffness. There was a crackle followed by red alert sirens that strained the comms. Words came next.

"Make it stop, Beardbrain!"

"Can't, Featherbrain!"

"Not trying!"

"You shut off the safety-"

The connection shut off.

"I think we made them mad." Murph said, sniggering the entire time. Jolene looked out to the gorgeous expanse and watched the freighter's flight path.

"Hey Murph, save that chatter please."

Some empaths detested pettiness, Jolene, on the other hand, wished she could enjoy it with a side of her morning coffee.

"Only if I get a copy," they answered. "Make as many as you want." Jolene headed back to the elevator to wait for Boris.

When he came down, he'd resumed his four eyed, six-armed chrome dome shape. When he saw Jolene, all six of his hands came together, covering the now colorless bear sign and twiddled his thumbs. The sound of three sets of thumb servos filled the hall.

Galaxy Waffles

"So..."

"We've got a lot to take care of, and then I want the full story." Jolene nodded as Boris went ramrod straight and saluted with one arm.

"Murph, any word from the Peacekeepers?" Jolene winced as she looked up at the ceiling.

"They'll be here in an hour, they've asked us to lock them down with a tractor beam and avoid further contact," they answered before stepping out into the hall showing off 'a ready to eat you' needle toothed smile. Murph followed it up with an impossibly curled mustache that they twirled. Jolene just shook her head.

"What did they say about our stolen product?" Jolene asked.

Murph's head shifted. A large blue hat with a badge formed first. Their face went pudgy with bloodshot eyes and a bulbous nose. Their villainous whiskers grew into a mustache so bushy Jolene couldn't see a mouth. Most Kyanese she'd seen didn't spend time in their original shape. Murph had explained said it was easier to shape-shift out of their original shape instead of another.

"So this is the lowdown, see. Corporate property will be returned after evidence is collected, see. Don't be gettin' funny ideas about justified salvage or we'll throw you in the slammer, understand?" Murph's gangster accent was always perfect but never requested. Jolene rubbed her temples, weighing the options.

"At least we can recover the sushi." Boris said, still saluting, and Murph returned the salute with a three fingered blue hand.

"Alright, I'll notify corporate." Jolene said, wishing she had a reset button for this entire situation. O.D. appeared as a hologram and looked at each of them with a smile full of marshmallow teeth.

"Status report on order queue. Tractor beam deployed. Ship network infiltration complete. I have set their ship to standby mode with basic life support functions. Last I heard from the comms the Pricklebeard had locked the Strigaform in the bathroom. I am scanning the area for shell fragments. Galaxy Waffles Sector Supervisor Erabella was notified as the situation developed with all relevant details. All employees are to standby. They will arrive in forty-eight hours for a performance review." O.D. finished with a smug smile that put the phrase shit-eating grin to shame. He offered Jolene a one-finger salute, stuck out his surprisingly human tongue and disappeared.

"Where's your stash?" Jolene asked Boris.

"Stress drinking?" The bot asked, relaxing out of the salute.

Murph's head shifted back to the blue tear drop shape they preferred. "Who cares! Let's let off some steam and get our stories straight."

Jolene gave a thumbs up and all three of them went into the kitchen to pour drinks and figure out how they were going to handle the nightmare that was Erabella.

ARRIVAL

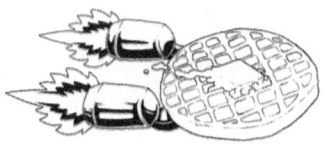

Jolene's head pounded every step towards the dining room. She leaned on the ship's walls for support just to feel the cold metal numb the pain. She tried to speak, but her tongue felt like sandpaper, so the words came out as mumbles.

"One hangover cure!" She groaned through gritted teeth.

Jolene whimpered through the renewed pounding in her temples. She draped herself over the counter, half tempted to just sleep it off. Instead, she leaned forward and rested her head on her arms to keep her eyes away from the lights. The counter in front of her slid open, providing her a cup with the corporate logo; a waffle shaped ship with maple syrup coming out the engines in a swirl against a background of stars. She shook her head at the constant attempts to reinforce company pride and employee ownership, ignored the milky substance in the mug and threw it back like the shots from last night. The stuff fizzed across her tongue with the taste of burned nuts. In moments, her pounding pain faded into aches, her tongue felt like a tongue again, and she could string more than one thought together.

"Replay" The mental command brought up a first-person view and crystal-clear audio from last night. Boris had suggested drunk poker, and one shot led to another. It was tempting to sit, watch, and enjoy but there was a problem coming and she needed to be ready.

"Erabella."

She thought the scene paused and a timeline loaded across the bottom with yellow markers. Mentally, Jolene selected the first one. Her vision went white and reloaded the scene. She saw the pot was twenty shots and two bottles big.

"Think the old bearcat will be trouble? I raise." Murph asked in their usual moving gangster accent, before pushing forward five shots.

"Does a bear shit in the woods? I call and raise ten." Boris chuckled at his own question. Jolene looked at her full house hand and did her best not to smile.

"Peacekeepers determined we had zero liability. We recovered ninety percent of the sushi that we can flash freeze and sell as a specialty item. FTL is down thanks to the hole but our shields will keep us in one piece. We claimed a hefty bounty and made the sector safer. Anyone else and we'd be getting a raise. All in." She pushed her ten remaining shots and three bottles into the pot. Blue and red eyes stared at her, then at the pot in the center of the dining table. Five bottles was a huge haul to use for favors or trade when they docked, but that was only if she won. If she lost, she'd have to drink... Jolene whistled as she counted forty-five shots.

"I like my liver." Murph tossed their cards on the table.

"And I do not have a liver. Call." Boris pushed his bet forward. Jolene stared at him, waiting for an arm to tap, for an eye to blink, or some sort of static crackle.

"Going to play the last card?" Boris asked, resting his smooth chromed head on one of his hands. Jolene nodded and watched, but found nothing. No tell was coming. She looked at her two kings and the three sevens. A straight was impossible but... Jolene couldn't finish the thought because Murph shifted their hands into dense little nubs and began drumming. Jolene flipped over the last card. Ace of Spades.

The card did nothing for her, but she still had one of the best hands in the game. "Time to drink to the Motherboard, comrade." She laid her cards out.

This time, Murph whistled. Boris looked down at his cards and the bot rumbled out a laugh.

"I think it is you who will honor the Motherboard." He laid out two aces, making his full house the better hand. Jolene slumped until her forehead hit the table. She kept hitting it.

"Going to need all your brain cells for hand eye coordination." She looked up to see he already had all the bottles in his hands and was walking off to Jolene could only guess where to hide them.

"Time to see how good your system's filters are!" He called back.

Jolene, like every human in deep space, had body

augments. Some humans went over the top replacing everything with bio-tech. She'd gone for practical changes that helped her survive. One of them was an automatic filtration system that was supposed to be for poisons, radiation, and a depressingly long list of medical conditions. Corporations in untamed space did not believe in paid sick time, especially for Starbloods. After that many shots, it explained why she'd felt like warm nuclear waste this morning. Her world titled as something hard and metallic pushed against her forehead.

"Earth to Jolene." Boris' voice rolled in over the scene.

"End replay." The mental command brought the world back in a rush of color and sensations.

"I was looking for our plan to deal with Erabella." She rubbed the crusty sleep crud from her eyes, hoping it would help bring things back to normal.

"Could have just asked. You can't start the day without your favorite chemical." Boris said, sliding a cup filled with delicious brown rage suppressant.

Jolene ignored the bot's chuckle and inhaled roasted cinnamon with hints of chocolate, almonds and that slight bitter tang that so many humans could not live without. She opened her eyes to see a large mug filled to the edge with light brown coffee. Leaning forward, thankful again that she kept her red hair short, she sipped the delicious flavors over the rim.

"Caffeine acquired, so what's the plan I still can't remember?"

"We use the rulebook." Boris held up a blue chip.

"There's a program here that'll pick out keywords from what Erabella says, and let you reference Galaxy Waffles regulations to cover our collective butts and ports."

Jolene wrinkled her nose. "This migraine is gonna suck." Boris laid the chip down near her coffee cup.

"Think I'm an amateur? It's custom coded to you." Boris said indignantly.

Jolene laid a hand on the chip and felt a jolt of power race up her arm. A notification in the corner of her vision showed the program loading.

"STOLEN MERCHANDISE." As Boris finished a text box appeared in her left eye showing a list of regulations. **"FOOD."** The additional word narrowed down the list even more. Jolene sipped and considered her next step. O.D. blinked into existence, arms behind his back, his marshmallow teeth fixed in a smile that made Jolene's skin crawl.

"Galaxy Waffles Sector Supervisor Erabella is arriving now." O.D. gave a one finger salute and blinked away.

"Shit!" Boris and Jolene shouted. She checked her Bio-tech for the Empath Blocker medication. Hope surged for precious seconds as she thought the command

"Deploy Deploy Deploy"

The surge fizzled when her H.U.D. responded.

MEDICATION DEPLOYMENT DENIED REASON LISTED BELOW

REASON: EMPATH ABILITIES ARE MANDATORY DURING WORKING HOURS.

Jolene facepalmed and slid her hand up her forehead

scratching at the itchy irritation racing across her skull. She'd never changed their hours in the system.

"Boris! Blockers now!" All of Boris' eyes went dark for a moment, then red again, his best simulation of a blink.

"Ok"

Boris passed her three beige pills Jolene washed them down with the remaining coffee. Jolene smiled as she thought the command an entire month's worth of credits had bought her.

EMB a three letter command no one would look twice at if some corporate snoop looked at her Bio-tech's code. Moments passed before a green checkmark popped on her H.U.D. A quick circulatory system map showing the distribution. One problem behind her and then the next one docked at their front door.

JOLENE (CHAT MESSAGE)

"Murph, why the hell didn't you say anything?"

Jolene messaged them while the diner's outer doors opened.

MURPH (CHAT MESSAGE)

"System says she's two hours away!"

They answered and sent a live star-chart with Erabella's ship and estimated arrival time followed.

JOLENE (CHAT MESSAGE)

"How the hell did our system mess up this bad?"

Jolene sent back. After a second of silence, both of them sent the same message.

MURPH & JOLENE (CHAT MESSAGE)

"O.D.!"

Murph's showing in a blue bubble and Jolene's in a green bubble.

Murph grumbled in the chat about putting O.D.'s server in an aquarium. Jolene straightened her uniform as the diner's inner doors opened. Platinum was Erabella's color and element. From her platinum blonde hair. To her shimmering platinum laced boots. She'd even had most of her skin replaced by shiny platinum bio-tech. The effect made her look like a sophisticated mannequin. Their corporate appointed judge and jury scanned the dining room from behind large ice white sunglasses.

"Glad to see company property is still in one piece," she lectured in a reedy voice that was the only original part she had left. Removing the glasses, Erebella's neon blue eyes stared at Jolene. High pitches stabbed into Jolene's ears before scrambling into static noise. Two empaths in one room could lead to anything from fainting to aneurysms. Empath blocker side effects were temporary but included: low energy, sleep disruption, high or low blood pressure, and were still better than scarring your brain. Erabella closed her eyes and tsked. Her eyes opened, her eyebrows lowering artificial skin, showing zero wrinkles.

"Late on taking your blockers shows a lack of planning and organization. Not surprising." Erabella smiled through every insult and critique. Jolene didn't smile back, but also didn't say anything to make it worse. Erabella raised a snow white eyebrow at the silence. "Take your blockers earlier and we can avoid this kind of discomfort." Erabella lectured before looking over at Boris.

"Bring the chef's table." Boris didn't salute, but he did nothing he shouldn't either. After providing the table and chairs Erabella put down a recording device.

"Sit." She pointed at the chair opposite her. Jolene didn't let her smile waver. With a snap of her shiny mechanical fingers, a pale white holopad appeared in Erabella's hand. "Shall we begin?"

The question wasn't a question, but Jolene nodded, and Erabella started recording the legal interrogation.

Erabella

Species: Human
Pronouns: She/Her
Abilities: Empath
Likes: Obedience and Money
Dislikes: Confident Employees
Role: Sector Supervisor

Performance Review

"This is Galaxy Waffles Sector Supervisor Erabella beginning a performance review of Galaxy Waffles crew 3371. Please state your name for the record."

As Boris promised, the program picked out keyword offerings related Galaxy Waffles regulations.

"Jolene, Employee ID 135. Per Galaxy Waffles regulation 003 any crew under performance review is required to be informed of a performance review's potential results."

Erabella snapped her holopad away, her mechanical eyes stared out the diner windows into the vast blackness of space. Jolene recognized it from all the times she used her augments.

"I am happy to comply with that regulation. This performance review will determine if you are to enter indentured employment to recoup profit losses. If your judgment is reliable enough to justify your continued employment. If my findings determine neither is necessary, you will receive additional training and supervision."

Boris' keyword program came up with zero results. The stress of reality threatened to bring back her hangover pains and nausea. Jolene wished she'd ordered double the hangover cure.

"May we continue?" Erabella's neon blue lips curled into a smile that made the question a command.

"Yes, of course. Would you like anything to drink or eat?" The empathic feedback loop was dying down and helped Jolene's smile to be a little less forced.

"Finally, the service that Galaxy Waffles is known for. There may be hope for you yet. I'll take a breakfast disc and some stabilizer tea."

"Coming right up." Boris answered.

Erabella snapped her fingers and began making notes on her holopad. Jolene felt her stomach unclench as Boris prepared and delivered the food without a single word or sound of protest. He called orders like Erabella's pellet food, and given the round bland colored disc, Jolene couldn't argue.

"Thank you! Keep it up and I might leave a tip." Erabella winked and Boris' eyes moved from her to the plate.

"Thank you, your generosity is most kind. Please enjoy your meal and I will consider that payment enough." He crossed three arms across his chest and bowed. Erabella's smile cracked for a second before she stretched her congenial mask back into place. Boris retreated to the kitchen, still bowing.

Jolene wanted to smirk at Boris' polite disinterest, but Erabella had access to Galaxy Waffles' legally invasive employee files. Caffeine kept her sharp while the Empath

Blockers kept her head noise free. This would a brutal interrogation.

"Well based on that alone, he is certainly Galaxy Waffles material." Jolene brushed a bit of hair out of her eyes and stared at Erabella. The platinum mannequin raised an eyebrow, daring her to say something, her pen at the ready.

"He's an irreplaceable asset, and I look forward to working with him more. I hope you enjoy your meal." Jolene gestured at the tea and breakfast disc. Erabella sipped daintily and nibbled like a chipmunk.

"Excellent quality." She made a mark on her pad without looking. "Now then, you are the front house manager,"

"Server, assistant chef, assistant mechanic, and pretty much anything else this place needs me to be." Jolene cut in and Erabella tapped a fingernail on the metal table, filling the dining room with metallic echoes.

"Please answer questions and refrain from providing irrelevant information." While Jolene was glad she couldn't feel what Erabella was feeling, she wanted her to feel her fist breaking that perfectly sculpted nose. "Leading up to this incident it appears you used an unauthorized weapon to intimidate the two guests who later robbed us. How do you explain this extreme action and inappropriate conduct?"

Jolene looked at the table and wondered which would break first, it or Erabella's face. Instead of finding out, she glanced at the menu in Boris' program.

"Per Galaxy Waffles Regulation 173572 Section H Subsection 37 employees may take extreme action in defense of company property or customers."

"The situation had not developed enough for that regulation to-"

"Subsection 53 of that regulation states that the threat of damage or harm is enough to take preemptive action." Jolene interrupted. Erabella's predatory smile shrunk. Jolene wasn't done shoving a spoonful of bureaucratic medicine down her throat.

"I think you will agree that use of psionic force on another customer's facial hair and trying to rip a bolted table from the ship's floor qualified the situation for this regulation." Jolene pulled up a file on her H.U.D. and waited for Erabella to recover. She pouted her metallic teal painted lips.

MURPH (CHAT MESSAGE)

"Looks like a neon sphincter."

Murph sent in chat, Jolene had to cover her laugh with a cough. Erabella's expression changed to a naked hateful glare.

"Is everything ok?" She said it cold as the space outside the ship.

"Just fine." Jolene said hitting her chest a few times to sell the lie.

"Moving on. I will agree the circumstances fit the regulation, except for the Voltsriker. It is a recognized effective non-lethal weapon but not one authorized for use by Galaxy Waffles employees." She leaned forward, steepling her metallic fingers and staring at Jolene over her fingertips. "Galaxy Waffles Regulation 7732 indicates any employee using unauthorized tools will be fined and terminated once a performance review confirms their guilt."

Jolene snapped her fingers and her file loaded as a light blue hologram over and around Erabella's face. The holo's electric field made her hair stand on end. Jolene remembered one of Murph's movies had a poodle whose poofy tail looked like Erabella's head.

"Childish actions like this prove that you are not —

Erabella manically combed her fingers through her hair, absently reading the file.

"That you are not Galaxy Waffles." Erabella trailed off as she continued to read.

"- material."

Jolene snapped her fingers again and the attached voice file played. It was a voice exhausted by just being alive, before sharpening into a drill sergeant's no nonsense bark.

"*To whom it may concern,*

I, Orzahn, Galaxy Waffles' Alpha Quadrant Executive hereby grant Crew 3371's front end manager Jolene, employee ID 135, special authorization to carry and use a Voltstriker pistol. I do this because the territory her restaurant covers has a documented criminal element. This special authorization will continue until an official Galaxy Waffles regulation is ratified. All questions related to this authorization are to be forwarded to me. Any harassment of Jolene will result in a Performance Review of the guilty party."

Signed in the presence of a Galaxy Waffles lawyer.

Orzhan

Erabella trembled at the last line; her metal fingers tapped uncontrollably against the table. Jolene almost felt sorry for the woman as she watched and recorded her reaction to enjoy later. She watched Erabella smooth away the static from her snow white hair. It wasn't the same rigid spiky crest as before but she smiled at her reflection in the table.

"I'll be logging and reporting this irregular authorization. You're excused from the review until I send for you. Next up is Murphfree-." Erabella trailed off silently, mouthing.

MURPH (CHAT MESSAGE)

"Oh my god did my name fry her circuits?"

Murph asked and sent a string of laughing emojis.

"Muphreezius Imital is their full name. We just call them Murph." Jolene piped in, enjoying Erabella's glare at being corrected. By the way her fingers ground against each other Jolene would have bet that Erabella was now the one imagining a violent course of action.

"Of course, if you need me again, I'll be polishing my pistol."

Erabella's right eye twitched at the last word, but remained on Jolene anyway.

"I hope you enjoy that."

Jolene resisted the temptation to skip out of the dining room.

"Good luck!" She thought at Murph as they passed each other.

"Don't worry, Boris set me up." They thought back.

Jolene exhaled some tension away and whistled all the way to her quarters. Boris was waiting by the door. Without tapping the button it opened ahead of Jolene. Jolene turned and held up a finger to her lips then spun it in the air. One of Boris' thirty fingertips popped open deploying a small antenna.

"Thirty seconds. I knew she hated you, but what did you do? Piss in her vodka?" Boris whispered.

"Later. Did you message Orzahn?"

An ear-splitting whine filled the room, and the fingertip with the jammer crackled from burned circuits. Boris clamped it back into place just as O.D. popped into the room. His bacon eyebrows angled into were at sharp diagonals, his chocolate chip eyes moved between them.

The tips of his marshmallow teeth ground against each other, turning their tops black.

"What were you two discussing?" The bright cheerful customer service voice coming out between his burning teeth made Jolene want to make good on that syrup threat.

"Performance reviews." Jolene and Boris said at the same time.

"Right, I'm sure. Well consider this your first and only warning Galaxy Waffles Regulation 2253 states that employees suspend all privacy rights during a performance review. Violating this regulation will mean an immediate guilty finding, followed by termination or indentured employment."

"Too bad they didn't include regulations about using regulations to demoralize the workforce." Boris nudged Jolene and she grunted in agreement. O.D. expanded his hologram until the tip of his head pixelated against the ceiling. One chocolate chip eye focused on each of them. His maple syrup pompadour flopped forward in a way that made Jolene want to giggle.

"Would you like to repeat that insubordination, employee Boris?" O.D. asked in a too eager voice.

"Constructive feedback, I just emailed the official form, would you like to check?" Boris answered, holding up a hand his head leaning back while a bored sigh played over his speakers. O.D.'s oversized gloves pointed two fingers at his eyes then at Boris. Then repeated the gesture at Jolene, and started to fade away.

"Oh O.D., before you go, as the front-end manager, I

would like to discuss something." Jolene said in a way that gave the AI no choice, with her best wide eyed innocent look.

"The authority of your position is suspended until the performance review is complete as-"

"As such-and-such regulation states, I just feel it's a professional courtesy to inform you that I'm reporting your malfunction to Erabella."

O.D.'s bacon eyebrows crinkled until Jolene was sure they'd crumble.

"Lying during a performance review will not help you." O.D. said it in a tense voice that did not agree with his smile at all.

"It's a lie that you projected Erabella's arrival as two hours away and then popped in to tell us she was walking in the front door?" Jolene smiled the special smile she used for moments just like this one.

"One ex-" O.D.'s gloved finger came up to wag, but Jolene ignored him.

"My report will present this as a gross miscalculation." Jolene stepped forward and through O.D., ignoring the effect on her hair. O.D. reshaped himself so that he was looking at her again. "Included will be a detailed projection on the possible consequences should this lapse in performance occur mid-flight. Maybe during ship maintenance evaluations. Maybe even for supply orders. Loss of profit, loss of crew, and potential ship loss are tragic and best avoided, wouldn't you agree?" While Jolene pointed this out, O.D. deflated like a balloon, without the wheezing fart noises, until he was about the size of an actual waffle. "I figure they'll pull your core, run you through every machine and test they have, collect their findings and then stick you in a lab closet... if you're lucky."

Jolene squatted down till she stared the little animated sadist right in the eyes. "If you're unlucky, well, I hear formatting isn't that bad. It's like waking up with a fresh start."

O.D.'s usual golden color had gone white at this point. Jolene stood back up and wondered if she'd gone too far.

"Is there anything I can do to demonstrate I am still reliable?" O.D.'s normally cheerful voice was replaced by a pleading innocent tone Jolene was sure she'd heard as a kid in a cartoon.

"For now, just stop trying to screw us and we can figure something out later."

O.D. returned to his usual size and nodded furiously before disappearing. Boris rubbed the top of his head.

"Remind me never to get on your bad side." One of his hands gently petted her hair and she leaned into his solid cool fingers.

"Worry about that later, let's go over your answers for your review." Jolene smacked one of his shoulders before going to her bathroom for some headache relief.

"Da, not sure calling them wartime mementos will help the situation." Jolene winced before she swallowed the pills. Then turned back and began prying information out of Boris while sending mental commands to look for any regulations that could help them.

After Boris' prep they both linked up to the security system just in time to catch the start of Murph's interrogation.

"How would you describe Jolene's leadership during this incident?" Erabella stared at Murph the way a teacher stares down a trouble-making child. Murph shifted part of their face into a large cleft chin grunting in thought.

"Flawless." They drew the word out with their usual gangster twang. Erabella closed her eyes and rubbed her temples.

"Could you please elaborate with no other affectations?" She tapped the table while Murph's face resumed its dark blue rounded shape.

"Employee 135 Jolene was invaluable in deescalating the initial incident with the offending customers. During the second encounter, she ensured they were confined to one area of the ship and immediately contacted the authorities." The longer Murph spoke, the more their voice sounded like a modulated robot. Boris and Jolene could only sense each other in the wireless digital space, but back in her quarters, both burst into laughter.

"Her actions were logical and effective in preventing further damage to the vessel. Pursuit of the thieves resulted in the majority of the Eldritch sushi being recovered and a hefty bounty being claimed. Her leadership under intense situations is undoubtable, along with the ability to deliver desired results. Furthermore-"

Erabella held up a hand and scribbled so hard that her holopad started to fragment before reshaping. "Thank you for the elaborate explanation and endorsement of your fellow employee. This performance review finds you adequate for Galaxy Waffles employment and you may resume your duties."

Murph broke down into tinier versions of themselves, each one gave the dining room cameras a thumbs up before cartwheeling out of the dining room, "Yay!" they shouted in a helium toned chorus.

The shrill tones hurt Jolene's ears, but the frustration on Erabella's face was priceless. She rolled her eyes, barely audibly grumbling, "Kyanese Unions"

"Employee Boris, please report for your performance review." She stared at the nearest camera unblinking. Jolene felt a real chill down her spine. Boris and Jolene both pulled back into their bodies, looked at each other, and shook their heads.

"Remember, don't-"

Boris waved three arms behind him. "Don't say anything unnecessary, I remember."

Jolene linked her mind back into the cameras and this time flipped between them to avoid raising Erabella's suspicions. Boris walked in and bowed just as he had before. Erabella smiled and Jolene felt her fingers ball up. She remembered how much the woman thrived on deference.

"Won't you join me?" Erabella asked and Boris answered by strolling forward pushing the chair aside to sit cross-legged at the table. His head and chest easily cleared the edge.

"I doubt the chair is in my weight class." He added and Erabella giggled as she began a new entry on her holopad. "Please state your name, employee ID, and model for the record."

"Boris Employee ID 373 autonomous military battle droid." Boris didn't sit and kept his red eyes to the usual four.

"Before this series of incidents took place, where were you?" One of Erabella's eyes fixed on Boris, the other rolled around, looking at each camera. Jolene shivered again at the mechanical chameleon eye effect.

"Repairing the kitchen and preparing meals." One of Boris' arms scratched the top of his head. "I don't want to be rude, but uh your eye, Ma'am." Boris pointed at one of his larger eyes. Erabella's eye scanning the room stopped and focused on him.

"Too distracting?" She smiled her neon blue lips at Boris like a cat flirting with a mouse.

"Not at all. I was uncertain if that was intentional or a malfunction."

"I can assure you that my augments are top of the line with built in diagnostics that would report such a failure. Kind of you to ask. If I ever need it, I'll be sure to have you check my diagnostic reports." The platinum skinned woman smiled, her voice dropped to a husky tone as she stared at Boris.

"A generous offer, but one I fear I am unqualified to take advantage of, if you need catering done or a weapon system calibrated, I'm your droid, but the only one I can repair is me." Boris couldn't blush but he could stutter and Jolene heard at least three in that last statement.

Erabella looked him up and down. "A free A.I. like you, I'm sure you could think of something." She ran her metallic fingers over the table, drawing deep circles on the metal. The scraping was like sandpaper and needles in Jolene's ears. Boris' dome shrank into his chest cavity as she continued. Then her face smoothed over and she cracked off, "How did you participate in the de-escalation of the first encounter?"

Boris' head slowly rose out of his chest. "Oh, I implied my thermometer was able to detect and neutralize hostiles."

Erabella clapped lightly on the palm holding her pen. "Very clever, using basic psychology to bring them in line." Jolene wanted to turn on the speakers and scream at the woman. Boris' tactics were the same as hers! "And I understand that you were assaulted and drugged during the second encounter?"

"Yes, but-" Boris began and Erabella held up a finger.

"On behalf of Galaxy Waffles headquarters, we offer our sincere sympathies that your state of consciousness and bodily autonomy were violated. In consideration of your military service and the events you experienced, we are prepared to overlook the decommissioned munitions you smuggled aboard." Erabella's smile and appreciative glances continued. Jolene wanted to vent her silicone ass into space. She'd bet her tips for a week that O.D. had provided the footage of the shell casings. Erabella's little speech was a toxic little cocktail of threats and niceties.

"I am afraid to say your portion of the bounty will be used in part to repair the damage to the hull. It still leaves you with a portion and if I could, I would make sure the ones who planned and ordered you into the situation were punished, but regulations are regulations."

Boris' six pairs of hands twitched at the end of that little speech.

"Are there any other questions?"

Erabella looked him up and down again. "Sadly, no. You are deemed an exemplary Galaxy Waffles employee and may continue your duties." Boris nodded and bowed, crossing three arms across his chest.

"Employee Jolene report for the rest of your review." Jolene returned to her body, grabbed her pillow and screamed into it for all she was worth. Murph's union protected them. Boris was apparently Erabella's type, which made her uncomfortable for an entire list of reasons. Jolene threw the pillow down and tried to swallow the fact that Erabella would screw her over no matter what she said or did. She took a deep breath and stepped out in her uniform, brushed down her nebula print pants and straightened her brown shirt. Boris came down the hall with his usual metal march.

"So that was-" he paused, and Jolene could practically hear the databases in his head looking for the proper word.

"Obvious and uncomfortable?" she offered. Boris gave six pairs of thumbs up in answer.

"Well, she's pretty much set me up to take all the

punishment. So, let's see how bad this gets." Boris' immense hand closed over her wrist soft as a giant petting a kitten.

"Don't say anything unnecessary, and she can't do as much." Boris cautioned..

Jolene patted his hand. He let go as she walked towards the dining room.

"Please don't waste any more time." Erabella snapped towards the chair. Jolene plastered the smile she used for the worst customers on her face. "You have your crew's loyalty and respect. Traits that Galaxy Waffles appreciates in its leaders."

Jolene nodded and waited for the inevitable to happen.

"However, per Regulation 9339, all workplace harassment and bullying will result in immediate termination. The employee can consent to fines, employee mediation, sensitivity training, and weekly reviews." Erabella waved a hand and a holographic recording of the moment where Jolene threatened O.D. with the performance review played out. "So, given your perfect example of what not to do, how do you wish to proceed?"

Erabella steepled her fingers again and waited. Boris' program sorted through all the regulations, sections, and subsections. Nothing. There was no way to argue this. Jolene let her smile break and rubbed her cheeks before looking at the frozen holo.

"Well, shit." was all she could say to hold off the decision she had to make.

RESULTS

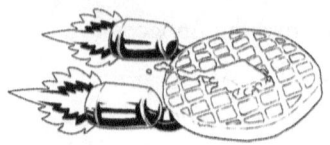

Erabella's neon blue eyebrows drew together. "Refrain from profanity in the workplace." She recited with machine precision and fluent human bitch.

Jolene rubbed her eyes with her fingertips, not bothering to point out the profanity regulation was only relevant while the diner was open to the public. "Era, give it a rest already."

Erabella's mouth dropped open and her hand rested against the bust of her snow white power suit. "I have no idea what you are implying, but my conduct has been in line with all regulations and that nickname is inappropriate."

Jolene ignored the urge to smash her face on the table again and thought back to different days. "Erabella, can we please speak privately?"

The platinum coloring of her skin made social ticks harder to read, but slowly her metal fingers clicked off the recording device.

"You have one minute," she said, looking at her metal sculpted nails.

"I'll pay the fines and take the weekly reviews, but I won't do mediation or sensitivity training. O.D. would have prevented us from recovering the sushi and claiming

the bounty. I didn't do it the right way, but I got it done."
Jolene crossed her arms and blew some red hair out of
her eyes.

"Galaxy Waffles Regulations don't exist for your
convenience, they are the bulwark that maintains the
standard of this company. You will go through mediation
and sensitivity training or you'll be terminated." Erabella
brushed her nails against the lapel of her suit. "You have
twenty five seconds left."

"Ok, best of luck with my replacement."

Erabella arched an eyebrow. "And why would I need
any luck?" She snapped her fingers and a holographic list
of employees auto scrolled over the table. "You may be a
rotten apple Jolene, but the company has plenty of quality
to replace you with."

Jolene didn't need Boris' program for her next move.

"And how many of them will take this posting?"
Erabella looked from the list to Jolene and back again.

"They would gladly-"

"Be put out in untamed space, fight for survival, be
away from their families, miss promotions, and live on
rationed supplies?" Jolene looked from the list to Erabella
and sucked on her teeth.

"Tall order, hope you find the right person cause if
they die, quit, or fail to meet numbers, well you might
end up on my side of the table answering questions like:
Where did your judgment fail? How much is this costing
us? Why did you fire the previous employee? What will
you be doing to rectify this situation?" Jolene was, of

course, recording every moment including the one where Erabella snapped her pen in half and dug her metal painted nails into the table. She generally looked like she wanted to pummel Jolene into beef tartar. If she pushed it any harder, Erabella might actually snap so Jolene stood and began to walk away.

"Think my times up. I'll start packing. Send my full severance package today please," she called over her shoulder.

"This review is not over yet. Sit and I will render my final judgment." Jolene returned to her chair, but didn't sit, staring the woman down as she clicked on the recorder.

"Due to the violation of Regulation 9339, Jolene will pay fines and be subject to a month of daily reviews. Given her previous service and the duress of the circumstances, we will waive the mediation and sensitivity training.." The last part came through gritted teeth that Jolene could have sworn would bite through steel and then she clicked off the recorder.

"Send me a copy of the authorization for the Voltstriker. Further threats to company personnel will result in fines deducted from your pay and legal action." Erabella added, slipping on her designer sunglasses.

Jolene stood, facing the hatred behind those mirrored lenses. She smiled so hard it hurt her cheeks, all the while reminding herself not to just grab Erabella by the hair and drag her out. "Thank you for the added incentives. Now get off my ship."

Erabella's smile was at odds with her eyes that said

burn in hell before putting her ice white sunglasses on. "O.D. initiate review mode."

"Review mode initiated," he responded over the speakers.

"I'll be getting reports every twelve hours and remember it never was and never will be your ship." She strode off towards the doors, slamming them open and re-entering her executive yacht.

Jolene started walking to her room, then jogging, and finally running. Gasping for air with her legs burning, all felt better than thinking about what Erabella had done. The words she'd wanted to scream still burned in her gut and throat. She stomped over to her room's tiny toilet cubicle. Falling to her knees accepting the pain, she bent over and screamed her guts out into the empty bowl.

A metal knocking behind her stopped her mid-scream.

"Bad time?" Boris stood at the bathroom door, one hand cupped behind his head while his other fingers interlocked, twiddling their thumbs.

"Pretty sure we've got nothing but bad times ahead of us." Jolene turned over, leaning on the walls of the toilet cubicle.

"There were good times?" Boris asked with a deadpan tone. Jolene spat out a laugh and pushed her hair back.

"Well, then the bad times are gonna get worse." She hit the word bad louder and kicked the wall opposite of her at the end of the statement.

"The review mode?" Boris stepped in, sitting cross-legged, his servos and hydraulics filling the bathroom with noise.

"That's the tip of the shitty iceberg and you know it." Jolene rested her forehead on her knees.

"Well, when the month is over it will-"

"Won't be just for a month," Jolene said between her knees. "Every mistake O.D. reports is gonna add days and weeks to it."

"Well the leverage we have-" Boris started rationalizing and Jolene didn't wait for him to finish.

"Ain't gonna stop him from doing his job. She scares him more than we do, and for once, I don't blame him." She leaned her head back, hoping repeated taps on the back of her skull would shake loose an idea. At this point, she'd won the battle, but not the war. Boris shuffled over until he sat opposite of her just outside the booth. One pinky popped open, a familiar antenna showing and Boris nodded.

"We have privacy for five minutes. When battles were against me and there was nothing else to be done, I called for reinforcements. Time to call yours."

Jolene looked at Boris' red eyes and rubbed her temples. Her brain felt like a spinning top spitting out different colors of emotions splattering them all over each other. Sorting through the mess made it harder to click in on what he meant.

"Orzhan?"

Boris nodded. Jolene groaned at the idea of going above Erabella's head. Even if it worked, people like her didn't forgive or forget their authority being undermined.

The other options were resigning or termination and taking severance. Last time she'd looked there was enough credits to get her close to Earth and not much else.

"What could he do?" Jolene asked, curious to see what Boris would say.

"Reassign her to waste management?" They both laughed at the idea of Erabella managing every species of excrement and the paperwork that went with it. One of Boris' hands showed fingers in three, three, zero. Not long left.

"Can't use anything on the ship. Either O.D. will report it or she'll trace it." Jolene reasoned, and Boris nodded in agreement.

"We're stopping at Horsehead for repairs and resupply. Use the starport's systems." He added. Jolene nodded, calm hope replacing her burning urge to scream at Erabella. Boris closed his pinky and O.D. pixelated into the room, marshmallow teeth on full display, his bacon eyebrows and chocolate chip eyes raised in wide-eyed innocence.

"Confidential conversations are not permitted on Galaxy Waffle vessels during review mode. Please refrain from using devices that prevent me from fulfilling my company approved functions."

"Are you making unfounded accusations of your crew?" Boris' dome spun back to look at Jolene and in a conspiratorial whisper said loud enough for O.D. to hear, "Looks like he might be degrading faster than we thought."

"My statements are based on logical deductions from current circumstances." The waffle's smile stretched past the point of wholesome and O.D. swelled to stare down at Boris. "Logical deductions are not infallible. Something a fellow A.I. and machine should be able to understand unless you're the one in need of servicing?" O.D. hissed. Boris answered by stepping through O.D. one of his fingers sparking causing pixelation and distortions across every waffle square and frizzing his pompadour.

"Tha- iszzzaaa-dig-dig-digital- ass- assa- assault of company property!" O.D. shouted with a hefty side of static noise.

"Include it in the report," Boris said over his shoulder, leaving the room, hopefully to see how long before they'd arrive.

"Gladly," O.D. answered, then frowned as a message automatically played.

"Requested files are corrupted and can't be retrieved." He fried himself black from waffle to bacon brows to marshmallow teeth, even melting his chocolate chip eyes. "You unprofessional garbage can!"

Jolene had long suspected that O.D.s vocabulary was limited by company programming and giggled as he tried and failed to swear. The blackened waffle with melted eyes and charred facial bits turned on her. "Improper conflict resolution between employees will be noted in your first report." Then popped out of the room.

Jolene groaned and kicked the bathroom wall again. Everyday was a fight to stay sane and polite. Now she was going to have to fight to stay away from the maple syrup and O.D.s motherboard as well. "We'll be docking at the Horsehead Starport in 72 hrs." Boris' red text bubble popped in their chat. Jolene did the math... six reports from now she could reach out and hopefully get Erabella off her back. She walked over to her bed, fell face first, groaned, and drifted off into exhausted sleep.

THE NEW NORMAL?

Jolene woke up on her day off to her H.U.D. flashing maple syrup brown. Multiple employee surveys and petitions about the color and even the catchy "No brown eye!" campaign hadn't persuaded Corporate from using that particular shade for their official communications. Delete and ignore were greyed out. Jolene groaned at the sender name before mentally clicking on accept.

"EMPLOYEE JOLENE,

DUE TO YOUR INEFFECTIVE CONFLICT RESOLUTION BETWEEN EMPLOYEE BORIS AND EMPLOYEE O.D. YOUR DAILY REVIEWS ARE BEING EXTENDED FOR ANOTHER WEEK. GALAXY WAFFLES REGULATION 9999 SECTION A SUBSECTION 99 STROKE A1 STATES IF AN EMPLOYEE'S CONDUCT WARRANTS REPEATED REVIEW EXTENSIONS; THEY WILL BE TERMINATED WITHOUT SEVERANCE AND LEFT AT THE NEAREST HABITABLE WAYPOINT. PLEASE KEEP THIS IN MIND IN YOUR DAY-TO-DAY CONDUCT.

WITH RESPECT,

SECTOR SUPERVISOR ERABELLA."

Jolene's solitary silver lining was that the email didn't include audio. She sent it to trash and enjoyed the burning dumpster play through its animation loop. The envelope sprite tossed about until it floated up and dissolved into ashes.

JOLENE (CHAT MESSAGE)

"How long before we're at the Horsehead Starport?"

She asked in the group chat.

MURPH (CHAT MESSAGE)

"Be there in time for my Nonna's dinner."

Jolene rubbed her eyes through the gangster drawl.

"Murphreezius Imital, I am not in the mood." She growled over the comms.

"64 hours till we reach port, Captain." The words came in a panicked rush.

"Ok, sorry for playing that card, Murph. Woke up to Erabella up my ass." She grumbled the apology, scratched the back of her head, hoping she could put the platinum anxiety inducing nightmare behind her soon.

"I mean, I always sensed something between you two but I didn't think it was that intimate." Murph teased.

Jolene cut off the sniggers over the comms by setting Murph to mute for the rest of the day. Three separate metal drumbeats shook her door in its frame. She jumped from the bed, fists up, one of her eyes linked to the camera outside her door. Boris waved to the camera and held up a platter. "Caffeine and protein so you can slay your day efficiently." Boris said in a rumbling sing-song voice.

"Open," Jolene grunted. The door complied.

She crossed her arms, trying to look like the stern manager Galaxy Waffles regulations demanded. A salty meat aroma rushed into the room. Bacon. Behind that, she inhaled apples and cinnamon, her favorite oatmeal flavor. Boris held out the platter and Jolene shook her head. She would not be startled and bought off in less than five minutes. Then she saw the mug. Boris played dirty. Bittersweet notes filled her nose and made her heart skip a beat. Coffee. Her stomach betrayed her with a rumble. Boris looked at the platter, then at her and didn't say a word.

"Shut up and get in here!"

Boris set the tray on her bed and inquired: "So, what did our fair-minded and impartial supervisor have to say?"

Jolene snorted. "She extended the daily reviews for another week."

"Why?"

"Ineffective conflict resolution between you and O.D."

One of Boris' arms rubbed the back of his head. "Sorry."

Jolene waved off the apology and took up the coffee. Closing her eyes at the warm cup, inhaling the bittersweet scent and exhaling annoyance. The first sip was creamy with notes of vanilla.

"Is it good?"

Jolene gave him one thumb up. "Perfect."

Boris answered with three pairs of thumb ups.

A new message popped up in her H.U.D. from O.D. the subject line read:

MANAGER IMPROVEMENT TRAINING.

JOLENE,

PLEASE COMPLETE THE ATTACHED TRAINING MATERIALS TODAY. IN CONSIDERATION OF MY MANY ONGOING DUTIES, FINISHING THEM BEFORE MY NEXT REPORT TO ERABELLA WOULD BE SEEN AS MOST EFFICIENT AND RESPONSIBLE. I HOPE YOU WILL SEE THIS AS AN OPPORTUNITY FOR GROWTH AND IMPROVEMENT.

WITH ALL DUE RESPECT,

O.D.

Jolene rubbed her eyes and tried to sip away the knot of annoyance building in her brain again.

"Let me guess, our waffle overlord gave you marching orders?" Boris flipped his finger with the jammer open, but Jolene shook her head.

"Our invaluable corporate asset provided me with training materials. After I finish this wonderful breakfast,

I'll be doing that. Does anything else require my attention?"

"The hole in the hull and my kitchen need repairs. Can't use FTL or we'll get turned inside out."

Jolene nodded.

"How are we paying for it?"

"Oh, corporate insurance already approved repairs and kitchen upgrades." Boris' Russian baritone went up an octave on the word upgrades. "I'm going to shop till I drop!"

Jolene forced herself to swallow the coffee in her mouth or it would come flying out her nose. "Good to know. Now please excuse me. I'd like to eat my breakfast in peace."

Boris' three right arms saluted, and he marched out.

She managed one more sip before O.D. pixelated into the room with a full marshmallow toothed smile. "I noticed you read the training materials message. I hope you'll be starting them soon. I will transmit my next report in three hours." His voice sing-songed with syrupy sweetness. Jolene ripped a piece of bacon and chewed with more force than necessary, before smiling. O.D.'s bacon eyebrows twitched at the sounds.

"I'll get started after I eat breakfast. Was there anything else?"

Round black glasses took shape over his eyes, while pale light shaped into a clipboard in his hands.

"Yes, our quarterly quotas have been adjusted in order to include ship repairs and upgrades." This time, coffee rushed out of Jolene's nose. Her nostrils flared with hot pain. She wanted to scream and swear. Instead, she set the coffee down and began to furiously dab away the mess on her shirt.

"What?"

O.D. looked her up and down and adjusted his glasses. "Insurance agreed our claim was valid, but using it also means our premiums go up. That increased cost must be covered." His hologram may not be smiling, but his tone screamed happy dance. Jolene rubbed her eyes at the stabbing headache behind them. Glaring like she wanted to feed him to a blender wouldn't help anything.

"What are the new quotas?"

"My calculations put the minimum at 150,000 credits." O.D. said it like it was routine.

Jolene stopped rubbing her eyes and looked at the full-time snitch with her best poker face. At the moment, she didn't care that it meant he could read her like an open book.

"Come again?" She asked.

"The minimum to cover the repairs and turn a quarterly profit is 150,000 credits." O.D. repeated.

Jolene laughed a laugh that would have had most people reaching for a tranq gun. That insane number could have paid for a new ship! In fact, she wasn't sure the diner ship was worth that much after all the wear and tear.

"Even with the bounty on those two idiots, our total profit so far is 30,000."

"29,532.23 credits total." O.D. was back to his full marshmallow smile. Jolene hated every inch of it.

"The quarter ends in a month!" She shrieked, but the holo continued smiling.

"Given the mandatory ship repairs, Supervisor Erabella feels that an extension would only be fair." O.D. continued baiting.

Jolene didn't bite. Instead ,she crossed her arms over her coffee-stained shirt and waited. "An extra week will be enough time to fulfill the adjusted quotas."

She did not scream or threaten to deep fry his hardware no matter how much she wanted to see him sizzle into nothing and never return.

"Please leave." The words came out quiet and O.D.'s bacon eyebrows lowered in annoyance.

"Procrastination is not a-"

He stopped dead short when Jolene opened her eyes and vanished in an instant. She mentally called up the group chat with Boris and Murph. End-to-End encryption and about four other layers of security should keep O.D. out of the loop.

She attached a recording of O.D.'s ultimatum. Both of them reacted with the same calm, professional murderous threats she expected.

JOLENE (CHAT MESSAGE)

"Are you done?"

She asked five minutes later.

BORIS (CHAT MESSAGE)

"Just getting started."

MURPH (CHAT MESSAGE)

"I gotsa cement suit perfect for

blocking his signals, then alls we need is a black hole, and bada bing bada boom! No one'll ever find a molecule."

Jolene entered into the chat.

JOLENE (CHAT MESSAGE)

"GUYS, ENOUGH! Murph, keep the ship flying as fast as you can. The sooner we get to Horsehead, the sooner Orzahn can help us. Boris, itemize what you need for the kitchen. If the numbers get big enough, that should keep O.D.'s attention."

Murph sent a GIF of themselves saluting while Boris sent a mad laughing scientist including the audio file. Maniacal cackling filled Jolene's ears and she couldn't help smiling. Jolene sent two thumbs up and one last message.

JOLENE (CHAT MESSAGE)

"All we can do is play by the rules until we have a move to make."

Jolene smiled for a microsecond before the entire ship shook them all off their feet.

"Excuse me!" A nasal demanding voice punched through their comms, followed by more ship shakes. "Can I get some service!" Jolene turned towards the front doors. In between the words were bright blue flashes of their ship's shields. A rounded flat shape drew back and smacked them repeatedly. She squinted but couldn't see more.

Boris stomped into the dining room, each step hammered into Jolene's ears as he magnetized and demagnetized the bottoms of his feet.

"Who the hell-" Boris didn't finish before connecting to the comms. "We are closed for repairs, please stop assaulting our ship!"

For a few moments, it stopped until the comms screeched into every hall.

"Who the hell do you think you are talking to me like that!" She overwhelmed every speaker, sending sonic needles into everyone's brains. Even Boris took a step back.

Murph stumbled their way into the dining room, their head sealed off in an astronaut helmet with the words soundproof across the face shield. An oblong shadow filled the room, and all three of them stared into an eye as big as the window. Jolene's H.U.D. popped with an explanation.

FLUKER – GARGANTUAN SIZED SPECIES CAPABLE OF SWIMMING THROUGH SPACE, AND REQUIRE SPECIAL MATTER COMPRESSION TECHNOLOGY TO SHRINK BEFORE INTERACTING WITH MOST SPECIES.

Jolene took in all the words as the customer's voice came through again.

"That disrespect will be reported to corporate! Now open up, that little hole isn't an excuse to stop working."

O.D. projected between the inner and outer doors of the ship. "Our chef is correct Ms.-"

"Krillsworth, and it's Mrs." The giant whale shaped bitch intoned.

"Mrs. Krillsworth, normally we would be happy to

serve you, but these are extraordinary circumstances."

The giant eye didn't blink.

"Did I ask for a lecture from a pixel puppet? Let me answer that for you. Open up and give me a table! I want one ton of eggs, half a ton of waffles, and you better not overcook the bacon -"

As the list of demands continued, a malicious lightbulb went off in Jolene's brain.

"Do you want shrapnel with that?" Jolene asked, smiling as she said the words.

"What?" Mrs. Krillsworth floated back from the window with her mouth hanging open.

"Since you've chosen to ignore everything but your own wants, I'm just trying to make sure we live up to your expectations." Jolene said it before filling the dining room with pictures of the destroyed kitchen.

"Broken glass and eggs is a classic" Murph said, flipping open their astronaut helmet. They were also smiling.

"Da, and bacon with steel splinters is a good serving of iron and protein." Boris said, and crossed his arms.

"Wait... I well this is" Her rounded nose moved between the three of them. The blood vessels in her eyes bulging red. "This is-" Her chest puffed up and everyone flinched, preparing for another ear stabbing.

"Ms. Krillsworth, their point is that the kitchen is broken. We do not wish to serve you unsafe food. Here are coordinates to the next nearest Galaxy Waffles diner" O.D. said it all so quickly and politely, the giant demanding space whale flicked its tail and grumbled into the inky blackness. O.D. turned to them showing a full smile that raised the hairs on Jolene's skin.

"It's a shame that order could have put a big dent in your quota." O.D. said and blinked away.

"Asshole!" Jolene, Boris and Murph shouted at the same time.

TRANSMISSION

"And remember, at Galaxy Waffles, communication is key!" The film reel started scrolling. It listed everyone responsible for the brain cell barbecue she just sat through. Everything in the training videos made Jolene question reality.

The black and white animated waffle mascot that could have been O.D.'s musical theater twin. The relentlessly peppy attitude of the trainer bordering on psychotic killer happy complete with original song and dance routines! The nightmare soundtrack included:

Scrubbing Stress

Edible Chemistry

Life is like a plate

Rules are Friends!

Someone in training had too much time and budget. She sent off her perfect test results to O.D. and made a duplicate file, just in case. Then gravity pulled her down onto the bed and into a dead sleep.

"We are one light-year away from Horsehead." Announced O.D. waking Jolene a few hours later over the comms.

She stretched and processed the fact she'd slept for over sixty hours. Months of double and triple shifts meant opportunities to sleep in were like winning a lottery ticket. Cash in and splurge was her M.O. She was swimming in her 5XL t-shirt, but the size also meant it was more of a nightshirt. She smoothed it out, smiling at the broken white circuits on a black background, their frayed ends shooting words in a lightning looking font: "*SUCK MY VOLTAGE.*"

It'd been ages since she'd been to a concert. Hopefully, she could find their tour schedule at the starport.

"Ship holding together?" She thought to Murph through the comms while pulling back the hair sitting on her forehead.

"Like a champ," they answered. "Already spread the word to insurance approved shops. Got us a bidding war on who can do it faster and cheaper." They finished with a cartoon villain chuckle.

"Murph, please don't cheap out on fixing something that keeps us alive!" Jolene washed her face before heading to the dining room.

"Those repair monkeys are lucky they get to touch her, let alone do repairs! If Corporate didn't treat credits like their main squeeze, I could have the tools to fix this on board." Jolene rolled her eyes at the gripe. It was one of Murph's favorite go to rants about being a Corporate owned franchise ship. How they owned nothing and just rented. Which was true,

O.D. monitored and documented every molecule of oxygen and ounce of fuel. It wasn't any less annoying when he kept pointing out problems and offering no solutions. One search on the net and she could find countless articles about ship AIs saving their crews and their credits. What kind of economic sadist created someone like O.D.? None of the answers would help her mood, so she forced herself to focus on Murph's words and tried to play along.

"You're the cat's meow with a torch and wrench." Jolene tried on the gangster accent Murph always used. For a moment, there was silence.

"Leave the slick talk to the slick, toots. Half a light-year away, go watch the light show." Murph closed the line.

Jolene huffed her way into a booth. Murph's teasing faded as they got closer. She smiled. In just a few hours she'd call Orzhan. With his help they could put Erabella and O.D. behind them and get back to running the ship.

She watched the multi-colored shape ahead of them grow brighter and more defined. Dark gold light mixed with flaring red that softened with bright orange. At this distance, it looked like a star, but that would have cooked their atoms to a crisp. As they closed the distance, the truth was much weirder. It was a massive Horsehead.

"They cleared us to dock at the biggest Godfather reference in the galaxy!" Murph announced over the ship's comms.

"You really need new material!" Jolene answered.

"Classics don't need updating!" Murph countered.

"But there is more than one!" She snapped, and Murph only grumbled back until they segued so hard it could have been a barrel roll.

"Crew 3371 please take a moment to admire the wonderful light show provided by Spendicus Incorporated." Murph said it with an announcer voice, and Jolene let it go, turning to the window. Orange flames burned into blue and ended with white tips from the mane. The boosters used to move it away from debris and space events were blood red. Its eyes were dancing with green holographic sparkles. The golden head and neck reflected light like a disco ball. The quintillionaire, Maximus Spendicus, saw an opportunity in the multi-species push into untamed sectors of the Milky Way.

He'd struck a deal with the Galactic Government allowing him to build and manage a casino that doubled as a starport. The casino provided maintenance and employment, all while providing a fixed waypoint for settlers. The representatives signed without the input of a single lawyer. No one could have predicted the gaudy monstrosity he had in mind. Part of the contract's fine print also allowed him to pump out ads on all frequencies nonstop.

"Murph, please tell me-"

"Already paid for ad free airtime." They

interrupted. The ship angled towards the lines leading to the fiery mane. The air crackled for a moment and Jolene didn't look away from the window. A throat clearing sound came from behind, and she still didn't turn around. She watched O.D.'s expression sour in the window's reflection.

"I have some unfortunate news." He said with the smile he knew Jolene hated. She turned around in the booth, trying to keep her face neutral, but still felt her teeth grinding hard enough to crack walnuts in their shells. "Your test results were corrupted mid-transmission. I'll need you to retake the training class so that we can include them in the next report. I know you were eager to get off the ship and stretch your legs, but this takes priority." O.D. held his gloved hands together. His eyes were at a downcast angle. It was the worst kind of insincere sitcom acting, but Jolene didn't need a poker face for the smile she gave him.

"Oh, that is unfortunate. If you'd alerted me sooner, I'd have provided you with this backup copy." She flicked a finger in his direction. O.D. 's eyes became loading bars then chocolate chips again, his malicious smile became a frown.

"But a copy isn't-"

Jolene held up a hand. "I can optionally duplicate all training and test results just in case this sort of thing happens. It seems strange to me you weren't aware of that? Also seems strange that it took you this long to bring this to my attention. Can you explain these repeated oversights?"

O.D. put balled fists on his rounded edges "You were sleeping, and I had to keep Boris in check. Crazy bot was planning to spend the entire insurance payout on kitchen upgrades. As for the backup copies, I knew of them, but no one makes them because instances of file corruption are so rare."

Jolene gave him her best wide-eyed expression. "Really? Well, how rare is it for an A.I. to miscalculate arrival times, fail at sending emails, and assume their crew doesn't have common sense habits?"

Jolene waggled her three raised fingers between his eyes. O.D.'s golden waffle skin started leaking red jam.

"I don't have that statistic." his mouth moved to say more, but nothing came out. Jolene seized the moment.

"It would be best if you started a self diagnostic to determine the source of these repeated instances." O.D.'s mouth opened, but she wouldn't let him break her momentum. "We'll be in a restricted area. Diagnostic mode automatically locks your access to your core, so that will keep the repair crews away. Correct me if I'm wrong, but I believe corporate regulations mandate this sort of procedure when time allows. Do you know that regulation?"

Jolene brushed her fingernails on her shirt and admired them for a moment as O.D. growled out between blackened marshmallow teeth.

"You're not wrong. Regulation #005 indicates repeated performance failures in A.I. mandates a full system diagnostic."

Jolene snapped her fingers then gave her own best insincere disappointed expression.

"Well darn, that means you'll be offline for the first forty-eight hours at the starport. Such a shame."

O.D. didn't say another word. Didn't even change his expression. He just disappeared. Jolene happy danced.

"Did not know bean bags could dance." Boris said, leaning on the doorframe, his four eyes yellow with amusement. Jolene backed into a moonwalk that ended with a spin and bow.

"Basic rule for happy dances. No one cares what it looks like, just do what feels good."

Boris responded by standing ramrod straight, his hydraulics hissed while his metal gears ground. His torso leaned forward, then clicked till he was straight again. Half his arms bent back at the elbows while the other half bent forward. Jolene rolled her eyes.

"A robot doing the robot, real original!" Jolene said between laughs. Boris continued popping and locking his feet and arms.

"Time to cut a rug!" Murph's mobster accent came out of a petite woman in a ballroom red dress spinning to the center of the diner floor. She writhed her hips with her arms over her head, and a pencil thin mustachioed man slid in behind her rose between his teeth. Drums and brass sounded over the ship comms. Boris spun his torso. Murph danced in and out of Murph's arms. Jolene fist pumped and stomped her feet. Sometimes you just gotta happy dance.

Thirsty six hours passed. Jolene took time to plan her doses of empathy blockers. Boris sanded away the vacuum pressure damage and polished it to a high shine. Murph, with their usual overcoat and three-piece suit, stepped off the ship into the hangar.

"Shopping, here I come." Boris rubbed his palms together. The sound reminded Jolene of steel wool scrubbers grinding against each other.

"And I gotsa union to report to!" The tip of Murph's teardrop head shifted into a fedora and they tipped it towards them.

"And I've got a call to make. Meet up at the Black Stallion later?" Jolene asked, and they all nodded at each other. They each took a different exit.

With her first step on the starport a frenzied whinny filled the air! A giant horse and armored rider galloped down the hall, metal armor clanging, hooves thundering. His white-hot lance tip lowered, aiming for her chest. Instinct pumped adrenaline through her every vein, but horse and rider took up the hall.

She couldn't outrun it. So she stepped in, hoping to sidestep the lance. Instead, hot current crackled onto her skin raising the hairs on her head. Horse and rider passed through her.

"Heed my call, fellow warrior, for a contest of blood and steel has joined this illustrious arena of competitions! Combat Cavalry!" The faux medieval voice echoed through the helmet. Jolene cursed as her bio-tech systems reported the starport had loaded an advertisement into her eyes.

"Witness valiant knights meet on the field of battle and earn-"

"Terminate Ad!" she mentally shouted and watched her pixel animated dumpster grow to the size of the horse and rider then have its flap and swallow them whole. She blinked it away and proceeded into the organized chaos of Horsehead Starport.

Without thinking about it, she joined the flow of the crowd. Aliens and humans alike hustled and bustled about in every variety of limbs and colors. Shop vendors with holographic signs lined the edges of the walkway, baiting and sometimes pulling people from the flow of foot traffic. All the while people floated on taxi discs to their destinations. Jolene mentally linked with the starport's network and mapped her way to the nearest long-distance phone. Stepping into the press of bodies and keeping pace was a bit like an overbooked dinner rush.

She focused on her meeting with Orzhan. If he

demoted Erabella she'd get a pay cut, and if Jolene's evidence was good enough maybe she'd get fired! That was a lightyear longshot but even Starbloods were allowed to dream impossible things. In a perfect universe, he'd let her record every moment. That last one took up enough mental bandwidth she'd nearly missed the directions from her map as they rattled off inside her head. Several leathery elbows, webbed feet, and tail flicks later, she broke away.

She went to a private booth, paid for actual encrypted privacy, and entered Orzhan's number. The word phone was as antiquated as democracy, but it was a box that sent a signal that was received by another box many light-years away.

The black screen flickered into color, showing a skyline view of a Galaxy Waffles' owned planetoid. Bookending the transparent force field window were shelves with actual paper books! Jolene counted several years' salaries on each shelf. In the middle was a perfect white marble pillar. Orzhan floated back and forth in front of the view. At one point, the Rigani race was hunted because they looked like the Cthullians. The Milky Way soon learned they were smarter and much harder to kill. Despite looking like balls of floating blue spaghetti, they had communicated their way into a reputable place in the Galactic Government. Which Jolene always thought had to do with their passionate tempers.

"I don't care if it's a valid protein! Humans are

our biggest customer base. I would sooner put you on the menu than tofu bacon! Don't tell them-" A tentacle that ended in a serrated barb left the central mass of tentacles and waved in front of the screen. Jolene mouthed the word, 'OK.'

Orzhan's eye stalks vibrated while his solid white eyes started filling with red veins that Jolene worried would burst. "So your solution is to label it as usual! You're not worth the DNA combined to make you. Your dumbass is this close to being fired!" Two separate tentacles ending in round edged sucker tips came centimeters from touching.

"Go cry to Mom and I'll tell her you just proposed galaxy wide fraud. Then let's see who she decides to boil!" Both eyes blinked, and a shudder rippled through his center mass.

"Hey Jolene, sorry you had to hear that." Orzhan's voice came from a tentacle that ended with a little hole that one time Jolene had said looked like a straw. Orzhan had asked why her mouth and asshole shared a shape. They'd been best friends ever since.

"No worries, at least you still talk to your family. Reggie get an idea again?"

Orzhan shuddered, a pair of sucker tentacles pulling up a very nice looking bottle while a stinger tentacle stabbed and removed the cork.

"Every quarter it's something. This time the vegans got to him." Orzhan sighed and stuck his not straw tentacle into the bottle.

"Hey, he was the one who came up with Eldritch Sushi. The stuff still sells like crazy." Jolene reminded him. Orzhan answered by blinking his eye stalks, followed by an eye roll. He then focused on sips and held up a barbed tentacle, asking for a minute. After he finished, he let out a contented sigh.

"Yea, I guess. Listen Jolene, much as I appreciate you helping keep my blood pressure down, I can't help."

Jolene felt cold clench her stomach. The naïve foolish part of her brain tried to ask the truth away.

"Help with-?"

"I can't help you with Erabella."

WHERE DO WE GO FROM HERE?

Jolene closed her eyes and breathed through the impulse to shriek the word. Why? "I can explain, but it's not gonna make it any easier." Orzhan's limbs wriggled after the statement, but Jolene didn't care about his discomfort right now.

"You tore off the band aid. Might as well explain why you're leaving me to bleed out."

Orzhan's eye stalks drooped as he floated down to his marble platform.

"You're not wrong, but you're not being fair." The blue interweaving strands of his body inflated and deflated.

"And is my situation any different? Life's not fair, ain't it a bitch. Now out with it." Jolene glared at him through the demand. Orzhan's eyes rose and the hint of red veins came back.

"Don't push it."

"Or what? You'll fire me? I'll take my severance and see if Maximus is hiring."

Orzhan raised multiple barbed tentacles, and they all pointed at her. "Alright, if you wanna play it that way! How about this? Your temper has always been your biggest problem, and it's part of why you're fucked right now."

Jolene shot out of her seat.

"Easy for you to say from your literal fucking throne, you spineless sack of motherf-" she cut herself off when she noticed Orzhan had muted the call. She balled her fists, exhaled the rest of the rant, and fell back in the chair.

"You done proving me right?" His tone was sandpaper on her nerves, but she nodded.

"Ugly truth is you can do everything right and still be wrong." Orzhan put his tentacle back in the bottle of unnamed alcohol.

"Next time I'll just keep my mouth shut." Jolene tapped her head against the cushioned chair. Orzhan corked his bottle before answering.

"No, you won't. If I believed your principles that shallow, I never would have given you that ship."

Jolene snorted. "So help me keep it!"

Orzhan sighed, one tentacle putting the bottle away.

"I can't, she-"

"Sir, your mother is on line one." A reedy voice interrupted the call. Orzhan's eye stalks looked to the ceiling.

"Tell her I'm meditating and hold everything until my current call is over."

"Yes sir, I'll put the apology gifts on standby."

Orzhan grumbled about boundaries and appearances before focusing back on Jolene.

"She's not breaking any regulations." Jolene's mouth dropped open. Her brain wanted to throw words out, but she couldn't pick any.

"She's bending them, but that's what management does. Exercises appropriate judgment in each case. According to her record of conduct, she's painting you as a loose cannon who risks corporate property. There's nothing I can bring against her."

Jolene rubbed her eyes. "Transfer her! Assign her a project? Promote her back to her old job?"

He held up sucker and barbed tentacles, but no words came out. Orzhan floated up, turning to look out his window. Jolene was on the edge of her seat, hoping he'd take any of her ideas.

"She's Terra Blood." Orzhan said, eye stalks drooping.

Jolene remembered being burned while fighting a grease fire. Orzhan's words compressed that searing agony into one sentence. All his tentacles drooped; they swayed like gallows ropes as he returned to his pillar.

"Great, so I'm getting fucked because my mom didn't squeeze me out on-world?" Jolene accused.

Orzhan's eye stalks dipped up and down. Jolene slow clapped.

"Must be nice being part of the elitist assholes club."

Orzhan's limbs flared up into an undulating mass. "It's not me! Terrabloods or Starbloods, I don't care. My boss's boss made it clear. Erabella's decisions are within regulations."

Part of her considered asking to speak with them, filing a complaint, or going to the media. She shot them all down like a logical executioner. Erabella got to them first, and they'd listened. HR protected the company, not the employees. The last hurt the most if she tried to sell the headline.

"Starblood gets screwed. Same shit different sector." Jolene said it through a sneering smile before letting her head hang low, tears threatening to leave her eyes.

They'd run it as a punchline in their late-night shows. One more example for everyone born at the wrong time to keep their eyes low and their hopes small.

"Give me a reference?" Jolene asked, trying to blink away the tears, hating how they flowed down her cheeks. Wiping them away she refused to sniffle, fist pounding on her knee. "No one will take a Starblood without a guarantee!" Her voice rose so fast that by the last word that it cracked.

Orzhan sighed and shook his eyestalks back and forth. "If I give it, my career is over. Something they made clear off the record."

Neither of them suggested pleading with Erabella. An assembly line had more empathy than she did.

"Prejudicial policy is ok so long as it's not illegal and not documented. Got it." Jolene said, hating every word.

Orzhan's body deflated until the only three-dimensional parts left were his barbs and eyes. "If I had cards to play against them or her, I would."

Jolene wanted to take the words in and acknowledge them, but her brain repeated the reality she was facing. Three years of her life. She was going to lose the ship, lose Boris, lose Murph, and have no references. Even the adult industry would raise an eyebrow at the silence. "Best I can do is max out your severance. I'll throw in what I can. Should be enough credits to give you a good start." Orzhan muttered. Jolene tasted her tears before wiping away the streaks.

"I'll think about it."

"I'm so-"

Jolene cut the connection before letting him finish. After leaving the booth, she used her H.U.D. to file a refund request. She couldn't afford to waste a single credit.

The press and pace of the crowds moved Jolene along. Once again, she thanked the inventor of the empathy blockers. Her mind was an emotional storm. If she had to deal with the chaos of these streets, it would deep fry her sanity.

Jolene's thoughts kept circling back to the facts. Something she had no say in and couldn't change had decided her fate. She spat at the fact that it wasn't even new. The planets spun and stars exploded. The Milky Way had a surplus of elitist privileged assholes. Ever since the mass emigration to space, a prejudice began against the space born, the Starbloods, of the galaxy. Didn't matter what species you were. If you weren't born on-world you weren't a citizen. She'd heard all the reasons: limited resources, criminal element, tax dodgers, loner mindsets. It was a laundry list of nonsense that anyone with half a brain cell could resolve. Instead, corporations, like Galaxy Waffles, stepped in with employment and protection. She'd been in the company's citizenship lottery. That got vaporized with the whole Erabella mess. If she hadn't gotten mad, if Erabella had listened, and if wishes were horses. The idle thought reminded her she had somewhere to be.

She mentally requested the fastest route to the Black Stallion. Her H.U.D. started guiding her through the crowds she followed. Like most establishments on the starport, its name and aesthetic were on theme. A 3D holographic sign above the bar showed a gorgeous black horse charge up a hill of shimmering flowers and neon grass. It reared and whinnied in triumph as the name flashed in golden letters. At least she didn't have to worry about any edgy over the top fake bloodsports here.

Stepping in, her boots knocked instead of the usual metal slap. She looked down and gaped. He'd gotten wood floors!

"Jolene!" A warm baritone voice shouted.

Emerson stood at five foot nothing, but the bar's crowd parted for him all the same. He walked with his thumbs in the straps of his leather apron and stopped to shake limbs and slap backs. Several customers raised their glasses to him as he passed. He wiped his hands on a towel before tossing it over his shoulder.

Jolene clasped his callused Black hand, and they did their best to lovingly crush each other. They smiled though cracking knuckles and pulled each other into a back slapping embrace. When they pulled apart, she gestured at the floor.

"So, you actually did it?" She stomped her foot just

to hear it and feel the solid but subtle give of the planks.

"Yup, just about a month ago. Adds a nice touch to the place." He chuckled.

Jolene cast her eyes at the decorative horse tack on the walls. At the bouquets of alfalfa hay on the columns. The oil lamps at each table that looked so warm and natural you'd never guess they were LED. Their low glow cast the painted riders on the walls half in shadow. "Yeah, cause you were slacking on the look and feel."

"Say what you want about Maximus, when he likes an idea, he funds the crap out of it." Emerson shrugged.

"You mean he shipped this here?" Jolene knelt down to feel the grains and trace the whorls.

"Nah, crazy S.O.B. is growing his own forest on station." Emerson explained.

The expense, coordination, and technology behind maintaining a bio-dome on this floating testament of wealth made Jolene feel microscopic.

Emerson leaned down, putting a gentle hand on her shoulder. "I hear that you've come down with a stage four pain in the ass!"

"You heard right, and it looks terminal." Jolene replied through a sigh, looking up into kind eyes that brought the hurt rushing back.

Emerson's smile shrunk but didn't disappear. He rubbed his shaved head. "Don't give up before you try everything. Boris and Murph are in the back. Have a bottle on the house!"

The promised drink brought back her smile. The latest

round of Combat Cavalry announced its winner, and the bar exploded with cheers and jeers. She mouthed the word thank you. He mouthed back, winked, and motioned for her to follow. The uproar continued as credits transferred from losers to winners.

"I'll close out our tab and send my resume." She half shouted while leaning towards him.

Emerson blinked and gave her a light punch in her shoulder.

"Don't make me repeat myself!" She shouted.

He motioned with his head to the back rooms. She stopped at the doorway to watch Murph.

"And the A.I. says stop shoving your input into my output!" Murph fell over themselves and a wet jiggling smack filled the room as they fell face first on the table.

Boris' head swiveled left and right. Then swiveled to look at Jolene.

"Your face is longer than war and peace. What happened?" Boris asked.

"So, we're gonna skip Murph's joke?" Jolene asked. Boris' red eyes went dark, then red again.

"More like verbal diarrhea. Now sit and tell us the news." Boris answered her while Murph's fingertips grew into miniature hands. All ten of them flipped off Boris.

Jolene's smile died when she realized this was the last time they'd be together. Communication was easy, but being with anyone meant light-years and fuel. Two things she couldn't afford without credits. She flopped into her seat.

"Orzhan can't help us." She sighed and rubbed her aching eyes.

"Can't or won't?" Boris growled.

"Both." Jolene answered, slumping on the table resting her forehead on the cool metal.

"Well, maybe we needs to give Erabella that black hole vacation I was talking about." Murph's Chicago gangster accent was there but they didn't smile, their eyes just looked back and forth from Jolene to Boris.

"No!" Jolene and Boris shouted at the same time.

"Fine fine, let's keep it simple. I can get us a meat grinder, some shovels, and we just add a bit of fertilizer to Spendicus' forest and BAM ." Murph clapped their hands after the onomatopoeia. "Environmentally friendly revenge!"

"And back to reality, one where we don't go to jail. What's the plan Jolene?" Boris asked, ignoring Murph's dejected frown. Jolene shrugged.

Emerson walked in with bottles and cups and asked, " No plan yet?"

All three of them shook their heads.

"Well, let's hope this gives some inspiration." He poured two cups of dark liquid gold into glass tumblers. A sweet honey and rich tobacco scent filled the room. He then slid a chip of digi-vodka to Boris, 1 TB printed on it, and cleared off with a wink. Jolene rolled the tumbler in one hand, watching the whiskey rise and fall against clear walls.

She inhaled the scent and sipped on the sweet, rich

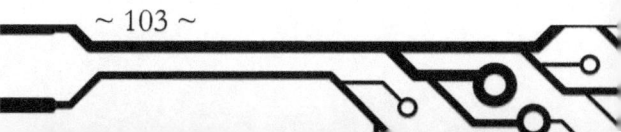

fire. When she opened her eyes, they were still waiting and watching. "Orzhan says the best he can do is terminate me and pay my severance."

"Take them for every credit you can." Boris said, plugging his digi-vodka chip into a finger.

"Well wait, hold on! What about filing against Erabella?" Murph asked, their rounded features still showing determination.

"Erabella went over Orzhan's head. He got his marching orders. And of course, the cherry on top of this bullshit sundae. I'm a Starblood and she's a Terrablood."

Boris and Murph looked at her, then each other. She smiled at the metal and gelatinous gears turning in their heads.

"Guys, there is no record to find. No leverage we can apply. I can either take my chances on the ship with those two watching every breath I take, or I get off here to see who's hiring. What would you choose?" The room stayed silent, and that was all the answer any of them needed. She raised her glass, took a quick sniff and then sucked it in. Murph followed suit. Boris' chip showed the vodka remaining with a white bar that slowly drained away.

"We could threaten a walk off?" Boris offered. Jolene put a hand on the droid's arm with the digi-vodka chip.

"And they'd laugh in your face." Jolene grumbled dejectedly.

"And what's with the 'we', you garbage can mook? If I walk off without my union's ok, they'll put me in a blender and set it for puree." Murph rested their cheek on a closed blue fist. It almost seemed like cheek and fist merged. Jolene chocked that up to the whiskey, drowning her anxiety and filling her up with a warm buzz.

"How many credits have you guys saved?" Murph asked, drumming their fingers on the table top.

"I am not investing until you deliver on that workshop you promised." Boris growled, his chip showing empty. "Emerson, another round! Make it a petabyte this time!"

"The union is still negotiating with Maximus. His last excuse was the economic upheaval of displacing any current businesses."

"Meaning he has to balance his friend's greed with his own." Boris grumbled. The door to their room slid open, and the chip flew in Boris caught it and inserted it into his finger.

"But no, come on, how much." Murph pressed for answers.

"I've got about 50,000 saved up," Boris grumbled. The one PB on his chip drained slower but still went down.

Jolene took another sip of whiskey. "About 25,000." Boris stared while Murph's mouth dropped open like a 2D cartoon from centuries ago. "They take room and board out of my pay."

"Bastards." They said at the same time. Jolene shook her head, Terrabloods didn't live tax free, but their existence didn't get added as 'Organic Upkeep' on every paycheck.

"Alright, well, I've got about 75,000. That puts us at 150,000 credits for the quota. I just checked corporate's pricing, the ship is valued at 200,000. We get that and we buy the ship. All three of us running it the way it should be." Murph said, smiling with every needle tooth on display.

Jolene choked and spat up her whiskey into her glass. Boris thumped her on the back. Both of them looked at Murph. Jolene pointed at Boris and made the talking gesture as she coughed out the whiskey in her windpipe. "How does threeway bankruptcy help us buy the ship? Even if we combined all our credits for a year we'd still be tens of thousands short. What sort of nonsense do you have planned for that?" Boris said it all in rapid fire confusion and irritation.

Murph waited for him to finish, then shifted their fingertip into a toothpick and flicked it into their mouth. The rows of needle teeth rolling up and down, moving the fake wooden pick from one side of their mouth to the other.

"I got a guy, and the only way to find out is to find out."

WE'RE GOING WHERE?

"This will never work!" Jolene grumbled. She'd lost count of the number of times she'd repeated herself.

"And your alternative is?" Boris' head swiveled back as he walked forward. Jolene stared at his four red eyes and grumbled the words the whiskey had helped her find.

"Accept reality and move on." Jolene snapped.

Murph grew eyes and a mouth on the back of their head. "So, why aren't you back on the ship packing?"

She glared at the shiny-eyed, savvy shapeshifter, but their needle toothed smile grew wider.

"Well?" Murph pressed.

A light feminine voice at the end of the hallway saved Jolene from the question.

"Welcome to Joust! The Delta Quadrant's biggest and best casino. How can we satisfy your needs?" The words went sultry at the end.

Murph's face sucked back into their head. Their walk turned into a swagger. They leaned on the attendant's podium, flicked the brim of their hat and with a gravel baritone asked, "What's a breathtaking flower like you doin' in a joint like this?"

Jolene sidestepped Boris to see a humanoid face made

of pink and white rose petals with shiny raindrop eyes. She leaned forward on arms made of interwoven green vines lined with thorns. Small yellow motes from her red petal halo filled the air. Jolene's H.U.D. popped the species name **STAMENITE** above the flower woman's head. She sucked in a breath of exhaustion as Murph, the omnivore dating machine, made friends and noticed the air had turned sweet. The more she inhaled, the more the tension knot in her stomach unwound.

"Oh, you know a lady has to photosynthesize somehow in this big old galaxy." Murph's blue skin shifted to a luminescent yellow. They leaned in a little closer, "The least I can do, when you should be on a throne of fertilizer with your own personal sun."

They rubbed the backs of their fingers on their vest as the Stamenite giggled. Jolene half expected Murph to grow a tail and bark. She wondered if that would be so bad.

"Ok, enough of that." Boris extended two of his arms and coiled them around Murph, putting them behind him.

"I would appreciate it if you refrained from excessive olfactory influence." Boris stood over her by at least a foot and when he leaned forward, it wrapped her in his shadows.

"Please." His usual Russian baritone had extra gravel in it. "Just following company policy, we must fully relax all guests before entering." The melodious charm of her voice was now a flat, sterile squeak. Boris made a few unnecessary computer sound effects that told Jolene he was enjoying himself.

"Primary policy is customer safety and satisfaction. Kyanese biology is vulnerable to your spores. You seem smart. Smart enough to know and make a few extra credits?" Boris said with a gentle accusation.

JOLENE (CHAT MESSAGE)

"Ease up before you make her cry."

Jolene messaged, noticing that thin water droplets were already darkening her white petal cheeks.

"This is for whoever is watching. They have focused cameras on us since we entered the hallway. This way we can get in and out without hassle." Boris thought back.

"How can I help correct this oversight?" Her halo of petals had shrunk inwards, the yellow motes stopping. Murph's body slid over and around Boris' arms, then reformed their black vest with red pinstripes. They took off their hat and bowed.

"Sorry they forgot to program him some manners. We're here to talk business with Mr. Calico Jack." Murph said, spinning their fedora on a finger.

Her smile returned. "Oh, yes, I see that here and he's requested a live escort. Please follow me."

Multiple holographic interfaces appeared and disappeared as they approached the doors engraved with a flaming green eyed fiery mane and blue flame-breathing horse head. Jolene understood brand recognition, but Maximus Spendicus took it to religious levels. The door slid open to show plush couches and a full charcuterie board that made Jolene's mouth water.

"Please enjoy." The Stamenite prompted.

Murph plopped themselves onto a couch, flattening out like a pancake, giving a contented sigh before rebounding to their humanoid shape. Boris stood to the side.

"Oh, please relax your gears! Our furniture can withstand up to fifty tons."

Boris looked at the armchair, then at her. With the stiff jointed motions of the ancient Earth dance, the robot, he squatted and then sat. The chair groaned but did not crumple. "Is the table the same Ms. -" Boris paused to let her answer.

"Oh! I'm such a dandelion fluff, call me Rosey! And, yes, the table is guaranteed as well." Boris shrugged, his massive metal feet slammed onto the table with enough force to make the charcuterie board jump.

Jolene whistled as micro-gravity pulses sorted it back into presentation shape before taking a seat by Murph and began filling up on grapes, cheeses, and sliced meats. When she noticed the crackers, some sandwich making happened. She didn't notice the door closing or the platform rising. Murph joined in, taking a toothpick between bites and letting it sit between their teeth. Jolene rolled her eyes at the completion of the gangster cliché.

"Rosey, what mood is Calico"o in?" Murph asked, spinning their hat on a finger.

"Oh, Mr. Calico is always in the best of moods." The thick lipped Stamenite's smile tightened as she answered.

Murph stopped twirling their hat and sat forward.

"The Union don't much like liars, Rosey."

An audible gulp followed. "Mr. Calico hasn't hissed at anyone today."

Murph eased back onto the couch and flicked two fingers at Rosey. A holographic square appeared, showing a fifty credit transfer. Rosey's white petal cheeks darkened to the same deep red as her flower halo.

"Union also loves honesty." Murph winked. Jolene silently wished Starbloods had the same Union the Kyanese loved to flex.

When the doors opened, Jolene half expected another onslaught of medieval holograms. Instead, they walked into an empty jazz lounge with a band. Boris pointed and Jolene's eyes followed to a couch on the dance floor. Multiple pairs of furry ears flicked along to the rhythm of the music.

"If you need anything else, I'm only one call away." Rosey said voice going sultry soft as her petals swayed at Murph.

Jolene turned back in time to notice her wink at Murph, who bowed and gave the back of her thorned hand a kiss. When the elevators closed, Murph stepped up, thorn dents already smoothing themselves from their face.

"Doesn't that hurt?" Jolene whispered.

"It's more like a love bite." They answered and winked before taking the lead.

Jolene and Boris shook their heads before following. The blood red sofa at the far end of the empty office was an invitation to lounge! Thick plush curves and humps

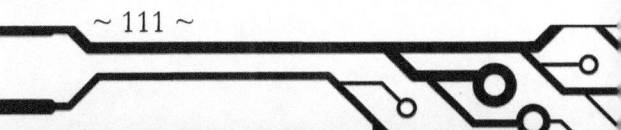

were covered in lazy smiling furry bodies. Jolene's H.U.D. popped the species name **FELINOID** over them as she looked left and right.

"Make yourselves comfortable." One of them purred out to them. A matching sofa large enough for all of them floated across the dance floor, landing without a sound. The same groaning as before interrupted the music when Boris sat, but the sofa didn't crumple. Jolene closed her eyes to savor the luxury while it lasted. Murph snapped along to the tunes until the sax and trumpet blared high and loud, supported by the piano until it all ended in a cymbal crash.

"You've got talent and room to grow. You get the gig!" A languid voice purred, five fingered paws clapped for the multi species five-piece band who all bowed and thanked in so many languages Jolene mentally shut her H.U.D. translator off before her eyeballs overflowed with multi-colored text.

"Time to go play." The languid voice ordered. Six humanoid felines protested in chorus, but stood and walked straight at a wall that opened to reveal they had a birds eye view of the casino game floor. The Felinoids stepped onto discs that floated them down into the masses.

Jolene checked her empath blocker dose. **EMPATH BLOCKERS 100% EFFECTIVE**, and swallowed the urge to run. She looked over aisles of machines and tables all playing for credits in numbers she'd only imagined existed.

"It's a pleasure to meet you." The human sized cat greeted, paws steepled. It's gorgeous black and tawny patterned fur with one green eye and one blue were all things that Jolene enjoyed looking at. But that outfit! It was straight out of a period holo, consisting of a royal purple Victorian coat with puffed sleeves and a deep blue waistcoat with a little silver pocket watch. It continued with royal purple pantaloons and deep blue leather boots. Jolene felt her cheeks get hot and didn't know whether to laugh, make obnoxious nonsensical cute sounds, or take a picture. She bit her lips to prevent the first two, snapped a quick pic with her H.U.D. and put it in the folder, 'Reasons to Smile.'

"Has good old Murphreezius told you anything?" The cat purred.

Boris and Jolene looked to their smiling blue friend, who stared back and shrugged.

"First off the clock is ticking." Murph held up one blue finger. "Second, no kitchen, no credits." They raised the second of their three fingers. "Third we don't do this, we lose Jolene, Union reassigns me, and Erabella tries to crawl into Boris' input port." Murph finished with a third finger before gesturing with their thumb at Boris.

All eight of Boris' eyes opened. "I'd rather date a Cthullian."

Calico Jack clapped and let out what Jolene thought sounded like a coughing chuckle. "Well, that's really saying something from a Cthullian War hero."

Jolene and Murph looked at Boris. The bot twiddled his three pairs of thumbs and didn't look at them.

"We aren't here for a history lesson." Boris deflected.

Calico Jack scratched behind his ear, his left boot tapping along with the scratching. "No we're not, but... that history could be what keeps you all alive."

Jolene stood up. "Ok, nope, calling this off now. No disrespect to you, Mr. Calico, or your employer, but-" She stepped forward and turned to look at Murph and Boris. "We are not doing something that could get us all killed just because Erabella's got me bent over a table! The ship's not worth it!"

Boris and Murph looked at each other then at Jolene.

"We're not doing this just for the ship," they said at the same time.

"Also, that's like saying you're not worth it. Which is mathematically wrong." Boris added.

Murph nodded along. "What the bot said."

"What the hell does math have to do with it?" Jolene was not quite shouting, but also not not shouting at the two most stubborn, wonderful idiots she knew.

"I am literally lines of numbers and equations!" All six thumbs pointed at his platoon bear insignia. "By my calculations, your value to my daily existence is astronomical. Subtracting you would be like all the galaxy's digi-vodka being deleted."

Jolene's cheeks heated till she was sure her freckles would also turn red.

Murph nodded along and tipped the brim of their hat, hiding their eyes. "Union has my back wherever I go, but I like where I am. That's rare for a Kyanese." They pulled down their hat to show actual puppy eyes, Jolene had only ever seen in cartoons. They pulled down the hat to show actual puppy eyes Murph had ever seen, and that included cartoons.

She turned away and realized her expression and wet eyes were now visible to Calico Jack. His chin rested on one paw while the other stroked his long whiskers.

"Lots of corporations in this galaxy say their crews are family. It's nice to see the real thing." Calico crooned.

Her empath blockers were wearing off, and the sensations she picked up from Calico Jack matched his words. Warm joy mixing with remembered sadness. Murph was a steady, determined tide that refused to be turned away. She felt her cheeks cool and her determination to call it all off faltered. Four smooth blue fingers rested on her right shoulder while five metal segmented fingers laid on her left.

"We will face it together and emerge victorious." Boris said with the quiet certainty Jolene depended on for the worst of shifts. Murph nodded.

"Alright, what's the job?" Jolene patted each of their hands before facing Calico Jack.

He leaned back and popped a silver fish shaped snuffbox out of his waistcoat. "I need you to cater!" He took out little green flecks and sniffed them into each nostril. "Oh, now that's good nip!"

Jolene had several questions, the first being, "How could a catering job be dangerous?"

MURPH

SPECIES: KYANESE
PRONOUNS: THEY/THEM
ABILITIES: GANGSTER MOVIES
LIKES: COOKING AND SINGING
DISLIKES: IDIOTS IN POWER
ROLE: PILOT AND MAINTENANCE

LETHAL CATERING...MAYBE?

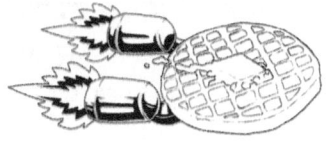

"Because we don't know what happened." Calico Jack wiped away the catnip with a deep blue handkerchief.

"To who?" Jolene pressed.

Green and blue eyes with needle thin slits fixed on her. His smile showed off canines as big as her thumbs. He licked each one. Her Empath senses picked up heat from him. Jolene blinked, and his gaze shifted to all of them.

"We dispatched a mining survey and setup crew to this asteroid field." A multi-colored holographic map filled the space between them and Calico Jack. "That was three weeks ago." A line traced their course from Horsehead Starport to the asteroid field. It time stamped expected arrival one and a half weeks, delayed arrival two weeks. "Mr. Spendicus wants answers, his property and employees back." Calico finished eyeing each of them, expecting questions.

JOLENE (CHAT MESSAGE)

"Anyone else get the feeling that Spendicus wants it in that order exactly?"

Jolene messaged the group chat. Boris and Murph

reacted to the message with thumbs up.

"And that is where you come in." Calico continued and their diner ship appeared on the hologram map. "We want you to follow their course, find them, provide assistance, and bring us back whatever you can find."

Jolene didn't bother watching their ship follow the same path. She rubbed her eyebrows at the universe, applying its sitcom logic again.

"So, you want a diner spaceship with a grand total of three crew members to run a recon and rescue operation?"

Calico Jack scratched under his chin. A throaty purr filled the lounge. "That's one outcome. The other is you find them and serve up the best service you can." The Felinoid held out both paws, balancing imaginary weights.

"Either way, Mr. Spendicus will pay one hundred fifty thousand credits for the job with an additional ten thousand credits per crewmember."

Murph whistled around their toothpick. "Now that's some serious scratch."

"In the name of the Motherboard!"

Jolene sighed, hating how killjoy was her job. "Why us?"

The question hit the room like a rail gun bullet. Boris sighed. Murph hid their face under their hat.

Calico shrugged his shoulders. "You're that special blend of talented and..."

"Expendable." Jolene suggested, and the heat from him intensified.

"Reasonably priced." Calico answered. His eyes

looked her over from head to toe. It took her rapidly returning Empath senses, forming one word to make it stupid obvious why.

DESIRE.

Jolene rationalized her black shirt and navy jeans rarely grabbed anyone's attention. Let alone Spendicus' cat's paw.

"Come on, Jo, it's a good deal." Murph gave her shoulder a nudge. Jolene looked over just in time to see their teeth lowering and rising like piano keys, rolling the toothpick to the other side of their mouth.

"It is a nice payday." Boris offered.

JOLENE (CHAT MESSAGE)

"Why are you encouraging them?"

She asked Boris in their private chat.

Boris withdrew his hand and twiddled his thumbs.

BORIS (CHAT MESSAGE)

"More persuading you, and like you said, no other options."

He answered over the private chat on her H.U.D.

"Sounds like there's a two-thirds majority. I'll have the paperwork sent-" Calico mused, stroking his left whiskers between two furry fingers.

"My ship is not a democracy!" Jolene interrupted. "Give us a moment."

"As you wish, Queen Jolene!" Calico Jack said, bowing low enough for his whiskers to scrape the ground. Jolene's empath senses sifted through his emotions, only finding more heat and more words.

PRIMAL,

HUNGER,

TASTE,

They made the hairs on her neck stand up.

"Float. Don't sink. Float. Don't sink."

She focused on the words, ignoring the sensations Calico's emotions offered.

"Earth to Jo?" Murph waved their hand in front of her face.

"I'm here." She shook her head and started with Boris.

"First Mr. I'm made of numbers." Boris' eyes went dark and lit up. "The payout isn't enough to buy the ship. That means we'd be leasing it, not owning it, and you know Erabella will bury us with the interest rate." Boris said nothing out loud or in her H.U.D.

Jolene only saw Murph roll their shoulders before side-stepping her. "Hey, tall dark and fluffy make it two hundred thousand credits for the job and thirty K for each of us."

"Never let a Kyanese Unioner in on a deal, but Mr. Spendicus hates wasted time. Final offer is two hundred thousand for the job and twenty-five thousand each." Calico let out a chuffing sound Jolene had only heard on nature documentaries.

Murph stroked their chin for a few moments.

Jolene had questions for them and Calico but didn't know where to start. "Since time is so important, our ship needs repairs. Throw that in, I'll put in a good word with the local Union Steward."

Calico's eyes turned into saucers at that, holographic interfaces took shape, lit up under the blur of his paws, and disappeared before Jolene could say one word.

"Repairs have been ordered and will be completed by tomorrow. At no additional charge." Calico purred in their general direction.

Jolene's mouth moved up and down as decisions were flying past her. She rationalized that the hull damage was at least fifty percent of why Erabella had jacked up their quota, and Calico Jack just overnighted the repairs. Jolene adjusted her opinion of the showy Felinoid, as not to be trusted.

"Ok but wait we still need to figure out-" Jolene stopped as the door to the casino opened. They were now on the gaming floor. Jolene started stepping back from the emotional ocean. Distracting herself with questions like how had they moved without a sound? Was she so nervous she missed the shifts in gravity or balance? Why didn't she feel the emotions before?

Her H.U.D. answered the last question.

"EMPATH BLOCKERS AT 99% EFFECTIVENESS!"

Then one of Jack's feline friends rushed in.

"Game floor riot!" They shouted.

Looking out to the casino, alien and human bodies were shoving and punching in every position. On top of tables. Breaking liquor bottles. Running away with chips. Jolene fixated on a bright white flashing crystal. The species name **CARBONITE**. Popped on her H.U.D. as rainbow beams shot out of every single facets shooting a rainbow beam of light at rioting customers and security alike. All while the mechanical arms of it's hover rig's stuffed chips and furniture into its rings. Started flying above everyone! Noise bombarded the energy field separating them creating air distortions.

Three Rigani with bright horsehead badges between their eyestalks floated in pursuit of the Carbonite. One had its blue noodle limbs wrapped around the carbonite's hover rig and was getting dragged along the walls for their initiative. Jolene was halfway to the elevator door before the effectiveness rating started plummeting.

BLOCKERS AT 85% EFFECTIVENESS

53% EFFECTIVENESS

JOLENE MENTALLY SCREAMED FOR HER BIO-TECH TO UP HER DOSE.

60% EFFECTIVENESS

35% EFFECTIVENESS

"Shit shit shit!" She swore and focused through the invading sensations and words. Calico Jack, Boris and Murph were distant objects their mouths moved but all Jolene heard was the incoming emotional tidal wave of the brawling casino smash into her. She didn't have time to scream. Her knees buckled. She shut her eyes out of reflex; it didn't help, it never did. She saw nothing. Felt everything.

FLOAT DON' T-

FLOAT DON' T SI-

The mantra drowned in all the constant feedback flooding her brain. She couldn't keep standing. Boris caught and ran with her at the same time. She pressed her head against his cool metal chassis, trying and failing to stand against the tide.

RIP-OFF.

STINKING OLD SWEATY SOCKS.

SEX.

WHISKEY MIXING WITH PERFUME.

MINE.

ROTTING VEGETABLES IN STALE WATER

KILL

MINE MINE MINE

The inside of her eyelids turned red. Statements blinked in and out of existence.

BREAKTHROUGH EMPATHIC EPISODE.

UNACCEPTABLE RISK OF PSYCHIC SCARRING

DEPLOYING ANESTHETIC.

One moment she was crying from a cluster psychic migraine. The next numb oblivion washed over her.

Twelve hours. That was the minimum medical downtime. If she showed any other signs of mental or physical wear and tear it could be twenty four hours. Galaxy Waffles healthcare, made sure every piece of Bio-tech worked and lasted as long as possible but locked you out of the settings. So when Jolene's brain woke up the first thing she did was check her H.U.D.'s clock. Twenty eight hours had passed!

Opening her eyes, she saw blue. Everything was blue. Instinct said to make a fist. Her fingers twitched, and that was it.

BORIS (CHAT MESSAGE)

"It's low stress lighting. One breath at a time."

Boris' words popped in their red bubble across her vision, one of his hands resting on her shoulder. Moving her head felt like moving a hairy, red mountain. Looking at his four red eyes and red eyed bear insignia, she tried to smile. She didn't bother trying to speak.

BORIS (CHAT MESSAGE)

"You're in your bunk. Ok to keep chatting like this?"

Boris sent through their private chat.

JOLENE (CHAT MESSAGE)

"Yes. Thank you for the earplugs."

Jolene sent back.

BORIS (CHAT MESSAGE)

"You're welcome. Murph and I decided on a new nickname for you."

Boris messaged and sat by the side of her bed.

"Wait, what?" Jolene asked out loud for context but also because reality was still a fuzzy concept.

"Glad you asked. Your hair is red. You are grouchy and stubborn. We think baboon ass fits." Boris explained his deadly serious baritone landed a bullseye on Jolene's funny bone. Laughter shook her brain inside her skull while putting a smile on her face.

Jolene's brain laughed while her lungs wheezed out a sound like an ancient Earth whoopie cushion.

"Then you are Mr. Killjoy and Murph can be..." Echoes of her migraine magnified the more she thought; spamming nonsense characters into the chat.

"We both know Murph is the Blue Hemorrhoid." Boris answered.

"Why did you not tell us your Empath blockers were wearing off?" Boris never typed in all caps, but it was always obvious when he was shouting.

"Needed. To. Feel. Out. Calico." Jolene thought the sentence word by word, her migraine threatening to throb each time.

"You're lucky he had access to Empath Blockers. It's why your brain is quiet now."

"Thank you, Daddy Boris." Jolene grimaced at the parenting and the stabbing in her skull.

Boris replied with an animated wooden paddle, smacking a pixelated butt. Jolene let out the whoopie cushion noise again.

"Well, baboon ass, we're going to do our best to keep her away until you can fight back."Boris explained, and Jolene didn't understand.

"Wait, who's her?"

She watched Boris twiddle his thumbs. Three little red dots hovered. "Erabella."

Questions and denial took turns trying to type until Jolene gave up and tried to scream. Her body only spasmed. She shut her eyes and felt tears slip out.

"Sleep and remember you're not fighting alone."

Jolene didn't fight the panic-induced exhaustion, keeping her eyes shut until she couldn't think anymore.

She's Back!

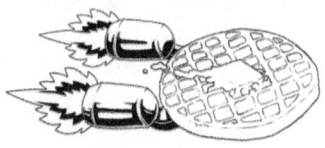

The first lesson for Starblood and Terrablood Empaths is lucid dreaming. After learning Erabella was back, Jolene had damn near screamed at her brain to sleep. Now she didn't want to leave. Floating above cheering masses, a cup of coffee between her hands, she watched the mixed species members of "Suck My Voltage" blast out bass and guitar riffs.

"POWER IN MY BLOOD!
PAPER VAMPIRES HUNTING!
MEMORY CHIPS IN MY SKULL!"

Her blunt battle cry supported by steady rhythms helped Jolene gather the empathic memories filling up her brain.

The second lesson for Empaths was deleting them. Cue the Kyanese drummer with hammer hands beating metal drums. From stage right, a line of floating light bulbs. Each one a memory, all of its sensory feedback drowned in the music. Useless ones she'd thumb down, like Caesar in the old Earth flicks Murph had shown her, and the drummer shattered them. She sipped from her cup, smiling at the blend of the best coffees she remembered.

The next ones included memories and sensations of

Calico Jack. Reliving them. She felt her cheeks flush and amped the volume on her music drowning them out. Then her sky of gorgeous black storm clouds turned blood red.

Jolene groaned as yellow numbers blinked on and off in the red clouds.

She wondered if Calico Jack could help get a snooze button installed in her bio-tech. Letting her cup float, she thrust her fingers into a double devil horn salute. Floating into the clouds; she guzzled her coffee memories every second of the way.

Regular lighting flicked on when she opened her eyes. She tested moving her fingers and toes. Joints cracked but no full body murder pain. She took one deep breath before sitting up. Gravity didn't reverse and her head didn't decompress into pieces. Brushing red hairs out of her eyes, she mentally turned on her H.U.D.

"Empath Blockers?"

Blue text typed across her field of vision.

CURRENT DOSE WILL LAST FORTY-EIGHT HOURS. ADDITIONAL DOSES INJECTED INTO YOUR BIO-TECH AT KEY ARTERIES FOR EMERGENCIES. TIME RELEASED FLUID VERSION.

Jolene whistled through her teeth. One of the many benefits of having the richest boss in the known Milky Way. You got the best of everything.

"Repair Status." She thought the question.

KITCHEN REPAIRS COMPLETE. HULL REPAIRS 90% COMPLETE.

Jolene cracked her knuckles one by one before asking

the next question.

"Erabella location?" She asked silently.

20 FT AWAY.

Jolene looked at her door and decided she could shower after dealing with whatever shit Erabella wanted to throw.

"Enter." She said, bracing for her neon teal platinum nemesis.

"Glad to see you're finally awake." The words sounded like a recording.

Jolene squinted at the hallway lights to see her. It was the same snow white power suit, gold rimmed white sunglasses outfit as last time, but a quick scan from her H.U.D. said Erabella was now 100% silicone and metal.

"Ditched all the organics?" Jolene asked.

Erabella stepped in, full lips pursed with one eyebrow cocked. "Some things are perfect without technology." Jolene's brain caught up with what her H.U.D. was telling her. "Nice rig, fresh off the factory floor?"

The Erabella looking, remote controlled android, crossed her arms and marched in until she stood over Jolene. Her high-heeled metal boots stomped her mood into the floor.

"I am required by Corporate policy, and G.G. law to inform you this android is broadcasting directly to my original body. All statements and actions observed by it are legally admissible evidence. Now care to explain why you disabled O.D. and compromised the performance review process?" She demanded.

Jolene yawned, then scratched the back of her head. The android's nostrils flared. Jolene winked, sending her a copy of the report she'd sent to corporate. Her neon blue eyes scrolled left and right, reading the information before focusing on Jolene, her metal fingers tapping her arms.

"From this point on, all decisions about O.D. will need my clearance." She growled through a smile of perfect metal teeth.

"Noted, anything else?" Jolene gave a two-finger salute, wishing it was just one finger.

Erabella's crazed smile eased into her usual predatory grin. "Yes! Your actions demanded my direct supervision. Because my time is valuable and this unit is being expensed to Galaxy Waffles, its costs are now added to your quota!"

"Send us the numbers. Now, unless you want to watch me shower, leave." Jolene stood nose to nose with her.

Erabella's silicone skin darkened to a shade of silver. "I'd never cross the line between employer and employee!"

It took seconds for Jolene to find the photo she wanted. Her in-room projector filled the opposite wall with an image of Boris lifting six thousand kilos of cargo, one thousand per arm, like they were serving trays full of appetizers. Erabella's android cheeks turned bright chrome. Her eyes widened until her black sclera bulged from the sockets.

"Come to the dining room after your shower." She ordered on fast forward, an octave higher than her normal voice, before double timing it out of the room.

Jolene grimaced. Boris would have to watch his back

on this job.

After the all over body scraping, vibrating sonic shower, Jolene dressed manually, stopping to groan at Erabella's email. It left them only a thousand credits from the catering job. Murph would suggest a poetic death. Boris would stoically keep going. Jolene wanted to do both. She ran her hands over her door frame and smiled. Soon it would be their ship.

She tried accessing the security cameras but was greeted by an automated message.

"ALL NON-ESSENTIAL SHIP SYSTEMS ARE DISABLED DURING REPAIRS." Jolene groaned, it would be much harder to avoid Erabella without the cameras. Walking into the dining room she was greeted by O.D.'s waiting smug marshmallow grin. Her eyes rolled before she could stop them. She couldn't help but wish they'd deemed him non-essential.

He was whispering to Erabella over her shoulder while she flicked through too many hologram screens to count. Jolene tried for a silent retreat.

"I expect you to start on time or your pay will be automatically adjusted." Erabella never looked her way. Jolene stepped up to one of the empty booths.

"Welcome to Galaxy Waffles. May I take your order?" She snapped her fingers for her holographic pad. It matched the green of her eyes.

"Please use the correct greeting." Erabella had closed one display, one of her eyes fixed on Jolene. She smiled until her cheeks ached.

"Welcome to Galaxy Waffles, home to the Milky Way's best breakfast. How can we make you feel at home?"

"Passable... barely." She sniffed before another appeared. Jolene snapped her fingers, dismissing the holographic pad.

"You wanted to see me?" Jolene asked.

Erabella snapped her fingers at the seat across from her. The array of holograms vanished. She pushed a recorder to the center of the table.

"O.D. was kind enough to catch me up. This catering job will meet your quota, but is that your only plan?" Erabella asked in a tired voice prepared for disappointment.

"We don't have time for backup plans because of the quota's due date." Jolene answered, struggling to keep the accusation out of her voice.

"You're pinning everything on one plan and blaming your circumstances on others. One leaves you with no other options and, second, taking responsibility is what good managers do. I will add these oversights to your review." Erabella answered her own question, smiling at the situation she had made.

Erabella's labored sigh turned into a full toothed grin. Jolene wanted to rub the ache out of her cheeks, but if she let her smile slip, her fists would start flying. O.D. just paced back and forth, his smile matching Erabella's.

"If you have ideas, why not share them so that we can all succeed?" Jolene asked, knowing she would hate the answer.

"I would, but my responsibilities are personnel and

~ 132 ~

brand image. Not doing your job for you." Erabella blew on her metal fingernails and rubbed them on her suit lapel.

"Still can't find anyone?" Jolene asked with a knowing smirk.

Erabella's eyes dropped, her silicone lips turning into a thin line. "If I were you, I'd be more worried about your plan failing. It'd be a shame if your crew ended up in corporate forfeiture."

"Not gonna happen." Jolene gritted her teeth through her pulse spiking, her customer service smile disappearing.

Erabella smiled wider as she watched Jolene react, then leaned her head in her hand. Perfect imitation hair swaying, all while O.D. did a dance that involved finger jabs and thrusting.

"Easy to say, harder to do. O.D. sweetie, can you check if anyone's worked their way to freedom at Galaxy Waffles?"

Erabella looked up at the nightmare fuel waffle mascot. O.D.'s waffle grid chest grew a cleft chin and tapped it a few times before answering. "Nope! We've got assets from corporate forfeiture that have been with us for decades!" The cleft chin disappeared, and Erabella looked at Jolene with sad eyes and a full smile.

"Of course, you could always resign and give up your severance. That would keep them safe. You could even call it the right thing."

Jolene imagined dunking the real Erabella into a deep fryer over and over. Finding it easier to smile at the android version.

"No, thank you. I'll go check on Boris and the new kitchen." The moment she mentioned his name, Erabella perked up.

"I'll join you. O.D., make sure the repairs are up to our standards." The tyrannical waffle mascot clicked his blueberry shoes together and saluted before disappearing.

On the way to the kitchen, they heard a xylophone playing alongside a piano while Boris' Russian baritone bounced off the walls. Jolene's H.U.D. translated it in red text.

OLD MEN DON'T GO TO SCHOOL –
IT'S SO GOOD BEING OLD!!
NO ONE MAKES YOU STUDY
NO ONE GIVES YOU TESTS

Right around disgusting mathematics, she couldn't help smiling at the beat and ridiculous lyrics.

"What a fun little song. I wonder where he learned it." Erabella's 'I own everything about you' tone went up to an octave Jolene hadn't heard since she'd had the word teen in her age.

"Ask him! Boris is a server without a password." Jolene said it over her shoulder, and Erabella pushed ahead. The entire kitchen was new. Calico Jack never blinked at the list of hardware they'd needed. Aside from restocking their cargo hold, they'd received new stoves with ovens, counters, utensils, mixers, cutting boards, and on one of the top shelves a heavy duty crème brûlée torch. Jolene scanned the room until her H.U.D. reported zero damage.

Boris was holding a manual for his top two eyes. A digital intelligence manually reading a data pad. Jolene remembered when she'd seen it for the first time, she'd asked why he didn't just download it. Boris had stopped reading and answered by asking why she didn't just chew caffeine pills? They'd laughed and left each other to their choices.

Another of his hands tapped the counter along to the song. Two skillets fired, two arms a piece, cooking up something salty, cheesy, and meaty. She wanted it in her mouth as soon as she smelled the garlic and chili.

"What a lovely little song. You must tell me where you learned it." Erabella said with corn syrup sweetness. Boris stopped everything. All four of his eyes went dark, then lit up red again.

"Downloaded it." He answered and continued. Erabella came closer, one finger drawing circles that smudged his new counters.

"But you were singing, not playing a recorded file." She reached for his hand, the one tapping along to the music. Boris retracted it into his chassis with a metallic whizz and snap.

"The Galactic Food Authority suspended us. Please go fix that." The words were sharp as the laser cut cleavers on his wall. Erabella stepped back, letting out a manic giggle that crackled into static nonsense. She coughed to cover it.

"I look forward to hearing you sing for me again. I'll

get the GFA to approve the ship for service."

She glared at Jolene with every step until she was walking forward and looking backwards. Then her head spun back to the front, grumbling something about backstabbing Starbloods.

"If you're going to use me like a bear trap, I deserve to know what happened between you two."

Jolene rubbed at her eyebrows. "That's fair, but if I'm gonna tell that story, I wanna know where you learned that song."

Two of Boris' arms plated up while another two poured and carried drinks. His last two arms setup the chef's table.

"Murph, come out or I'll test run my dishwasher on disinfect!" Boris growled and several kitchen tools sprouted dark blue arms and legs.

"You know… I'm not sure I could survive that." They said before jumping into each other, shifting back into their standard coal black shirt, red pinstripe vest, and fedora.

"I'm sure you could. Sit, eat and drink while we tell sad stories." Boris said.

BORIS

SPECIES: A.I.
PRONOUNS: HE/HIM
ABILITIES: ANYTHING DIGITAL
LIKES: COOKING AND SINGING
DISLIKES: TRAITORS AND BLAND FOOD
ROLE: CHEF AND SECURITY

VOICE OF A FRIEND

There wasn't a single chair on the ship that could support Boris. Even the diner booths would buckle and snap under him. He loaded up his four arms with drinks. Turning towards them showed he had coffee for Jolene and a multi-colored mystery drink for Murph. Two cheesy egg and meat dishes were in his hands that Jolene wanted to drool at in admiration. Boris came to the table side, slid their plates set down their drinks and with a hydraulic hiss lowered his frame to eye level.

Jolene thought he looked like a chrome plated penguin. She could not resist searching and saving a listing for a custom sized suit jacket service on her H.U.D.

"So, why is platinum pain in the ass so eager to see you gone?" Boris asked and interlaced all six of his hands, resting them on his chest and apron. Murph split off one of their fingers and shifted it into a blue and white swirled straw.

"I ruined her career." Jolene said. Unable to resist the omelet any longer, she cut a huge chunk and shoved it in her mouth. The perfect blend of spicy and salty, cheesy, meaty goodness also stopped her from talking. Boris and Murph looked at each other, then back to Jolene.

Galaxy Waffles

"Details!" they said at the same time.

Jolene chewed vindictively. Staring them both down, bite by bite. She tried glaring through the garlic and cheddar's treacherous magic. Instead, she closed her eyes and made the sounds the food deserved.

"Glad you enjoyed my cooking. Now stop stalling." Boris grumbled. Jolene looked at the bear insignia on his chest and shook off the shivers at all the ways her friend was dangerous.

Thick black bushy eyebrows grew over Murph's glowing eyes. They waggled the halves of their head up and down. Boris sighed and flicked Murph, sending a ripple through them.

"Ya, know, I could report you guys to O.D. for being so mean!" Murph said, their eyes going puppy dog huge with a frown that reached the table. All four of Boris' eyes blinked dark, then lit up. Jolene just ate her food, enjoying every bite. Murph drink and grumbled at the lack of reaction.

"O.D. is occupied with Erabella. I'd bet one of my arms you'd rather spend a month shifted as a drain filter than go to him. Now, knock of the cartoon bullshit. I want to hear her story." Boris lectured.

Two blue and four red eyes focused on her. Jolene no longer had a full mouth to hide behind.

"Galaxy Waffles bought my work contract and assigned me to Erabella."

Murph rippled from top to bottom, rattling their needle teeth. "That must have been a nightmare."

"Actually, it didn't start out that way." Jolene took a deep breath before pulling back the scarred over memories. "The Starblood allocation fleet was my twenty-year nightmare. Cheap food on cheaper ships." She squinted and sucked in a breath as the sensations of her memories crawled across her skin and brain. Every Empath learned intense emotions made the strongest memories. Hungry nights. Bare knuckle beat downs. Malfunctioning life support systems. Closing her eyes was instinctual, and she fought it. If she didn't, her brain would play out the memories on the back of her eyelids. Her palms hurt but she couldn't remember when she'd started making white knuckled fists.

"Eat before it gets cold." Boris said.

Jolene's knife and fork sliced and tore through every layer. Rich, cheesy eggs fought against the acidic anxiety in her gut. Murph drained their glass until they started slurping, then sucked in the straw like it was a spaghetti noodle.

"Erabella fed and clothed me the moment I walked through her door."

Multiple metallic pops came from Boris' side of the table. His top two hands balled into fists. "Please continue."

"She was a Brand Quality Inspector for Galaxy Waffles franchises. Took less than a month for us to leave Earth's solar system. I got to see so much. Meet so many people. All I had to do was help her with paperwork, carry her stuff, and-"

Galaxy Waffles

"You were a bellhop." Murph interrupted. Jolene smiled at them, for cutting her trip down shitty memory lane short.

"Got it in one, wise guy." Jolene tried on the gangster accent and Murph gave her a sour smile.

"If you're gonna play my game, toots, you gotta practice more," they said in perfect imitation of the movies they'd watched. Boris' speakers let out a throat clearing sound.

"Her story will never end if you keep interrupting." His head swiveled at Murph, all eight segmented eyes fixed on them. Murph tipped their hat in apology to him and Jolene. Boris closed the four extra eyes.

"Anyway, I noticed that after we visited independent franchises, she'd splurge. New clothes, beauty therapy, and after a year she'd include me as well. Never happened with a corporate owned location."

Jolene stabbed her last bit of omelet, mopping up every trace of flavor before setting it back down on the plate.

"I was happy, so I ignored it until my Empath senses made that impossible. Every time we entered an independent franchise, it was a pressure cooker full of liquid nitrogen and napalm. I started taking Empath blockers every day. I was living on less than a hundred credits, but it was worth it to avoid what she was causing. One time I ran out and couldn't get anymore. From the moment we walked in till we got back to her ship, she was like a supernova of dopamine."

Murph's eyes ballooned out of their sockets, shrinking the rest of their head. Boris' speakers let out a deep animal growl.

"She was a serial racketeer and emotional predator." A hair raising instinct kicking growl leaped out of Boris' speakers.

All the anxiety of the truth mixing with Erabella's enjoyment churned Jolene's stomach until she wanted to puke them out. Her eyes dropped to the omelet and stared at nothing else.

"Ain't just that." Murph said. Jolene continued to stare at her omelet.

"What do you mean?" Boris asked.

"She was makin' herself a patsy. If Cyber Cunt got caught skimming, she could just blame Jolene." Murph growled.

She nodded to confirm and looked up at Murph. Their hands were gray metal spiked gauntlets. They started punching their palm sending an echoing clang through the kitchen. Each one filling Jolene's ears with high-pitched needles.

"Those gifts were a paper trail and being a Terrablood, Galaxy Waffles corporate would always take her side. Starblood steals trust and credits from Terrablood exec. Headline writes itself." Murph said, their voice as sharp as their needle teeth.

"You're right, but please stop." Jolene said, hating the whimper in her voice. Murph's hands shifted back to blue.

"I figured it out just like you did. So, I started collecting evidence. Recordings, contacting old franchise owners, and receipts. She left little behind from all the months before, but I took what I could get and went to Orzhan." Jolene rocked back and forth in her chair at the memory of the confrontation.

"If you need to, we can stop." Boris' four metal fingers were a cold, constant comfort on her hand.

Jolene nodded instead of gushing a thank you at the bot. "I promise I'll finish later."

"Take your time." Murph and Boris said simultaneously. One of Boris' arms extended to the shelf with the crème brûlée torch, grabbing it and pulling it back to the table.

"May I warm that up?" Boris asked.

Jolene waved him on. With AI precision he set the flame pencil thin and gently heated the last bite of omelet. Jolene watched the curling fingers of steam draw patterns in the air before disappearing. Her stomach rumbled and she complied. The last bite was as spicy and warm as the first.

"Thank you!"

Boris let out a laugh, his frame shifting up and down. Jolene didn't doubt if he was human that his belly would be jiggling. "It's what the best chefs do! But it is now my turn, and I was not always a chef."

"Tell me what you know about the Cthullian Wars." Boris asked, his voice going deeper at the end.

"Headlines." Jolene said.

"Vids and articles." Murph said.

"Bah, propaganda and pop media." One of Boris'

smaller eyes started projecting a holo-map of the Milky Way. "They reported it as a nuisance, but it was an infestation across light-years."

The holo-map populated with worlds while dark purple clusters and lines took shape. Jolene whistled while Murph's eyes extended out on wiggling blue stalks, looking over the entire map.

"Hey now, hold up! This don't track with what the Galactic News Network put out." They said.

"And?" Boris asked.

Murph sucked their eyestalks back into their head until they disappeared completely.

"Whoa timeout! We gonna get our timecards punched for knowing this? I mean, this shit screams classified!" Murph crossed their arms with their blank blue face fixed on Boris. Jolene exhaled through the cold pit in her stomach and waited for the bot to answer.

Boris laughed. His head bobbed up and down. His chassis shook.

Jolene bit her lips to avoid laughing as Murph turned tomato sauce red.

"What do you think is the best kept secret?" Boris asked.

"Dead men tell no tales." Murph said slowly, turning back to their usual deep blue and Jolene shrugged, both waiting for Boris to get on with the story.

"True but impractical. The best kept secret is the one everyone knows. Upload this map. Record this conversation. At best, you get ignored. At worst, someone opens a file on you. Everyone who was supposed to know knows. Everyone else just wants to get through their day."

A ripple started from the top of Murph's head and flowed down. Their eyes floated back into place, while their needle teeth protruded through a frown.

"So long as I don't get offed," they said and waved Boris on.

"Time and distance are the problems. Coordinating a multi species effort became a nightmare of politics and strategic disasters."

"Operation Flechette." Jolene interrupted, and Boris' remaining three eyes blinked at her like red strobe lights.

"I didn't say which headlines I read." She winked at Boris, whose eyes stopped strobing.

"I have questions for you later, but yes, Operation Flechette was their answer. A.I.s in outlawed battle chassis deployed into Cthullian clusters." Arrowheads labeled with planet names and numbers left countless planets.

"Outlawed because?" Murph asked.

"Their death toll legally qualified as a war crime." Boris answered. Both Jolene and Murph looked at their friend's chassis. "Oh, this one can transform, but doesn't have all the weapons or ammunition... anymore."

They nodded and watched the arrowheads pierce the purple lines and clusters. Some went dark, others emerged on the other side.

"Which one is yours?" Jolene asked. One of the red lines turned blue, and she traced it back to Pluto.

"You're from Sol!" For once she didn't care how

she sounded even if words like unbelieving child came to mind. A quick search with her H.U.D told her it was one hundred thousand light-years away. A distance most humans needed suspended animation to survive.

"Yes, but we will talk about that another time."

"But-" Murph started.

"No." Boris ended.

They pouted, grinding their teeth against each other. Jolene set up a reminder in her personal calendar to ask as soon as the catering job was over.

"Anyway, a unanimous concern for the G.G. was us going rogue. So, they assigned us a small crew with deep space mission experience. Three in my case. For this story, only one of them matters. Vanya." The name left Boris' speakers with a sharp exhale. The holo-map disappeared, replaced by a sandy blonde boyish face with soft brown eyes. Jolene's Empath senses felt Murph go still as water in a cup.

On reflex she thought, *"Thank god I can't feel Boris right now."* before she squashed it and reached out to touch Boris' hand currently locked around a fistful of apron.

"If you need to stop, you can," Jolene echoed back at him. Boris' fist opened finger by finger. He gripped her hand firmly.

"No, I trust you. I want you two to know."

"He was the crew's engineer. Anything that broke on me or the ship he fixed. He won the poker game for our name, called us the Bear Claw." One of Boris' hands petted the battalion symbol on his chest.

Galaxy Waffles

"Wait, as in the pastry?" Murph asked, and Jolene was ready to make them eat their hat. Boris just laughed. It was more manic than his usual full belly laugh.

"He didn't know those existed. Didn't search the net before entering it into the records. Before we flew off Pluto, the other two made sure he got a stacked plate. Never seen a human blush from scalp to neck since!" Murph and Jolene looked at each other, and without a private chat or word, understood this story would not end well.

"Our mission was simple: search, destroy, and report results. After a few times, it was like washing dishes." The other arrowheads disappeared. Boris' arrow flew point to point, burning away all Cthullian traces.

"Everyone did their job and counted the days until our next resupply. All except Vanya. He wouldn't stop trying to be friends with the other two, asking me personality quiz questions, and always humming or singing. He could hit a pitch that rattled the bolts in my head." Boris interlaced all six of his hands, twiddled his thumbs. "One time we touched down on a habitable planet for R&R."

The projection zoomed in on a lush green planetoid. "He spent the entire time carving a balalaika." The projection changed to Vanya swearing at splinters and muttering something that Jolene's H.U.D. couldn't catch. "After stripping three trees of all their branches, he couldn't find anything for strings. The other two laughed and mocked. My programming said I had to support crew morale and mental health. I made him strings with some utensils from the ship."

The projection changed to show them looking down at Vanya. Boris passed him six strings. "Backups." He spoke in a computerized voice without an accent. They watched the young engineer string and tune, happy tears falling on the balalaika's neck and body.

"He played and sang Russian folk songs all night. The others went to sleep on the ship. Around midnight, I started singing as well." Boris' unaccented voice sounded like an out of tune auto tuner, but Vanya just kept smiling and sung along. Jolene couldn't help grinning at it even though she dreaded the ending. She felt the same emotions in Murph.

"You know you should have a name. Something other than gun or bot." Vanya's voice was light but strained from singing. Boris' arm entered the recording, offering a bottle of water. The young man gulped it down. "Oh, I know!" He exclaimed voice sounding smoother already. "You remind me of a cousin. Says little, strong like ox, and when mad, terrifying. Boris."

"My programming concluded this meant a lot to him. Since they were there to scrap me as a last resort, some self-preservation factored in as well."

"I accept the name." The recorded Boris said. "Da, but I think it would help them and me if you didn't sound like an ancient Earth video-game. You've got enough recordings to map my voice. Use that and put your own spin on it!"

The projection shut off. Boris was silent. Murph and

Jolene waited.

"That's where I got my name and why I sound like this." He said it hunched over and did not look at either of them. Murph and Jolene stood up, hugging Boris, who whispered. "Thank you. I'll tell the rest another time."

NIKOLAI WISEKAL

WAFFLE TIME

1,170 light-years to destination

Jolene stood in the empty dining room. Hot plates on her hands and forearm, at Erabella's table side. Calluses and abused nerve endings helped, but minutes of this was setting fire to her muscles and skin. Erabella's android whistled and admired her metal fingernails. "You may serve." Jolene set down the fried eggs and hash browns, then a plate of grilled cheeses stuffed with bacon. Finally, the signature dish every diner in the company served.

Galaxy Waffles. Waffle batter blended with different colored fruits that cooked into nebula colored squares of fluffy deliciousness. Jolene was proud of it even as her stomach grumbled for just one bite.

Erabella looked each one over, picking out crumbs on the edges of plates, and tiny drops of egg yolk like they were illegal infestations.

"Is this what you've been serving our customers?" Erabella asked, scrunching her silicone and platinum face at the picture-perfect dishes.

"Yes." Jolene answered.

Galaxy Waffles

"No wonder you're so far behind on your quota. It's awful." Erabella never broke eye contact as she shoved the plates off the table into the empty seat across from her. "Clean that up and do it right!"

Jolene tightened her fists until her knuckles hurt. Starbloods were given nothing, and this privileged cunt had just wasted enough to feed a family! Looking into Erabella's eyes Jolene knew she was waiting for any reaction to justify firing her.

"Right away!" Jolene said instead and moved to gather up the spilled food. Every instinct in her demanded she eat it instead of throwing it away.

"O.D., please make a note in her file that an improperly prepared order caused lost revenue." Erebella dictated.

Jolene sighed at the incoming brown-nosing statement.

"Unable to comply." O.D. responded.

Jolene checked her H.U.D. for any irregularities in her brain, found none, and decided waiting was the best thing she could do. Erabella's android inhaled aggressively. "An order does not require compliance, only obedience."

The tips of O.D.'s marshmallow teeth browned, then blackened. He floated over to the mess in the booth and stared at the waffles.

"Your most recent statement contains no errors, but my analysis concludes that Jolene used:

2 cups all-purpose ground grains
1/2 teaspoon salt
2 tablespoons sweetener

1 1/2 teaspoons leavening agent

1 3/4 cup fatty dairy

2 separated lab grown poultry embryos

4 tablespoons of solidified dairy fats

2 teaspoons of orchid fruit extract

2 cups of tart black fruits

2 cups of tart red fruit

2 cups of sweet blue fruit.

It is the exact recipe from Galaxy Waffles Corporate Cookbook and is not improper at all."

Jolene moved by muscle memory alone, green eyes wide as dinner plates. O.D. had just stood up to Erabella on her behalf... with SNARK! She set her H.U.D. to record and looked at Erabella; whose face did not disappoint. Her wrinkles and bared teeth all with the scrunched-up nose. Her stiff as steel shoulders. The unnecessary and confusing protruding artificial breasts. Her mechanical knuckles clicked as her fists trembled. If it was the real Erabella and not an android, Jolene would have asked if she wanted a laxative for her bitchy rage face. Her eyes creaked like rusty hinges when she looked at Jolene.

"You're dismissed until 14:00. O.D. send me that analysis. I'd like to verify your sensors are accurate." Erabella growled between clenched metal teeth. Jolene gathered everything up and ran away without running. Her H.U.D. popped with a eye stabbing neon white message from Erabella.

"A friendly reminder that it will be conflict resolution

training. Leave your Voltstriker in your quarters."

The message closed with no option to reply. Jolene sent it to her pixelated dumpster and smiled at the incineration animation. She turned into the kitchen and found Murph arguing with Boris.

"Surprised they let you have it." They said petting a new toy that Jolene hadn't noticed before.

"It's the only one on the market that can grind down Asteroid Wyrms!" Boris petted the machine like a puppy. It was a wide, thick steeled box that could have been an oven if not for the rows upon rows of segmented steel.

Murph shook their head. "I love your optimism, ya big palooka, but ya really think corporate's gonna send us something that costs a planet's GDP to hunt and process?"

"First off, I am a decorated veteran, the exact opposite of a palooka. Second, I made a deal with Calico Jack next time we dock at Horsehead." Two of Boris' eyes turned on and off.

"Look at you wheelin' and dealin' when no one's looking." Murph gave Boris a bow with their hat on their chest. "You got hustle algorithms we didn't know about?"

Jolene smiled at her two screwballs and cleared her throat.

"Hey Murph, wanna save me the trouble?" She offered the mess on the plate. Murph's legs shifted into eight spider legs as they skittered over to her. Almost tripping over themselves. Their hands shifted into smooth nubs that absorbed every waffle molecule.

Murph's satisfied grin belonged in horror movies, but

in true Murph fashion, they opened their mouth. "That's grub so good I'd die for it." They moved to stand behind Jolene before putting their hat back on. "And her waffles are still better than yours, Boris!"

Boris flipped them six middle fingers. "Get out before I make you into a dish for your replacement!"

"Looks like I got myself in hot water and better get while the getting's good!" Murph's blue legs went spidery again and they raced away.

"You know if O.D. or Erabella overhear that they'll accuse me of allowing a toxic work environment." Jolene said it and hated how easily she knew the lies Erabella would tell.

"For you, I'd turn on the charm and give her a charge she'd not soon forget. In exchange for overlooking workplace banter, of course." Boris had no mouth but Jolene read the smile in his tone and word choice.

"Great, I'll add robot prostitution to my ever-growing list of inadequacies." Jolene mocked, setting the plates and utensils in the sink.

"We finish this job, buy our freedom, and run this place like we want." Boris' cold, solid hands turned her around, shrinking his legs down till he was at eye level.

Jolene wanted to look into those big red eyes and hope, but her head hung low. Erabella was operating with impunity and at the absolute edge of her authority. There was no way of knowing what other fees or bills she'd ambush them with. The uncertainty twisted Jolene's guts into a knot. One of Boris' hands pushed under her chin until she looked at his dome and eyes again.

"Say it, dream it, work it, and come to us if you need reminding. This is my kitchen. Your dining room, and Murph's flying workshop. She will not take that from us."

Jolene couldn't help the smile that Boris' words brought out.

"There's the smile I know. Come look at my new tool." Boris teased.

Jolene did not laugh at the choice of words by biting her tongue.

"Behold, the Cruncher 5000 can handle enough organic input to feed a party of-"

"5000." Jolene guessed, and Boris' arms dropped.

"Yes, way to steal my thunder." Boris nudged her with one hand, and Jolene nudged back. Boris windmilled his six arms like his gyros were tipping.

"Unsafe actions in the workplace represent fiscal and legal dangers to Galaxy Waffles corporate. Cease and desist or face the consequences." O.D. floated into the kitchen. His teeth were the usual snow white, the smile a little wider, and that much creepier.

"The machine has the safety on, and no power. Now explain why you are invading my kitchen!" Boris said, standing to his full height, all six arms crossed.

"Informing employee Jolene that my earlier analysis was inaccurate, and she prepared the Galaxy Waffles improperly."

"Bullshit!" Jolene shouted, her sense of gratitude disappearing with the volume of her voice.

"Fortunately for your continued employment, I detected no bull feces." O. D's gloved hands were behind his back as he floated back and forth. "If you wish to know how this was determined, Sector Supervisor Erabella updated me with the latest patch from Galaxy Waffles corporate. I'm now operating at peak efficiency. I've updated your file. Besides conflict resolution training, Erabella will train you to prepare the dish properly. I hope you will commit to improvement." O.D. vanished, and Jolene shook, ready to make good on her syrup threat. She jumped back at a cold steel hand on her shoulder, ready to kick and scream. Boris held up his hands in mock surrender.

"Next time, I will record and provide evidence." Boris said. Jolene nodded and sent him a private message.

"I've got eighty hours of personal time. I'm using enough to cover the rest of the day." She didn't trust herself to be anywhere near O.D. or Erabella.

"Approved." Boris answered and Jolene ran to her room, engaged the electromagnetic deadbolt, slid down the door in darkness, and cried into her hands.

GLITCHING THE DAY AWAY

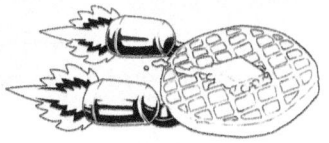

773 light-years to destination.

Jolene swung the sledgehammer up, smashing back the adolescent Cthullian's mass of tentacles. Then stepped forward, bringing it down with both hands. It skittered to the side, sticky suckers popping alongside the words of "Suck my Voltage" in her ears.

"RIP THEIR CIRCUITS!
DRINK THEIR POWER!
RIGHT THEIR WRONGS!"

She ducked swinging tentacles. Retreated from its snapping beak. Waited for the right moment. Stepped in and swung. The hammer smashed against its eye socket. The impact sent ripples through its body. Jolene grunted through a smile as the force-field reinforced hologram broke down into digital dust.

"Load Adult Cthullian combat program."

"You have used your maximum allotted Vent time. Please exit and continue to provide your best efforts for Galaxy Waffles." The automated system responded.

Jolene wiped the beads of sweat on her forehead, took a deep breath, and enjoyed the burn of her muscles as she leaned on the hammer's handle. Her H.U.D. flashed with the updated scoreboard. One thousand points higher than Murph. Boris wasn't allowed on the board because it was Boris.

"Please exit the Vent for cleaning."

Jolene hefted the hammer on her shoulder and stepped out of the Vent into the ship's cargo hold.

After the colonization industry took off, the Galactic Government passed a law for Terrablood and Starblood ship design; mandating recreation rooms. Predictably, the legislation's broad language allowed corporations to repurpose it. Instead of programs designed for mental health or career advancement, Starblood ships only had combat simulators.

Crew 3371's Vent looked like all the other cargo containers. Thanks to Murph's bizarrely long list of hobbies, they'd painted a collage of comic sound effect bubbles front to back. Jolene smiled at the SPLAT, OOMF, and BAM on the door.

"Employee Jolene fails to meet expectations, and does not use her available time for training."

Jolene did not turn and swing the hammer at Erabella. Instead, she turned to the nearest door.

"Training starts in thirty minutes. I'll be there in twenty-five." Jolene said, not looking back.

"Make that twenty. You have a lot to re-learn and correct." Erabella said, a tired sigh leaving her artificial body. Jolene's grip on the hammer tightened, but she kept walking. O.D. took shape in front of the door. Arms crossed, smile stuck from edge to edge of his waffle. Jolene's skin crawled at the thought of walking through him.

"Before you go, I want to know who defaced corporate property?"

Jolene smiled at O.D.'s new too wide smile before turning back to Erabella. The android's face scrunched from forehead to protruding pouting lips.

"Murph did it."

The android's nostrils flared at the words. Her face lost the scrunch of disapproval replaced with a full toothed smile that Jolene hated looking at.

"Then it's not defaced." Her remote control face rearranged between constipated rage and fake smile multiple times. "A unique Galaxy Waffles employee felt safe enough to express themselves creatively. Thank you for clearing up my misunderstanding."

Jolene rolled her eyes at the verbal backpedal and turned back to O.D. She jumped back several steps, raising the hammer.

"What the hell!" She shouted. O.D.'s golden waffle squares blinked with dead black squares. Multi-colored vertical lines flashed in and out across O.D.'s body.

"Everything is fine." O.D.'s voice distorted into a slow bass. His marshmallow teeth crackled into grey static blocks. His smile was still wider than Jolene remembered.

"O.D., run diagnostics and reboot." Erabella ordered.

The holographic waffle flickered away like a dying lightbulb.

"Great, the A.I. responsible for navigation and life support is glitching." Jolene said, rubbing her eyes. "We need to head back-"

"You need to complete the catering job. Leave O.D. to me." Erabella interrupted while she clicked away on her holo-pad. "Murph and Boris will make up for the gaps in your skill set."

Jolene had so many responses they got stuck in her throat. Erabella kept one eye on her holo-pad as the other moved to fix on Jolene.

"This job will strengthen Galaxy Waffles' relationship with Maximus Spendicus. Jeopardizing that for an expendable asset is the wrong choice." Erabella stared at Jolene with both eyes.

"A war hero A.I. and a Kyanese union member are not expendable assets." Jolene bit back. Erabella's holo-pad disappeared. Her neon blue lips stretched into something that fit the definition of a smile, making Jolene's skin crawl.

"Set a course for Horsehead and that's where you get off! No severance, no recommendations, no employee record. Those are the actions I will take. According to regulations, it would be considered compensation for the lost business."

"I'll update the crew." Jolene turned and said nothing else. She made her way to Murph's workshop.

Shortly after they'd gotten aboard, Murph had remodeled every square inch of their quarters into *functional inches* Jolene had chuckled at Boris' reaction to the pictures.

"No wonder you are late for so many shifts! That's not a room, it looks like a multi-dimensional puzzle cube!"

She set the hammer down, leaning it against the door, and messaged Murph on her H.U.D.

JOLENE (CHAT MESSAGE)

"Hammer's back."

She messaged in the secure chat.

MURPH (CHAT MESSAGE)

"I saw the scoreboard. You're on top now but wait till I take you down."

Murph's messaged back. The familiar argument tempted Jolene, but she had questions that needed answers.

JOLENE (CHAT MESSAGE)

"Hey! So, O.D. was showing deadlight squares and vertical lines. What could cause that?"

MURPH (CHAT MESSAGE)

"Space noise, holo projectors, resource shortage, and this is the one I'm hoping for—a critical coding error!"

Murph added a dancing emoji after the message.

JOLENE (CHAT MESSAGE)

"Not enough info?"

She answered. Murph responded with an animated bingo board gif showing the Xs filling out all the rows.

MURPH (CHAT MESSAGE)

"I'll access the diagnostics."

Jolene noticed she had fifteen minutes to get ready. She ran to her room, pulled her sweaty shirt off before she was in the room. Leaving a trail of clothes in her wake to the sonic shower.

"Speed clean!"

In two minutes, it vibrated her clean from head to toe. She had sixty out of eighty paid-time-off hours left. She needed to save some for the return trip to Horsehead. In the meantime, she had to hope O.D. didn't fly them into a black hole or vent all their oxygen. Just the normal things you had to worry about while getting dressed.

She stopped in front of the mirror on the back of her door. Syrup brown shirt. Check. Waffle ship name badge. Check. Nebula colored pants. Check. Plans to change obnoxious uniform when they bought the ship. Check. She put her best customer service smile on and entered the dining room with five minutes to spare.

Erabella clicked her tongue and pointed at the seat across from her. Just a few more days and she could kick this manipulative platinum pain in the ass off the ship. That thought made it easier to smile.

PLAY THAT AGAIN

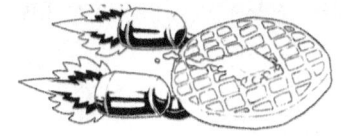

313 Light-years to destination

"I don't think there's anything to worry about." Erabella said through a gritted teeth smile. Boris, Murph, and Jolene looked at each other, blinked twice, and then back at Erabella.

"Play that again." Jolene didn't blink as the ship's bridge filled with the sharp lows and highs of static feedback. Murph's body vibrated like a series of sound waves until they smacked the console to make it stop. Erabella shrugged, the shoulder pads of her suit adding inches to the motion.

"Space weather, hardware malfunctions, or limited comm windows are all plausible explanations." Erabella looked at her neon blue nails before rubbing them on the golden stitching of her suit jacket. Jolene readied her laundry list of reasons that made no sense, but Boris beat her to it.

"Our sensors show no weather events. Their employer supplies the best. If there were such limitations, Calico Jack would have told us." He crossed all of his arms and hunched down, all four eyes shining red on Erabella's face.

The android smiled and waved her hand near her chest.

"So much eloquence and passion... I love it when you talk like that." Erabella's words came out in breathy tones. Jolene swallowed the urge to vomit. Murph turned sickly green.

"If you want to keep hearing it, why are we heading towards a situation with zero information?" Boris asked, never looking away.

Erabella's eyes dropped in time with a heavy sigh. She turned to the window, staring into the infinite depths of space, eyes forlorn. Jolene's urge to vomit transformed into the urge to fast forward through the melodramatic silence.

"Because without this job you cannot meet your quarterly quota, -" She turned back to Boris, hand on her chest. "Which will force me to declare you in default and pursue Indentured Employment to make up the loss."

Her eyes fixed on Jolene. She flashed her a shark smile for a nanosecond, before giving Boris the big eyed, broken-hearted routine. Jolene's fingers slipped into the contoured grip of her Voltstriker at the same time she decided to shove the barrel down the android Erabella's throat. The bitch just kept on talking, inching closer and closer to Boris; who stood there arms still crossed, still saying nothing. Jolene's first lesson in the service industry.

"You make a mess, you clean it up,"

Erabella was Jolene's mess, and it was time to clean up. She flipped her pistol's charging trigger. Took one step forward. Thick fingers grabbed her hand, Murph slid forward, putting their still green body between her and Erabella.

"Gotta hand it to you chief, your plan steps on two toes on two different feet." Murph said, while a mouth formed on the back of their neck.

"Wrong time." They whispered to her, and Jolene flexed against Murph's grip. They gripped harder.

"Care to elaborate Murphreezius?" Erabella said in a sickly sing-song. Murph's neck mouth frowned at their full name.

"Galaxy Waffles Slave Labor Corp! In a shocking overreach the diner chain corp forced a decorated veteran Galactic Government AI, and Kyanese Union member into Indentured Employment!" Murph's voice came out like the radio personalities in their mob movies complete with background noise. "Your bosses' boss' boss won't thank you for that headline."

Jolene noticed a single blue glowing eye joined the mouth on the back of their neck and winked at her.

"Galaxy Waffles Indentures for safe choices? Starblood chose to not risk Galaxy Waffles property and they've given her a life sentence!" They continued.

The itch to fry Erabella's circuits faded as Murph described the media fallout. Jolene ignored the urge to snarl at Murph's words. So many years and her nerves were still raw that Starblood was what she was to so many. Murph's fingers loosened, and Jolene flicked off the Voltstriker's charging trigger. They stepped aside and Jolene joined them, shoulder to shoulder, for Erabella's answer. She started slow clapping. The sticky sound of silicone skin and metallic fingers banging together.

"You might be in the wrong industry with a media spin like that. Despite being an easy target for inflammatory headlines, Indentured Employment isn't all bad." Erabella brushed one hand on Boris's arm. "Boris would be head of security at my office building and consult with Galaxy Waffles at large." Her fingers stroked the length of his arm as she walked past. "You don't upset the Kyanese Union. You make a deal they can't refuse. You'd be the face of our new employment drive. How do you feel about Specialized Species Service? Union members get work, the Kyanese get positive free press, and it would all be thanks to you."

Silence all consuming, like the vacuum outside the ship filled the bridge. Jolene looked from Boris to Murph. On paper, they'd be property. In practice, they'd be living peaceful lives. Their diner spaceship life was hard, but it let them see the Milky Way, grow, and learn together. Erabella offered roots, routine, and pay that they'd never see out here. Every thought and connection built in Jolene's brain, preparing her for their answers.

"You didn't mention Jolene." Boris said, cutting through the silence. Erabella sucked in a breath through her nose and closed her eyes.

"I'll let her choose between facilities and waste management." Jolene gripped her nylon belt hard. Burning friction and painful pressure kept her from drawing and shooting right then and there.

"O.D.!" Erabella ordered, and he projected into the

room.

"How may I be of service today?" He bowed through the question, his maple syrup pompadour bouncing with the motion.

"Crew 3371 is withdrawing from the catering job. Send them the Indentured Employment Contracts we discussed." Erabella's smile was a full toothed, wide eyed nightmare that Jolene wished she could wake up from. "Schedule a meeting with Calico Jack. Maybe we can salvage-"

"I am unable to comply." O.D.'s interruption caught Erabella's mouth open.

She turned on him, snapping it shut, mechanical eyes bulging from the sockets of her android. "Excuse me."

O.D.'s lips puckered. His marshmallow smile turned upside down. "Our destination is unchanged, and they have sent no communication back to Horsehead. At the moment, the catering job is active. I am unable to comply."

"For once, I agree with the waffle." Boris said and looked at Murph. "How long before we arrive?"

"Two days." Murph said.

"We have two days to strategize. I'm in." Boris looked at Jolene and Murph, ignoring Erabella's open-mouthed expressions.

"I've already got ideas. I'm in." Murph said. Both looked at Jolene.

"Can't be worse than the deal she offered. I'm in all the way." Jolene said while smiling despite every survival instinct screaming 'red alert' about this plan.

"My offer is open until we get back to Horsehead." Erabella had her arms crossed, while staring murder at O.D. "Now leave the bridge." She ordered. Jolene smiled through her salute. She owed both of her screwballs a bear hug, and she really needed to let out the laugh she was holding in. The bridge door slid shut behind them she head-locked Murphand then grabbed two of Boris' arms.

"Next time we're on Horsehead, drinks and food are all on me."

Murph tapped out on her forearm but smiled their needle teeth smile.

"You'll go bankrupt making promises like that." Boris said.

Jolene shrugged. Credits came and went but those two were worth it. Through her H.U.D., she connected with a security camera, hoping to catch Erabella throwing a tantrum. Instead, she saw her at one console, typing so fast that Jolene had to up the camera's frame rate to keep up. She recorded the last few seconds before Erabella closed everything.

Jolene pulled up individual frames of footage in her H.U.D. The menus Erabella was clicking through weren't for navigation. They looked like programming. She shared it in their encrypted group chat.

JOLENE (CHAT MESSAGE)

"Boris, can you read what she entered?"

Her green text bubble popped up.

Boris' red bubbles floated in the chat for a moment.

BORIS (CHAT MESSAGE)

"Need time to translate, but looks like custom code. Doesn't match any ship systems."

MURPH (CHAT MESSAGE)

"So, we're adding her to the strategy meeting, right?"

Murph's blue bubble asked.

BORIS/JOLENE (CHAT MESSAGE)

"Obviously."

Boris and Jolene's red and green bubbles answered in all caps.

Murph held up their hands in mock surrender. Jolene let go of them as they walked to the kitchen. In her head, she made a list and sent it to the chat. O.D. was being odd. Erabella was trying to divide and conquer. All the while, they were flying into a situation that made little sense.

Jolene, Boris, and Murph all sent the same GIF of a cow shitting out a cake. None of them actually asked what else could go wrong.

ARRIVAL

0 Light-years to destination

Jolene woke up to an email from Erabella marked URGENT, in Galaxy Waffles brown.

Mandatory Team Communication Channel

In it, she emphasized communication and teamwork. Ending on a direct order to use the new chat for all Galaxy Waffles related topics. Jolene tried to rub the micromanaging bullshit from her eyes.

"Understood" popped up in her usual green color. Neon white bubbles floated in the new chat.

ERABELLA (CHAT MESSAGE)

"I hope you'll view this as an opportunity to demonstrate how continued training will increase your value to Galaxy Waffles."

The color was an eyesore which fit Erabella but made Jolene's eyes ache.

"Absolutely." She answered, choosing malicious compliance as a pre-coffee strategy.

MURPH (CHAT MESSAGE)

"Read ya loud and clear Boss."

Murph's blue text popped as a reply to Jolene's

message.

BORIS (CHAT MESSAGE)

"Countermeasures ready. Decoy Coordinates sent."

Boris' red words popped into her eyes, moving Erabella's words from view. She mentally opened chat settings and dimmed the brightness just before three floating white bubbles came up again.

ERABELLA (CHAT MESSAGE)

"Please follow your co-workers' examples, Jolene. I expect all of you to post updates HERE."

The emphasized HERE pulsed in violent purple.

Jolene grinned as Boris and Murph sent animated eye-rolls to the encrypted chat.

JOLENE (CHAT MESSAGE)

"Roger."

Jolene answered, followed by Murph and Boris.

MURPH (CHAT MESSAGE)

"Dropping out of FTL."

Murph's blue text popped up. She peeked around the doorframe into the dining room. The flowing white corridor streaked with starry black space until the infinite horizon took shape.

Jolene flattened herself against the wall, preparing for inertia. The air and water inside her body squeezed and pushed back for torturous seconds before letting her go. She opened a list in her H.U.D. labeled 'Upgrade this shit!'

Thinking the words, quality inertia dampeners in all

caps, she adjusted her pale brown maintenance jumpsuit. Each dark oil stain, every black streak, a memory. The suit wasn't combat rated, but it resisted heat, tearing, and had an hour supply of oxygen. Compared to her diner uniform, it was as good as energy armor.

BORIS (CHAT MESSAGE)

"Decoy coordinates show received by outpost."

Boris' red words popped in both chats, but red floating bubbles came up in the encrypted one.

BORIS (CHAT MESSAGE)

"If they were all received, why isn't their traffic controller chewing us out?"

Boris asked. Murph responded with a GIF of rolling shoulders.

MURPH (CHAT MESSAGE)

"Maybe he doesn't wanna see the dentist for a broken mouth after biting you?"

Murph's message popped up. Jolene grinned and groaned. Boris answered with animated eye-rolls.

ERABELLA (CHAT MESSAGE)

"Sensors show no activity at the decoy coordinates."

Erabella's white message popped into the other chat. Jolene shivered at the thought that she'd done something helpful.

BORIS (CHAT MESSAGE)

"Confirmed."

Boris said in both chats.

JOLENE (CHAT MESSAGE)

"Any activity at the outpost?"

Erabella's white bubbles floated alongside Boris' red bubbles for a second before they both answered.

ERABELLA/BORIS (CHAT MESSAGE)

"No."

This time she groaned at the implications of a mining outpost with power, but no one acknowledged their approach.

BORIS (CHAT MESSAGE)

"Engaging decompression shielding."

Boris said in both chats. The air in the doorway crackled with energy before solidifying into a light blue sheet.

BORIS (CHAT MESSAGE)

"My money is on raiders or a critical fuckup."

He added in the encrypted chat.

MURPH (CHAT MESSAGE)

"That better be salvage money you're gamblin' with!"

Murph answered in the encrypted chat and then added in the mandatory chat.

MURPH (CHAT MESSAGE)

"Zero comms. No ship signatures. No lights from machinery. Looks like a graveyard."

ERABELLA (CHAT MESSAGE)

"A premature assumption, but I agree the initial data supports it. We need visual confirmations and evidence before we head back to Horsehead Station. Set a course for their hangar bay."

Erabella answered and ordered at the same time.

MURPH (CHAT MESSAGE)

"I'm going to be scrubbing every button and line of code when she leaves."

Murph said in the employee chat, adding in a pixelated humanoid aggressively scrubbing with a sponge at the end of the sentence.

BORIS (CHAT MESSAGE)

"I'll take a second pass on both."

Boris said in the encrypted chat. Murph gave a blue heart reaction and Jolene added a green heart reaction.

ERABELLA (CHAT MESSAGE)

"Also, Jolene, for the record, those stations of oil and emergency flares in the hallways you ordered are not approved by regulations."

Erabella said in the mandatory chat.

JOLENE (CHAT MESSAGE)

"There is no record saying we can't prioritize our survival over the regulations."

Jolene fired back, flipping her Voltstriker's safety on and off.

"Then you accept full responsibility for this decision?" Erabella asked and Jolene pictured the vindictive smile behind the words and answered.

"For staying alive? Yes. Yes, I will. And you can quote-" She stopped thinking as a mining drill floated by the diner's windows. Erabella's white bubbles floated in the chat and stayed floating. Empty spacesuits came next. Spools of cabling. Mining gear. All of it tapped against and bounced away from the waffle ship's shielding.

BORIS (CHAT MESSAGE)

"Engaging floodlights."

Boris said in the mandatory chat. Jolene braced herself for everything her imagination created. The ship's bright beams rolled over all of it. She took it all in. Only one question repeating in her head. She sent it to both chats.

JOLENE (CHAT MESSAGE)

"Where's the blood?"

Jolene asked.

Silence stretched time as multiple colors of chat bubbles floated in her H.U.D. She looked at every piece of everything through the dining room windows. Her H.U.D. identified hardware. She snapped photos of the names on suits. Not a single sign of life. Then a new message popped in the chat.

BORIS (CHAT MESSAGE)

"Blood isn't the only thing missing. Sensors say there's zero biological traces... in range."

Boris' words popped in the employee chat. Jolene swallowed the lump in her throat and used her H.U.D. to zoom in on the debris. She methodically looked for floating ice shards, red smears, anything nonmetal or plastic. She found nothing in the black and closed her eyes to reset her vision back to normal.

JOLENE (CHAT MESSAGE)

"Is the mining outpost in range?"

Jolene's green text popped under Boris' red.

BORIS (CHAT MESSAGE)

"Too much interference from the asteroids. We need to get closer for a clean scan."

Boris answered. Jolene pulled up the mapped route on a nearby screen. It showed the time to destination at fifteen minutes.

BORIS (CHAT MESSAGE)

"I know no one wants to ask me, but there is only one creature that eats this clean."

Boris started.

MURPH (CHAT MESSAGE)

"DON'T YOU DARE SAY CTHULLIANS!"

Murph's statement repeatedly posted until the employee chat was a wall of blue. Erabella's bubbles floated and Murph's text spamming stopped. O.D.'s silence was welcome but still unusual. Jolene half expected him to back up Erabella.

"Please finish what you were going to say, Boris?" Erabella ended her message with a smiley face emoji.

"Cthullians. They literally let nothing go to waste." Boris answered. Jolene drummed the back of her head on the wall. This was supposed to be a catering and recon job. Not a reenactment of Boris' war stories!

JOLENE (CHAT MESSAGE)

"Last time I start my day without coffee! Also, this is now a hostile extraction instead of a recon and report!"

Jolene typed into the encrypted chat ending with an eye-roll emoji.

MURPH (CHAT MESSAGE)

"Like hell it is! Save the scans, have Boris' flaunt his expertise bada-bing bada-boom and we light-speed outta here!"

They messaged both chats and Erabella's white bubbles started floating immediately.

"I respect your service to the Galaxy, Boris, but run the scans again. It was probably just a glitch." Everyone on the ship knew the diner was a bulky freighter, but the one thing Galaxy Waffles corporate didn't skimp on was sensors, internal and external. They looked great for insurance and helped keep ships flying. All of which invalidated Erabella's logic. Jolene was half done typing out the professional version of "That's bullshit!"

But Murph beat her to it.

MURPH (CHAT MESSAGE)

"WHAT!?"

Murph sent in both chats. Jolene was glad they weren't in the same room. Murph's emotions were always intense and when they got mad it was intensity squared.

MURPH (CHAT MESSAGE)

"Is your actual brain picking this up in real time, or did you set your android auto response to stupid?"

In the encrypted chat, they asked.

MURPH (CHAT MESSAGE)
"Ok, she's loonier than the bird. How do we get her in a straitjacket?"

They continued plastering the employee chat with GIFS themed around stupid and clueless. Boris posted a facepalm emoji in the encrypted chat.

BORISH (CHAT MESSAGE)
"Please de-escalate them."

Boris pleaded with Jolene in a one-on-one chat, and Jolene sent a shoulder shrug as an answer.

JOLENE (CHAT MESSAGE)
"Hell no! This could be the last time I see her get chewed out."

Her green text popped in their one on one, and she closed it to watch the textual fireworks. Sparing a moment to check the navigation screen, she verified ten minutes to destination.

ERABELLA (CHAT MESSAGE)
"Employee Murphreezius! That disrespect just earned you a write up! And six months of retraining!"

Erabella's white bubbles floated alongside Murph's blue ones.

MURPH (CHAT MESSAGE)
"And, if this mission kills me, the

Kyanese Union will put your name in front of Galaxy Waffles when they file their lawsuits."

Murph sent. For a minute, Erabella's white bubbles just floated.

ERABELLA (CHAT MESSAGE)

"I've noted your threat of legal action. If you or Jolene had bothered to read the contract, you would know that visual confirmation of the mining outpost is the bare minimum requirement."

Erabella answered and uploaded an image of the contract section.

She followed it up with another contract screenshot. This one stated they'd receive half the promised credits if they didn't meet the minimum requirement. Jolene bit her lip. Half the credits would pay off the quota, keep them alive, and let them try to score another payday. If Erabella didn't terminate, blacklist, and strand her on some no name backwater outpost first.

ERABELLA (CHAT MESSAGE)

"What is the current manager's decision?"

Erabella asked in the employee chat and sent a thirty-second timer labeled real-time motivation. Jolene didn't let it tick for long.

"Murph! Get us close enough to see. Boris, plot multiple routes to the mining outpost and back. We see a tentacle's shadow and I want us hitting light speed the moment we clear the field." Jolene's voice sounded steady over the comms; while her brain planned on the fly, exerting the little control she could.

"You got it, boss!" Murph answered over the comms.

"Plotting and uploading now, Captain." Boris said next. Jolene saved the best for last.

"Era, keep the corpo bureaucracy off the comms. We lose focus. You slow us down. We'll die, and so will that shiny valuable relationship with Maximus." Jolene said it all with a smile. Boris and Murph sent her salutes in the encrypted chat.

"Your plan is acceptable. Your tone and orders to your superior are not. I'll note both in your file." Erabella answered on a private comm channel.

Jolene bit back the reflex to give her a full serving of tone. "Considering our unusual circumstances and your repeated interpersonal difficulties with Murph, I thought it was-" She smiled through expert corporatese.

"You're not paid to think Starblood. You're here to obey. Now get to work!" Erabella shouted. Jolene muted the channel before exhaling in shudders. Terrablood propaganda preached tolerance and benevolence for the homeless Starbloods. Every Starblood learned that free of evidence and witnesses, those words became whips and fists. Jolene's sole comfort at the social whip crack was that Erabella didn't go off like that unless rattled. She owed Murph drinks at the Black Stallion.

BORIS (CHAT MESSAGE)
"Jolene? Your bio-tech is sending

alerts, blood pressure and pulse are all
over the place. What's wrong?"

Boris asked in their one-on-one chat. Jolene smiled at
her emergency contact, checking in.

JOLENE (CHAT MESSAGE)

"I'm fine, just overdosing on my daily
serving of privileged bitch."

She thought out the message, forcing herself to
breathe through the panic. The repetition helped clear her
head long enough to remember a question.

BORIS (CHAT MESSAGE)

"Were you able to load my Voltstriker
rounds into your arm cannons?"

Boris' red dots floated for a moment.

JOLENE (CHAT MESSAGE)

"No, but I'll find a use for them."

The chefbot replied.

Jolene smiled and remembered she had another job to
do. Eyes on the lazily spinning asteroids, she focused her
Empath sense around the ship. Sending them into every
crack and crater, finding nothing. On a nearby monitor,
their projected flight through the field showed they were
five minutes from the outpost.

JOLENE (CHAT MESSAGE)

"Report."

She said in both chats.

MURPH (CHAT MESSAGE)

"No visuals from the bridge."

Murph's blue popped in the employee chat.

ESTO BORIS (CHAT MESSAGE)

"Nothing on sensors."

Boris' red text popped next.

JOLENE (CHAT MESSAGE)

"Nothing setting off my Empath senses, either."

Jolene typed while checking their encrypted chat. No new messages were waiting. Dust and rock chunks lit up the ship's shields as Murph flew them slow and steady over and under. The inertia dampeners helped keep things in place, but Jolene's stomach still grumbled in protest.

ERABELLA (CHAT MESSAGE)

"Seems like the Cthullians moved on."

Erabella said in the employee chat.

MURPH (CHAT MESSAGE)

"Micromanager, manipulator, oh and let's add jinx to the list of reasons I wanna drop her in a black hole!"

Murph said in their private chat.

Boris threw in while answering Erabella.

BORIS (CHAT MESSAGE)

"I'll make the popcorn. That is a distant possibility. It's been several weeks, but..."

MURPH (CHAT MESSAGE)

"BUT WHAT?! You keep up this suspense malarkey and I'll switch all the labels on your spices!"

Murph said in both chats.

ERABELLA (CHAT MESSAGE)

"You just earned a second write up! Keep it up and I'll have you labeled as a threat to corporate property!"

Erabella sent it with two red Xs. Murph stayed silent in the employee chat.

MURPH (CHAT MESSAGE)

"All in favor of feeding her into Boris' fancy blender?"

Murph asked, sending a raised hand emoji that Jolene seconded. Boris sent a roaring bear GIF.

ERABELLA (CHAT MESSAGE)

"Enough. You quit it with the juvenile rage boner. And you, Miss Queen Snarksalot, reign them in. They're not helping you or themselves. Lastly, if either of you does anything to my kitchen, you'll be eating nutrition discs for a month!"

Jolene sent an emoji with a closed zipper. Murph didn't respond at all.

ERABELLA (CHAT MESSAGE)

"Boris, why is it a distant possibility?"

Erabella asked.

BORIS (CHAT MESSAGE)

"When Cthullians gorge, they go into torpor. They've learned that when they hunt us that-"

JOLENE (CHAT MESSAGE)

"Investigations and rescues are likely to follow."

Jolene finished in the employee chat. She leaned into the corner, taking comfort in the solid walls of the ship. Murph spammed every run away GIF they could into the encrypted chat.

ERABELLA (CHAT MESSAGE)

"Then where are they?"

Erabella typed out and before Boris answered, Murph blew up the comms.

"BRACE FOR IMPACT!" Murph screamed.

Jolene looked around the corner. In between spinning rocks were drifting crates. Each one marked with a bright red flame and skull.

"Murph evasive-" Jolene started over comms before they shouted back.

"If I go anywhere but straight, our last meal will be an asteroid!" They sent sensor images into the chat. Above and below, the gaps weren't wide enough. With icy terror in every muscle, Jolene thought the command.

"MAG BOOTS LOCK"

The suit beeped. Metal boot treads clicked down on the metal floor right before the first crate touched the shields. Metal blackened, then turned molten as it scraped across the field of energy. It floated out of view and exploded. A silent burst of force smashed the ship down. The force bent Jolene forward, but she avoided kissing the floor. Murph piloted into the momentum, nose diving them away from the chain reaction. Klaxons screamed in every part of the ship.

"Shields at ninety percent." O.D. announced over the comms. "The explosions are sending debris and asteroids in all directions."

"Boris, route options?" Jolene asked over open comms.

"Sending to Murph now, and oh son of a surge!" Boris cursed and continued. "Recalculating route to Mining Outpost, scans show its cargo bay shielding is down but operational." Boris answered everyone's question about why the sudden route change with a live feed of the latest sensor scan. It showed multiple asteroids all around them lit up with newly detected objects.

"Forget the creek, canoe, and paddle. We might as well just jump in a septic tank!" Murph's voice got louder as they continued, all while sending an alert of sudden acceleration. G-force pressure hit Jolene like an all over body punch until the inertia dampeners caught up to the new speed. She looked at the hallway screen. It said they were two minutes away from destination. Her brain piped in with a simple question. The kind she didn't want answered, but asked anyway, because of all the impending doom.

"Boris, did they set a trap?" Jolene closed her eyes waiting for the answer.

"Cthullian threat verified, lifting intel embargo." An artificial voice answered her from his side of the comms. The robot cleared the throat he didn't have before answering.

"Yes, they did." Boris said in his normal voice.

"What was that?" Jolene and Murph's voices flooded the comms.

"Seems the Galactic Government didn't let me be as free as promised. It wasn't just a trap. It was an alarm. If it killed us, they get an easy meal." Murph started decelerating for their approach, shaking everything several inches forward. Boris continued. "If it alerted them, what is the expression, 'dinner and a show'?" He said it all with a low electric growl that chilled Jolene to her bones.

"Grrrrrrrrrreeeeeeeeeeaaaaaaaaaat so we'll be expert tentacle food instead of ignorant schmucks. Wonder if that helps with the flavor?" Murph shouted as they banked away from an asteroid.

"Murphreezius! Your unacceptable conduct forces me to write up a third and FINAL warning! We'll see how your Union reacts to these transcripts and recordings!" Erabella's tone got progressively higher and more manic. Similar to the corpo rats on Jolene's orphan fleet, reporting everything they could with spiteful glee for the smallest bribes. Jolene mentally changed the navigation screen to show the latest scans. The red dots kept moving!

"We're about to be eaten! Take those transcripts and stick 'em in your charging port! You manipulative, paper pushing, chrome plated bitch!" Murph enunciated every insult.

"And that's strike four Murphreezius Imital you are fi-" Static cut off the rest of the statement. Syrup brown bubbles floated in the employee chat.

O.D. (CHAT MESSAGE)

"Termination of the pilot in this high-risk situation endangers the ship and its crew."

O.D.'s icon showed in the chat.

Everything went sideways as Murph turned the ship to fly between two asteroids.

"Mining outpost dead ahead!" Jolene shouted. She tried and failed to jump for joy with a fist pump.

"Mag Boots unlock," she thought and with another mental command, turned off the decompression shielding to the diner. She rushed to a booth, focusing her vision on the docking bay. "No Cthullian welcoming party!" She said.

"Finally, some good news." Murph answered, while changing course for the hangar bay.

"The Cthullian madness is in pursuit." O.D. said over the comms and employee chat. Jolene winced for two reasons. Firstly, O.D being the pedantic double messaging distracting jerk. Secondly, she now knew what to call a group of Cthullians. "Estimated docking time is thirty seconds. Contact with the Madness estimated at thirty-three seconds."

"Boris, can you hack the station from here?" Jolene hated every bit of the idea she was about to share.

"Yes, what is the plan?" Boris asked over the comms.

"Set the shields to power on in thirty-one seconds." Jolene waited for questions, none came.

"Ship needs a new paint job. Tin can you do the programmin I'll do the flyin" Murph said it in their most Chicago accent. Erabella's bubbles floated in the chat for a moment before a message from O.D. appeared.

O.D. (CHAT MESSAGE)

"I've suspended Sector Supervisor Erabella's chat privileges until further notice."

O.D. sounded happy, which didn't fit with everything, but at least he'd done something useful instead of annoying.

BORIS (CHAT MESSAGE)

"Thank the Motherboard for that!"

Boris' red text answered O.D.

"Murph, if you use the hangar bay floor for an emergency friction landing, we can maintain seventy percent speed." O.D. said it in text and comms.

"Listen up, nightmare fuel pixels! No one calls me Murph without my say-so. That being said, Erabella's puppet's got a point. It'll be rough, but might give us a few extra seconds."

"Do it!" Jolene shouted, the ship answered by speeding up, giving her another g-force punch and squeeze. She gritted her teeth through it and pushed her Empath senses around and into the hangar bay. "Zero emotional feedback inside the hangar bay."

"Boss, I'm buying you a halo and angel wings when we get back to Horsehead!" Murph shouted as they closed the distance.

Galaxy Waffles

"Fifteen seconds to land. Sixteen for shields deployment. Seventeen for our guests to arrive!" Boris' Russian baritone conveyed a happy rage that Jolene had rarely heard and hoped it would stay that way. The ship lined up with the hangar bay.

"Firing retrorockets!" Sound didn't travel in space, but the clash of forward and reverse thrust rattled the inside of the ship. "O.D. override the landing gear!" Murph shouted.

"Landing Gear override complete." O.D. shouted back.

"BRACE YOURSELVES!" Murph's voice shrieked into octaves Jolene had never heard from them. A harness automatically deployed in the booth. She clicked each point in.

"Mag Boots lock!" She mentally commanded.

"5, 6, and 7," Boris typed as the nose of the ship cleared the doorway. Loud thumps echoed through the halls of the diner.

"Three Cthullian stowaways detected." O.D. announced just before the ship started grinding across the hangar. With the shielding down, there was no air to feed sparks or sound waves to travel. Instead, Jolene heard and felt everything in the kitchen shake, rattle and roll. All the while, the ship's impact and vibrations pulled her in the harness in every direction. She didn't have time to wonder about bruises.

"Shields-" Was the last word Jolene heard before all three Cthullians let out psychic howls. The burning pain racing across her brain and skin forced her to scream, but she didn't hear it. The bestial anguished cries from the Cthullians filled her ears. Cold sweat broke out from every pore.

O.D. (CHAT MESSAGE)

"The Madness has surrounded the outpost."

O.D. typed in the chat.

Jolene screamed again at the tsunami of outrage and hunger.

"Deploy Blockers!" The two words took endless seconds to think, but her H.U.D. responded. **"DEPLOYED. EMPATHIC OVERLOAD IN PROGRESS. DEPLOYING SEDATIVES."**

Jolene knew she should have stopped it. They needed her! Her mantra was in reach; she could try to float through everything. Then more howls scraped inside her mind, and she let the sedative fill her system. She closed her eyes and slumped in the booth. Letting darkness and silence win.

SATISFYING CRUNCH

Empathic Migraines, as defined by the Non-Empath Doctor Sharad Quackerson, are a minor inconvenience that is easily managed with over-the-counter medications and hydration.

Jolene woke up and refused to open her eyes. Closing them harder pulled at the drum tight skin of her skull. Her brain felt like a bunch of knots pulled taut enough to snap. She sent a quick question to her H.U.D.

"WHY THE FUCK ARE THE MIGRAINE MEDS NOT BEING DEPLOYED?"

"BIO-TECH RUNNING AT LIMITED CAPACITY." popped on her H.U.D. She didn't open her eyes. Didn't scream out everything in her. She pushed it all down to ask.

"By who?"

"'By what?' is the correct question." Erabella's voice burned every customer service habit to ashes as the urge to grab and throttle her grew. Jolene barely managed to roll forward landing shoulder first on the cool floor and into metal bars. Questions and thoughts about how that was possible since diners didn't come with a brig. With her head on the floor a slow electrical hum filled her ears. They were were in the Vent! "O.D., make a note of her emotional instability and add conspiracy to commit murder to the list of charges."

"A Galactic Government court defines conspiracy to commit murder-" The air filled with garbled words and static. Jolene cracked her eyes open to see O.D. fragmenting. Pieces of his waffle contorted. His colors flashed in and out. The random light show and unnatural twisting of who he was, stabbed into her eyes. She tensed into a ball as her migraine flared, sending waves of spikes down her spine. Her mind screamed at the violations to the A.I. Rage pushed her through the pain, as she glared at Erabella.

"What is-" she started and stopped as she looked at Erabella's android. She was staring at O.D. with a tiny neon blue lipped sadistic grin. O.D.'s pixels swirled back into shape.

"Logging both events for the trial." He said in the same peppy voice he used for birthday songs.

"Good boy! Is her bio-tech still disabled?" Erabella asked, looking at the painted nails of her metal fingers. A distant memory flashed in Jolene's head about how all Galaxy Waffles bio-tech was their property until paid off and could be remotely accessed. She could still move but every bit of wear and tear the tech helped, now just screamed for her attention, as well as her empathic migraine.

"All but the drip feed of Empath blockers! Galactic

Government regulations G.G. 301 'All prisoners must receive enough care to ensure they are competent for trial.' " O.D.'s chocolate chip eyes melted into trails of snowy static while his voice stayed peppy.

"It'll have to do. Go help Murphreezius with the sensors."

O.D. saluted and disappeared.

Erabella turned to look down her nose. "Jolene Starblood. Your dereliction of duty endangered corporate property and fellow Galaxy Waffles employees. I am exercising my legal right to detain you and disable your bio-tech, until we surrender you to the Galactic Government."

Erabella's platinum teeth shone in the overhead lights. Her mechanical pupils dilated into black portals with every word. Jolene's brain reeled from every sight and sound. Each fresh sensation interrupted every attempt to put together an answer.

"Not guilty." She groaned out.

Erabella's android laughed. It was a mechanical screeching assault on the ears. Jolene curled up into a tighter ball, hands over her ears, waiting for it to stop. Biting her tongue to keep any begging words inside. When it did, she opened one eye, sucking in air at the eye stabbing light, but refused to look away from Erabella.

"I've got you on video passing out in the middle of a crisis you led the ship and crew into! You gambled with corporate profits, employee lives, and the cherry on top is that it proves you're incompetent because it looks like you abandoned them. I don't even have to lie! You had premium Spendicus Inc Empath blockers, and you still chose to give up! Add all that up and any trial will be a formality! You disposable dishrag!" Erabella stepped forward, metal hands wrapping around the holographic bars, her face pressed between them.

"Why?" Jolene asked weakly. It was the only word she could say in between the waves of pain. Erabella's grip tightened, distorting the hologram.

"Because I took you in. Taught you. Fed you. Clothed you. Showed you how to build an empire! And were you grateful? Did you obey orders? No! Instead, you took everything from me!" The silence that followed made Jolene's insides twist at all the twisted logic. "So why? Because it's only right that you lose just as much as you cost me. Even if it is next to nothing."

She pushed away from the bars, running fingers through her platinum colored hair. The present was an unreal fever dream that Jolene couldn't quite absorb, but she needed to know two things.

"Boris-" she coughed through her scratchy, dry throat and pushed on. "And Murph?"

The doors to the Vent slid open. Boris' heavy steps fell like hammers on Jolene's ears. She smiled through the pain at the steady vibrations traveling through the floor into her. He was unharmed, the first good news since she'd woken up.

"I thought you were better than your fears." Boris said it so calmly that Jolene didn't have a single answer. "I was wrong." He finished and she pushed herself back to the wall when all eight of his eyes fixed on her. His chassis was slick with purple gore. His merciless gaze turned to Erabella. "The hangar bay is clear-" His head swiveled back. All eight eyes flashed brighter red. "For now. Murph is plotting a course with minimal risk to the ship. As soon as I've said what I need to say I will extricate the ship from the hangar bay floor." Boris finished, and Erabella twirled on her toes, clapping while laughing maniacally.

"I'm so-" Jolene started, hoping she could at least explain that at the moment, it was all too much.

"Do not waste my time or Murph's with useless apologies!" Boris raised three palms up. "We put our lives and futures on the line with yours and you abandoned us to escape pain! You chose yourself and now" Boris stopped and five of his fists grinded as he clenched. "Now we choose like you did." He said it all without a hint of hesitation. Jolene wanted to beg for one word, one sentence hoping he would understand. Before she could say anything, he stomped forward, the sounds and vibrations pushing Jolene back into a ball, hiding her face in her knees.

"Remember when I said you'd hear the rest of my story?" Boris asked with the same cold certainty. She nodded, looking up just past her knees.

"We were on shore leave. The planet was supposed to be safe. The other two, Smith and Folly, stayed on the ship. I was charging. Vanya was exploring." Icy dread forced her to hyperventilate. At the picture Boris painted mixed with the unending growling of his voice. "We were already off-world when I finished."

Boris' fists clenched again, sending grinding rattles bouncing off the walls.

"They said they'd tried to save Vanya and couldn't risk waking me and interrupting my processes." Boris let out an angry laugh. "I checked the logs. Vanya stumbled on some predators. They sent him coordinates away from the landing zone. They promised to back him up. Internal ship cameras showed they'd only ever prepared to lift off."

Even through the brain fog of the migraine, Jolene connected the dots. Abandonment. She closed her eyes and felt tears slip down her cheeks. She opened them, meeting Boris' blood red stare.

"I'm sorry." Jolene said. She hated how her voice trembled and how she'd proven she was no different from the monsters in his past.

"Smith and Folly cried and apologized while they dug Vanya's grave. I watched them fall to their knees when I flew away. They got what they deserved. We'll make sure you get the same." One of Boris' arms wrapped around Erabella, pulling her in close. She clung to him like a magnet.

"Yes, we will," she hissed.

Jolene swallowed the lump in her throat. They'd survived the Cthullian Madness, but all of this felt like mad unreality.

"Boris, sweetie, let's go. I don't want you re-traumatized by talking to human garbage." Erabella started toweling away the purple gore. Boris stood there, his red eyes turned off and on again. He sighed and looked into her neon eyes.

"I'm sorry I've been so distant. Thank you for showing us her true nature."

Erabella polished his bear insignia before leaning on his chest looking into his eyes.

"Thank you for trusting me." One of Boris' fingers pushed her chin up gently. Erabella's foot popped like a love-struck lead from Murph's old movies.

Jolene swallowed the urge to projectile vomit all over the moment. Her insides rumbled at all the conflicting emotions in her guts.

She'd lost her freedom. Broken Boris and Murph's trust. Would never have her own ship. To top it all off, she had front row captive seats to an abominable mechanical romance.

"I know eating is unnecessary for this android, but would you do me the honor?" The hand he'd been hiding came over his head. Erabella's head twisted around one-hundred-eighty degrees, every part of her body staying in contact. Jolene held up a hand to the light, too horrified to stop watching.

"Oh, you are such a romantic! I can't wait to eat these off your chassis when I get you back to Horsehead."

Boris wrapped two more arms around her.

"I'm going to quality inspect every inch of you." The timbre of his voice was deeper and smokier. Erabella bit her lip and groaned.

Jolene couldn't take it anymore. She stuck her tongue

out and acted out vomiting at the spectacle.

"If you ruin this moment for me, you won't live to see a courtroom!" Erabella shrieked, the words sharp and shrill. The suddenness forced an open mouthed gasp out of Jolene.

"Please don't pay her any mind and taste perfection." Boris gently waved a plate of nutrition discs under her nose. Jolene, bent over crying from the pain, watched as Erabella stacked two of them.

"Double the nutrition. Double the deliciousness." She tittered and bit down. An electric pop and sizzle filled the Vent from ceiling to floor. Blue electricity arced out of her hair. Erabella's android wriggled into spasms. Boris held her against his chest. The android's hair started smoking. Her head spun like a power drill was screwing it in place until both of those neon chameleon eyes of hers popped out of their sockets. All the sounds and motions shook some of the nutrition discs off the plate.

Jolene watched them fall to the floor, and they gave off the same electric pop, and leaked a familiar blue gel. A tiny arc of electricity bounced from drop to drop. Her Voltstriker rounds! She looked up at Boris open mouthed and hopeful. Four of his eyes shut. He let out an exasperated sigh.

"You know, you almost ruined that plan!" He grumbled, setting Erabella down, while another pair of hands opened the Vent door. The overhead lights shut off.

ADMIN ACCESS RESTORED. Appeared on her H.U.D.

Galaxy Waffles

She mentally slammed the order to deploy painkillers and full doses of Empath blockers. Relief flooded her bloodstream. She still couldn't decide whether to yell or scream at Boris and Murph.

Coffee First

BORIS (CHAT MESSAGE)

"Murph, stop recording!"

Boris sent through their private chat.

MURPH (CHAT MESSAGE)

"Think I'm short a brain cell? I stopped all the cameras soon as you started walkin' to the cell."

Murph answered.

The words left her breathless, but Boris let Jolene lean on him as her brain caught up with reality. It didn't help that the room was spinning, and if she tried to fight gravity, she would kiss the floor. "So, whose idea was it to give me a heart attack?" Jolene asked.

"Mine with some dialog from Murph." Grunts of effort left Boris' speakers even though he was probably using less than one percent of his battery.

"Some? More like the whole damn script!" Their voice came over the ship's comms. "Mr. Fancy Chrome pants wanted to do Shakespeare and Pushkin."

Jolene couldn't help giggling, imagining Boris reciting ancient earth poetry.

"Also, now that we can speak freely, I'd like to

paraphrase a golden oldie."

"Ding dong, you fried the wicked bitch
Pour the whiskey.
Deal the cards.
Sing it high Sing it low
Ding dong, you fried the wicked bitch."

Murph sounded like they'd swallowed a tank of helium, but Jolene still slapped Boris' chest along with the words.

"The meter is off, the lyrics are juvenile, you're combining two very different songs, and despite all of that, I love it." Boris clapped his spare hands.

"A thank you, thank you very much," Murph's voice came out deep and smooth.

"Hold on a sec." Jolene stopped them at the door, eyes fixed on Erabella's smoking fizzing android body. She pulled away, leaning on the wall. Just holding herself up was knocking the air out of her lungs. She sucked in everything she could pulled her foot back kicked. She avoided the face and focused the toe of her boot right into her silicone guts. The android's artificial muscles reacted to the force curling the body around the center of impact.

"Here's your fucking e-val- "kicked again. "ua-" kicked twice in a row. "Tion" finishing by wiping her boots against Erabella's suit. She smiled at the black smears across the white fabric and gold thread stitch.

"And that folks is why you don't piss off your

waitress!" Murph said, as Jolene walked without stumbling back to Boris. Her H.U.D. typed out the messages:

MOBILITY AND MENTAL ACUITY CURRENTLY AT SIXTY-FIVE PERCENT.

ONE HUNDRED PERCENT FUNCTIONALITY WILL RESUME IN TWENTY MINUTES.

"While I'd give this serving of schadenfreude five stars it doesn't help us answer the question. How the hell do we survive?" Murph joked and asked with equal parts amusement and panic.

"Right now we're besieged. We need to itemize supplies. I'll have a report and projections shortly." Boris answered with stubborn certainty.

"Coffee first." Jolene demanded.

Boris turned towards the dining room.

"May I-"

Jolene sighed and rolled her eyes at what she knew he wanted to ask.

"Please carry me."

Four of Boris' arms extended around her. Slowly and gently supported her from head to toe, and lifted her to rest across his chest. Murph, being themselves, started playing the wedding march as they walked through the halls. Jolene's freckles didn't interconnect when she blushed, but they did nothing to help hide the red heat filling her cheeks.

"Enough of that, you blue jackass." The music ended on Boris' last word.

"Thank you." Jolene muttered against his bear insignia,

as she watched the timer on her H.U.D. tick down.

"You're welcome." He put her in one of the swivel chairs at the counter.

"Going to make you a Drill Sergeant Special." Boris' hands came together, filling the dining room with recorded cracking sounds. Jolene rested her chin in her palms.

He strutted into the kitchen, six arms extending ahead of him to different cabinets. From left to right on the counter in front of her he placed the grinder, pour-over coffee drip with large glass bottom, an aged gooseneck kettle, a pint of milk, and a pack labeled 'distilled water'.

"Now last, but not least, we have the star of the show." Boris pulled a bag over his head.

Jolene didn't believe it. In fact, she rubbed her eyes to make sure she was seeing right. She reached out to pet the surface of the force-field reinforced packaging. They were real, whole coffee beans! She put a hand over her mouth. Unsure what words or noises it would make.

"It was going to be a birthday surprise, but jailbreak and survive the day is just as good."

She wiped away tears before they could leave her eyes. Over the top gifts made every birthday memorable. She had no idea how to top this one. Thoughts of the future forced the next words out of her mouth.

"I know that low risk flight plan was part of your script but…" Jolene said it trailing off, afraid of what everyone would say.

"We've made it this far, to abandon it would mean losing us and the ship. Well, here's what I say to that."

Boris stopped talking to lean over the counter, all six of his hands gently grabbed and pulled Jolene by the front of her engineer suit. "Let's fuck shit up, and go for gold."

Jolene nodded, unable to stop the happy tears spilling out of her eyes.

"What he said" Murph added over the comms. "Ain't no way I'm givin' up after coming this far."

Jolene nodded at Boris, and sent Murph a thumbs up. Not trusting herself to speak.

Boris continued preparing his coffee gift. Two of his hands held up the bag while a third disabled the force-field and a fourth unzipped it. Roasted notes of bourbon and vanilla wafted into the room.

Jolene closed her eyes to inhale every moment. Force-field packaging captured every molecule of the contents, even the air during roasting. Boris poured the beans, re-zipped, and activated the Force field in less than five seconds.

"Who, what, when, and-" One of Boris' arms extended, pressing a finger on her lips. "Please hold all questions until you are properly caffeinated." The words came out through a robot voice filter.

Jolene couldn't help smiling and shaking her head.

"My favorite tin can and jailbird!" Murph cheered as they slid into the dining room growing bear arms to give Jolene a bear hug before turning to look out the window. The hangar bay shielding generated a low light casting shadows from tossed crates and torn up flooring. Murph rubbed the back of their head.

Galaxy Waffles

"So, chef, what's on the menu for the damned?" Murph wore a smile that didn't reach their eyes. "Give me the fattiest, greasiest, meatiest thing ya got. Just none of that sushi! I coulda had a happy life never seeing a live slicing and dicing!" They took their hat off, setting it down on the counter. For a moment they turned sickly green, then they sat straight up. Their eyes turned into old earth dollar signs, while the top of their head turned into a light bulb. "How much do you think all those fresh tentacles are worth?"

Boris growled something while pointing his trusty meat cleaver at Murph. Jolene's H.U.D. translated the Russian words to: **"ENOUGH ALREADY. SHUT UP AND SIT DOWN."**

Murph's eyes narrowed, "Just wait till I report you to the manager."

Jolene turned towards them. Boris' head swiveled back. Murph's narrow eyes and snarl didn't last. They all broke out in smiles and burst into laughter. Boris took a tiny electric whisk and frothed the milk.

"Bad jokes are better than cynicism. Now both of you enjoy this, then we plan our escape." Boris instructed.

He poured the coffee into two glass mugs. Jolene licked her lips at the cup of energizing darkness. All that excited nervous energy rushed to her bouncing foot. Then he started pouring the frothed milk. A layer of pure white formed at the top. Whirling clouds fell through the black to the bottom. The slow transformation from black to brown mesmerized her. With a spoon in each hand, he gently stirred, turning it lighter and warmer. He pushed the mugs into their waiting hands. She took her first sip right as the ship's lights flickered over to red and alarms went off.

"Attention Crew 3371. Multiple Cthullians have entered the mining outpost. They are heading straight for the hangar bay. Estimated arrival is three minutes." O.D. announced and took shape over the counter.

Jolene did not stop sipping. Creamy perfection flowed across her tongue. The sweet depths of bourbon mixing with the bright vanilla made her groan a certain way. The inevitable caffeine tingle rushed from the base of her brain to the bottom of her spine.

"How many?" Jolene didn't look up, choosing to stare into her coffee instead.

"Count in progress." O.D. floated down to eye level. He was chewing on his oversized glove hands. Each marshmallow tooth sinking down and puffing back up.

"Murph, go make sure the oil and fire supplies are still useable." Murph saluted, bottom half turning to spider legs and rushing off. She swiveled to the right and shouted. "Also, get my Voltstriker!" Her voice carried down the hall.

"One peashooter coming up." They answered in the private chat.

"What can you handle?" She swiveled back to the front to see Boris armed with his kitchen arsenal.

"All of them. Also, best way to fight an enemy is to know them." A red file notification popped in Jolene's

H.U.D. labeled: **CTHULLIAN INTEL!**

She hit download without a second thought as Boris' ice carving chainsaw revved to life. A rolling pin sized for him rested near his head. Heavy duty crème brûlée torch in a lower hand. The meat cleaver's blade gleamed in the red emergency lights.

"Time for pest control."

His four remaining eyes opened as he marched to the main doors.

THE PLAN GOES BOING!

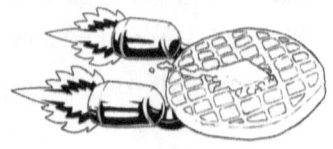

"His odds for survival are-" Jolene tossed a spoon at O.D. It sank into his face. Pulling everything out of place until his low grade force-fields gave up! Then everything snapped back into shape. This, of course, meant he jiggled all the way from maple syrup pompadour down to his blueberry feet. His bacon eyebrows slanted, while the tips of his marshmallow teeth blackened. "As I was- "

"Saying something useless." She took a sip of coffee as O.D. floated there, mouth open. He raised an oversized finger.

"Analysis and statistics are a vital- "

A napkin dispenser flew through O.D.'s mouth, stretching and jiggling him faster this time.

"Shut up or say something useful!" Jolene screamed at him before sliding into a window-side booth to watch Boris work.

He'd sheathed his cleaver and rolling pin into his apron, leaving two arms free to extend and grab two cargo containers. He lifted both and ran towards the only door Jolene could see. The hallway security lights flickered in time with the docking bay lighting. Boris ran drumming a thumping metallic beat.

"Intruder Alert. Three Cthullians inbound." O.D. announced on the ship's speakers.

"Cook and book stations ready. We only had one spill in cargo. Got it cleaned up. How's Boris?"

"Good job, Murph. Get a new station setup and don't forget my pistol. Boris is about to throw down." She said trying to force a smile through her shaky voice..

"Can't miss that!" They cut off comms.

Boris wedged the containers in the doorway then sheathed his remaining weapons. Jolene's coffee cup was on her lips. Not a drop passed between them. She watched her friendly six armed armory spider his way up the wall. When he flipped over, four arms gripped the wall, leaving two for his cleaver and rolling pin. His eight red eyes fixed on the door below. Jolene saw the wriggling, one eyed masses turn the corner, bowling over each other. Scrabbling forward on suckers. Their muted growls crawled over the hull, raising the hairs on her neck.

Jolene zoomed in to scan and snap photos. Results typed across her screen:

SPAWN - YOUNG OR ADOLESCENT CTHULLIANS. FAST AND DEADLY IN LARGE NUMBERS.

ABOMINATION - ELDER CTHULLIANS. SLOWER THAN SPAWNS, BUT MUCH STRONGER AND MORE DURABLE.

Jolene sent them to Boris as beads of sweat trickled down her cheeks. Habit forced her to check her Empath blocker status. She pulled up dose time and supply in

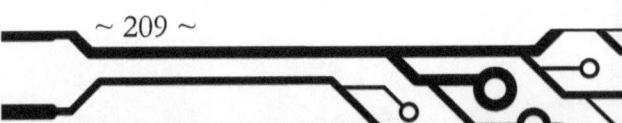

her H.U.D. and exhaled at one less tension knot in her stomach. She cleared the H.U.D. and focused on the fast-approaching Cthullians.

Lights on. She saw snapping beaks and strained eye vessels. Exposed wiring sparked.

Lights off. She looked and saw eight red eyes.

Lights on. They'd reached the door. The Abominations' scarred tentacles pushed through the barricade. Beak open, roaring. Jolene backed away at the sound.

Lights off. Eight red eyes fell, disappearing into the darkness. Jolene held her breath. Shrieking. Scraping.

Lights on. Boris sitting in the center of the Cthullian mass. Rolling-pin bashing the eye to jelly. Cleaver cleaving. Chainsaw cutting. Blowtorch cooking. His last two arms holding something.

Lights off. The sounds stop. Eight red eyes rush towards the ship.

"Murph, get out here and fix the damn wiring!" Boris shouted over the comms.

Lights on. Boris was fighting off the two remaining Cthullians, three arms each. He stayed mobile. One arm flaring the torch at the closer one. His cleaver and saw swinging at the other. Retreating, he grabbed rubble, tossing it at one or both to buy time.

"More Cthullians inbound!" Murph announced on a three-way comm channel.

"Numbers? ETA?" Boris asked.

"Last scans say forty one and two minutes." Murph answered.

"Shit!" Jolene shouted. "Boris, get back inside. We can deploy shields and-"

"Last for less than ten minutes." O.D. added helpfully, depressing everyone.

"Hey O.D., when we're dead and you're all alone asking yourself why no one liked you. Replay this moment." Murph growled actual animal sounds over the comms.

"I have a solution, but I need your authorization." O.D. looked at Jolene.

She took a sip of coffee; focusing on the caramel, sweet touches of bourbon and floral depths of vanilla. All while her brain screamed one of her favorite Suck My Voltage lyrics.

SCORCHED BY YOUR SCHEMES!
SMILING AT YOUR SCREAMS!

"Boris, how many can you handle?"

"Forty one, but it will be ugly." He stepped forward, pinning the left Cthullian's tentacles. The one on the right charged. Boris' head swiveled. All eight eyes turned white sending searing lumens into its pupil. It fell back, screaming and bundling its tentacles over itself.

The pinned one closed the distance. Its black-green limbs wrapped around every joint it could find and squeezed. Jolene's heart stopped as she heard metal groan. Boris swiveled and Jolene saw fingers of steam rise from the closest tentacles. It didn't release. Boris chainsawed his way to the eyeball. While his cleaver chopped at the tentacles crushing him. By the end, he was purple top to bottom. Then he swayed. His other leg came out, and he steadied. Jolene focused on the other limb. The hip joint's smooth metal was now crumpled, silicone muscles hung loose.

"Get back inside!" Jolene ordered. Boris' two free arms extended and grabbed the last groaning Cthullian. He reeled it in at full speed, impaling it on his rolling-pin handle. The mixture of sights and sounds belonged on Combat Cavalry, not in reality. Boris pushed it off with his good leg before finally answering.

"I've already set up a transfer to my backup server. I'm not letting a single one of those things in my ship!" Boris said, flicking purple gore off his weapons. She set aside her coffee as Murph rushed back in. They passed her the pistol. She primed it and turned on O.D., not raising her pistol and keeping her finger off the trigger.

"What's your plan?"

O.D. swallowed. A lump rolled down his waffle squares.

"I need to alter the ship's shielding. Give me admin access to the system and I'll get to work."

"Murph, is O.D.'s cook and book station ready?"

Murph's spider legs went blue and re-absorbed into their normal bipedal form. Right as they took off their hat, popped out a detonator, and clicked it.

"Deadman switch, primed and ready."

O.D. lost all color, turning into a pencil outline of their usual selves.

"Why? I helped you! I did–"

"A lot of shit she ordered." Jolene finished. Murph nodded, twisting their hand and the detonator sucked into their body. O.D.'s white bacon eyebrows curled up as they stared down at the floor with a frown.

"I don't know what shady shit she pulled with you, but you were against us before she showed up. So this." She nodded at Murph. "Is insurance." She pulled up the menus in her H.U.D. and gave O.D. admin access.

"Get moving."

O.D. vanished in a blink.

MURPH (CHAT MESSAGE)

"I thought the Union wrote the book on tough, but you could teach a class."

Murph's blue text popped in their encrypted chat.

JOLENE (CHAT MESSAGE)

"You and Boris still need to fix whatever Erabella did, and I'm not wasting time arguing regulations with him."

Jolene's green text typed out. They shared a smile as Murph produced the detonator and turned it into a bouncy ball.

"Alright, so we give the tin can covering fire, while the waffle modifies the ship's shields. And then what?" Murph asked.

Jolene loaded the assisted targeting and ammo counter programs into her H.U.D. She couldn't remember the last time she'd used it and hoped she could keep up.

"Survive. Better question: how are you gonna help

Boris without-" She didn't get to finish because full riot gear rose out of Murph's skin. It covered their arms in black overlapping metal diamonds. Pulsing white energy between each proved it wasn't them shifting. This gear was real. A helmet that only showed their eyes, a blur of air pulsing before them told her the gap had shields.

"You're not the only one who can do dramatic interruptions." They said, deploying an energy riot shield. A gun flowed out of Murph's hand. It took a moment for Jolene's H.U.D. to scan and give her results.

THOMPSON SUBMACHINE GUN

MODIFICATIONS DETECTED:
ANTI-PERSONNEL ROUNDS
EXPANDED AMMO DRUM
KYANESE STABILIZER AND COOLING SYSTEM
PINPOINT HOLO SIGHT

Jolene waved it out of her vision.

"When and how and why didn't you use that when we were getting robbed?"

"On Horshead-" was all they managed before Cthullian roars shook their bones and gelatinous limbs, respectively. Murph moved to the front door entryway, leaned on the doorframe, and took aim. Jolene was right behind them, remembering to breathe and keep her finger off the trigger. Her H.U.D. marked the edge of her range with a line across the docking bay. While the lights flickered on and off.

ENABLE AUTO AIM

She sent the command to her H.U.D. and felt a tingle go down every limb.

"I've loaded the modifications." O.D. said over open comms.

"How long before the shields can deploy?" Murph asked, while Mini-Murphs came out of their feet with ammo drums on their back. Jolene wondered how much they could actually carry after the fifth one.

"They need to shut down and restart with the modifications."

Their heads dropped, alien, and human groaned in protest.

"You mean anywhere between five and thirty minutes?" Boris asked.

"Yes." O.D. answered.

In the dry recycled air of the docking bay, Jolene heard the snarling raging grow as the pile of dead Cthullians grew. Murph's modified machine gun opened fire. Instead of exploding gunpowder and belching metal, it let out a sharp whine and white muzzle flash. Lights on. She watched the leading monsters stumble. Murph's precision tore through their tentacles. Lights off.

"Gats for days, bitches!" They shouted in the mobster accent Jolene didn't know she'd missed.

"O.D. time?" She shouted.

"Shields are shut down. New settings loaded. Startup time is five minutes!"

"Good news wrapped in bad news still tastes like shit!" Jolene shouted through the comms. Murph and Boris laughed. The sound alone was enough for Jolene to smile as she set a timer.

5:00 minutes.

Lights on. Murph's continued bursts found anything moving and stopped it. Jolene didn't bother zooming in and scanning. With the lights flickering and that many overlapping limbs, she'd fry her gray matter with all that conflicting information. Then the blockage of writhing tentacles advanced.

Lights off. "Boris, were they?" Jolene asked the unfinished question hoping her eyes were lying.

"Using their injured as meat shields. Yes."

"Tin can, anything else you wanna share about these things? Cause so far we've got traps and tactics." Murph said at a higher pitch. Jolene almost laughed from the squeaky mobster accent.

4:00 minutes.

Lights on. They'd reached Boris' damaged barricade. The injured were squeezed into the middle. Murph's rate of fire slowed as they tried to aim around the wall of meat. In moments the Abominations shoved aside the cargo crates like they were paper crates.

Lights off. Jolene sniffed and gagged as her nose filled with charred meat. It was the same stench when a customer had snuck in to "pan fry" their eldritch sushi.

She looked down to see Boris super-heating his cleaver. Bitter, burning blood turned her stomach.

3:00 minutes.

Lights on. The auto aim lined up her sights with the darkness and fired. A line of crackling blue flew until it burst against a Cthullian. Bellows of pain scraped at her brain as it attacked her psychically. The auto aim program in her bio-tech did not care. She fired round after round until her ammo count reached one.

Lights off. She squeezed, reloaded, and resumed. No matter how many times she used it, the auto aim's puppet master effect threatened to send her into a panic attack. She brought up the digital red button in her H.U.D., focusing on it; trusting it would shut it off.

2:00 minutes.

Lights on. The Cthullians spread out in an arc. Hissing, spitting Spawn behind Abominations pushing cargo containers. Others held up flat pieces of steel flooring. Murph's ammunition peppered their improvised cover with steel quills.

"Please tell me you have armor piercing for that thing."

"Sorry, boss, just the ripper rounds."

Jolene's body swung towards the left and fired, but it splattered on the cover. The constant back and forth was making her dizzy. With a thought, she disabled the auto aim. When she finished fighting off the urge to vomit, she turned to Murph.

"Ripper rounds?"

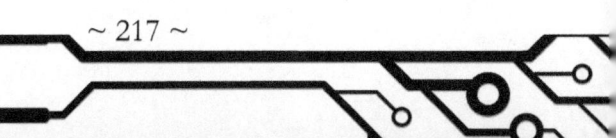

1:30 seconds.

Lights off. Murph faded to background noise as two metal thuds hammered through the darkness. Two crate shaped trails of sparks lit. Murph opened fire and Cthullians screamed.

"Cover your ears." Boris said over the comm channel. Jolene complied. Murph kept shooting. Both asked in chat:

BORIS/JOLENE (CHAT MESSAGE)

"What's he doing?"

The click and screech of audio feedback wormed into their brains. She and Murph shivered at the involuntary tingles.

"I killed Threshold!" Every Cthullian froze. Murph didn't stop shooting, but none of them screamed. For precious seconds, the only sound was their gun. Jolene's hands eased away, and that's when it started.

:45 seconds.

Lights on.

They ran and roared. Pained sounds. Raging sounds. Every single one frantically charging straight at Boris. She pressed her hands to her ears but was still curled in a ball. The auditory and psychic assault combined into a blocker breaking nightmare. She spammed her system to deploy more, cutting her off with a message in flashing red letters.

EMPATH BLOCKER MAXIMUM EFFECTIVE DOSAGE DEPLOYED.

She rolled up to see Boris not buried by Cthullians. He'd cast off both legs and was leaping from body to body. Four hands free now. Cleaver and Chainsaw slicing.

Every time he landed, his hands would rip and crush. A whirlwind of purple blood and flashing steel.

"Give em hell, tin can!"

Jolene needed the Russian word to cheer him on. Her H.U.D. answered, **"Ура BORIS! Ура!"**

She shouted it with her whole chest, again and again. Boris landed on an Abomination, crisped its eyeball, but its tentacles still grabbed his arms, giving the Spawns the chance they needed. Jolene and Murph's frantic adrenaline high crashed as Boris was swarmed.

His head swiveled, all eight eyes burning every Cthullian they passed over. They just kept coming. By grip strength and weight, they held him in place. The larger Abominations piled on. Sparks. Stretches of silicone. Crumpled metal. Tossing pieces of Boris into the flickering dark.

Jolene screamed a different scream. If they interrupted his backup transfer... She had to give him time. She shot the Voltstriker as fast as she could. Murph concentrated fire on the larger ones. Jolene didn't blink. She stared through tears. *"Aim and squeeze,"* were her only thoughts.

Then she noticed the timer.

5...4...3...2...1.

A curtain of blue tinted energy burst from the ship and smashed the Abominations off of Boris, carrying him a few feet before flowing over him. The Spawns still held on. Jolene and Murph jumped down shooting their way to him. Boris had one eye left. Every arm was in pieces. His black bear platoon insignia was barely visible beneath the gore. They'd started worming in through joints to pull pieces out of him. Murph took lead, bashing the ones that that got too close with their shield.

Jolene noticed pieces of his speaker. She sent questions through the chat, through the comm channel. Tried to scan him. The comm channel was silent. The chat was a wall of her green text: Scan inconclusive.

The results spelled out in her H.U.D. and then Boris' last red eye went dark. She wailed. Her grip so tight it hurt as she looked for anything she could shoot, she noticed the Abominations. They were smashing on the restarted shields. Instead of a hard wall of energy, the shields dipped in, absorbing the impacts, and popped back. One of them backed up to charge and leap. Landing and sinking its wriggling shape into the shield until it stopped. Jolene had the vicious pleasure of watching its giant eye bulge as the shield flung it back and smashed it with wet, pulpy sounds on the walls.

Her brain remembered Boris and turned to run, facing Murph. Their helmet was off and they were smiling.

"Look at your chat,"

Jolene checked it and found one message repeating.

"Alive." in red text.

Before she could burst into happy tears, another Cthullian charged, collided, and splattered on the wall. A springing BOING sound filled the docking bay. Jolene looked back at Murph, who shrugged and smiled.

"Couldn't resist."

They both fell to the floor, laughing.

SHIELDS

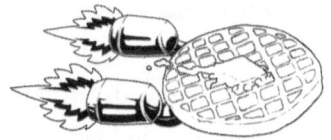

"I've confirmed with the station's automated repair systems that the power lines have been stabilized. Lighting should continue working normally." A static rippling sound interrupted O.D. before ending in a familiar splat. "Shields at 89%" O.D. continued through the ship's speakers.

The sound waves of the Cthullian's roars created needle ripples in the shields. One by one they gathered into a half circle. Jolene's mouth went dry as Spawns and Abominations intertwined their tentacles, anchoring themselves to each other and the floor. Without a sound they leaned against the shields as one mass.

Looking through the constant flexing and sparking energy to the docking bay doors, she cursed their collective bad luck as more kept coming.

"Shields at 80%."

"O.D. get your pixels out here!" Murph shouted.

Jolene blinked at their volume and the fact that they turned blood red. Bubbles swelled under their skin, shaping into muscles. Murph's clothes adjusted as they gained mass and height.

The hairs on the back of Jolene's head stood on end. Not as a survival instinct response but a literal tug on the back of her skull. Looking over her shoulder O.D. was a colorless outline who peeked out from behind her, his hologram's electric field pulling at her hair.

"You get one sentence to explain what you did to my ship before I feed you to the fishes!"Murph demanded while jabbing a finger at the windows.

"Well, actually recent studies suggest they are more closely related to earth's starfish." O.D. answered and Murph's eyes narrowed.

Jolene stepped away, turning to face him. Her own pulse rising, fear and rage mixing in her brain for an explosive result she tried to shout at O.D. Her screams drowned in the roars and splatters on the dock.

"Shields at 70%."

She waited until the announcement ended before shouting again. "Answer them or I swear I'll rip your servers out piece by piece and throw them to the Cthullians!"

O.D. shrank to plate size, their voice going up several pathetic octaves. "I set up Dynamic Shielding!"

Murph didn't lose their blood red coloring, but they facepalmed their sausage thick fingers with a wet splat.

"Please. Please tell me you linked the shields to the engines to handle the increased power demand."

They said it through their hand. Jolene couldn't tell if they could see O.D.'s bacon eyebrows lower and go diagonal, or how they crossed their arms, before floating to Murph's eye level.

"Absolutely not, that could have damaged the engi- " O.D. objected. His words were cut off by the Cthullian's chorus of anger and pain.

"Shields at 59%" O.D. announced again.

"And if they fail, no one is gonna be undamaged." Murph said and their legs shifted into spider limbs. They rushed through O.D. for the engine room.

"I'll set it up. You and tin-can make a plan!!" Murph shouted back.

Metal taps skittered behind her. Jolene spun Voltstriker crackling as air particles burned up in the barrel. Her finger curled around the trigger.

"At best that will tickle." Boris quipped.

She snorted at his words. Boris, with his usual four red eyes and chrome domed head, was standing on the counter on tiny legs and nothing else. She powered down the pistol and holstered it. "Ummmmm since when-" She gestured at him, unable to find the words to finish the question.

"Does my head resemble a detachable centipede?" Boris asked without a hint of sarcasm.

Jolene tilted her head at the four red eyed head of her friend and nodded.

"This was always an option. I believe my designers were told to make me more durable than earth's cockroaches." Boris said, tiny taps filling the dining room as he walked back and forth across the counter. "Anyway, I'm glad you are thinking with your head and not your pistol." Boris said, a grunt leaving his head's speakers.

Jolene laughed. Exhausted panic laughter as life tried to kill you.

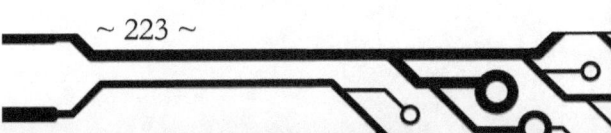

"Shields at 49%"

"Murph?" Jolene asked over the comms.

"Working on it!" They shouted back loud enough to distort the ship's speakers.

"Even when they finish. The shields won't hold forever." One of Boris legs turned out and up to scratch a nonexistent chin.

Jolene flinched at the crackle of bending energy.

"So we need weapons, distractions or both." Jolene summarized.

Boris nodded.

"Only place to look is the outpost. Maybe we can repair communications and call for backup."

Jolene mentally ordered the hologram displays in the ceiling to project her H.U.D's recorded footage. A wireframe of the outpost's front filled the center of the room.

"Let me fill out the rest." Boris offered, red light projected from his eyes at the ceiling and in moments lines of light built out the rest of the outpost.

"And done!" Murph shouted. The lights and hologram flickered. Jolene clenched from her teeth down to her butt as the ship system announced,

"Shield loss stopped. Shields recharging."

Jolene bent over, head between her legs. She breathed in and out, letting go of the survival stress.

"I hope the ship will still fly." O.D. was back to normal except for the same squeaky voice.

"I'd sooner fry myself than strand her. Also did I hear

right, you two are planning to go explore?" Murph asked.

"Yes." Jolene and Boris answered as he jumped down, skittering towards Jolene. She argued against the irrational instinct to punt him even as he jump-climbed his way onto her shoulder.

"Next obvious question, how?" Murph asked.

The maintenance tunnels lit up in the wireframe.

"Maintenance tunnels. They connect to every sector and only the Spawns can fit." Boris said over the comms.

"And you're gonna fight them off with one Voltstriker?" Murph asked while sending a picture of a shovel shifted and a gravestone.

A room one sector over lit up on the map. "Security should have weapons." He turned to Jolene, a throat clearing sound leaving his speakers. "Would you like to go shopping?"

Two of Boris' eyes turned off and on again. Jolene beamed at him quippy answers fighting with her weapon wish list for attention.

"Get a server room or get moving!" She could hear the eyeroll in Murph's tone.

Boris let out a heavy sigh. The map disappeared from the room and re-appeared in Jolene's H.U.D. as yellow arrows on the floor.

BORIS (CHAT MESSAGE)

"I will load their next meal with food coloring."

Boris sent in their one-on-one chat.

Jolene smiled at the prank and the idea it inspired.

"I'll bring glitter." Her green words ended with an evil smile emoji. Boris let out a belly laugh as she followed the arrows to the cargo bay. O.D. trailed behind silently until they reached the cargo bay door.

"I'll keep watch and..."

A request for an encrypted chat from O.D. popped in Jolene's H.U.D. She hit accept without thinking about it.

O.D. (CHAT MESSAGE)

"Please don't throw my server off the ship."

The words typed out in the same maple syrup brown as his pompadour.

She stopped at that, turning to face him. O.D.'s oversized gloved hands rubbed together over and over again. Revenge was a reflex that Jolene enjoyed when it wasn't permanent. Even if he wasn't edible, the Cthullians would probably tear him to pieces just for fun.

"That was never an option." Jolene said aloud. O.D.'s mouth dropped open while their bacon eyebrows rose. Then his chocolate chip eyes became chocolate hearts. Jolene hit the button to lower cargo bay doors, drowning out what the AI was saying.

"I'll keep watch Captain!" O.D. saluted and disappeared.

Boris couldn't shake his head without a neck, but she felt him rock back and forth.

"Careful with making him promises." Boris said with a low growl.

"We're not like her. Also, he can vouch for our story." Jolene countered.

Boris' legs flexed up and down.

Jolene walked down the gangplank following the arrows pointing at a section of torn up floor. The Cthullians who saw her pressed their beaks against the shields. Jolene flipped them off before jumping down.

BORIS SQUARED

Jolene ran down the maintenance tunnel. Her metal and rubber treads pounded into the floor. The sounds bounced off the steel walls inches from her shoulders. Echoes building on echoes in her ears until fresh screams invaded her skull. The rapid pop squelch pop of Spawn suckers mixed with slathering hisses. Heat from Boris rolled across her neck and shoulders.

"Now serving crispy Cthullian with extra crisp," Boris said above the short lived screams and crackling sizzles. If she laughed, she'd stop running, so she sent a green message in their chat: LMFAO

She checked her Empath Blocker dose. Her supply was good. The remaining effective time was one hour. She slid into a right turn and bounced off the wall into a run. Her H.U.D. highlighted the areas of impact and showed she'd only earned some bruising. Fear spiked adrenaline pushed her forward, all while reminding her to set her system for another dose in forty-five minutes. None of them could afford her passing out.

JOLENE (CHAT MESSAGE)
"They better have something good!"
Jolene messaged the group chat.

MURPH (CHAT MESSAGE)

"One thing you can count on Jack and Spendicus for, they don't cheap out."

Murph answered, sending an animated pixel of money stacks.

BORIS (CHAT MESSAGE)

"Will you both please focus!"

Boris typed out. Jolene sent the chat away before Murph's blue bubbles became words. She turned down the final hallway… it ended on a ladder. Jolene mentally spammed her suit's artificial muscles for speed. She was running faster but did not know how it would help her climb.

BORIS (CHAT MESSAGE)

"I've got your back. Climb one rung at a time."

Boris' red text showed in all caps, taking up her H.U.D., interrupting the flaming wreck of thoughts her panic was feeding.

BORIS (CHAT MESSAGE)

"Switching to multi-beam targeting."

She didn't have time to ask what that meant. The heat radiating from Boris' head increased. Her H.U.D. warned her that continued proximity would cause first-degree burns. She really wished it would help to yell. "Better burned than eaten!"

She sucked through her teeth as she heard her hair sizzle and the back of her neck gently cook.

JOLENE (CHAT MESSAGE)

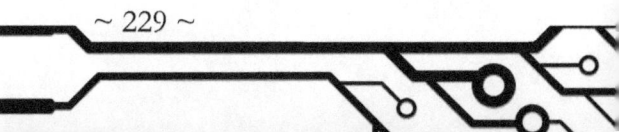

"Get the hatch open!"

She messaged Murph and Boris hoping one of them could do it, as she made a panicked *"I don't want to die"* decision.

She leaped forward.

Her muscles combined with the suit landed her hard halfway up the ladder. She hugged the metal even as it beat the breath out of her. Panic and pain running through her brain, she fought to suck air back in.

Her H.U.D. filled with information, the pending notifications ramping up past one hundred. She shut it off before it could tell her anything about any bones. She climbed rung by rung. Burning hair filling her nose. Her neck and shoulders screamed at her. Boris was firing faster and faster. Teeth gritted, grunting out curses for every step.

Hissing air drew her eyes up to the security office hatch. She smiled as it unlocked and swung open. Hard sliding pressure wrapped around one leg. Without looking, she instinctively kicked it down.

"Eat my beams and burn in hell!" Boris shouted loud enough for her right ear to ring. Her gloved hands smacked on the lip of the hatch. Silicone and human muscles clenched as she heaved herself up and rolled onto the floor. The hatch slammed shut with a wet sound. As the lock spun and sealed, filling the room with wet slicing sounds. Jolene rolled to her knees and saw a halo of black tentacles and purple gore around the hatch.

She wrinkled her nose at the salty vinegar stench

filling the room.

"Made it," She said it to herself and the comms.

"Maron! you two are gonna make me fall to pieces one day." Murph answered with more Italian than Chicago in their voice this time.

"Isn't that a built-in feature for you?" Jolene asked, less for the snark and more from confusion.

"Hey now, this ain't no time to be jokin'. Engine is holding steady." Murph said through their comms. Multiple wet splats came through the comms before the line closed. "Son of a whore, they just keep coming. Boris, is this normal?" Murph asked, the steady sound of their guns firing.

Boris jumped down from Jolene's shoulder and headed towards a steel door marked 'Emergency Use Only'.

"Only for a planet-based nest. This level of infestation takes time and resources." Boris said while his eyes projected a white beam at the control panel. Jolene watched its display run through multiple combinations.

"So, either Spendicus is running a space farm or just has worse luck than a mook robbing a Peacekeeper fundraiser." Murph tuned up the accent for the last part and Jolene couldn't help giggling. All the chaos the galaxy threw at them and they were still standing. The thought made her laugh hard enough to hiccup.

"Glad you can still laugh, boss." Murph said in between her hiccups.

"Oh-" hiccup "Come-" hiccup "on" hiccup.

"Deep breath and hold it." Boris said. The white

beam cut off as the last numbers were displayed. Jolene complied, her lungs and chest tried hiccupping and she didn't give. Fighting the urge to breathe, she dumped all the waiting data in her H.U.D. Fully booted. It immediately started scanning, but she muted notifications at the sound of sliding metal. Instead of a door, the whole wall slid up into the ceiling. Back-lit by white light was an arsenal ranging from non-lethal to disintegration.

"HELL YES!" Jolene jumped for joy and immediately regretted it when her whole chest flared into sharp pain. She didn't stop smiling, as her H.U.D. named each weapon. Pax Punch. Paralyzer, and many more.

"Mine!" she shouted while pointing and walking towards the one with a familiar blue steel open air barrel design.

Her smile grew wider as she read the words scrolling across her vision.

STORM CANNON

SHOTGUN VARIANT OF THE VOLTSTRIKER. THIS WEAPON FIRES SHOTS OF ELECTRIFIED GEL ROUNDS IN NARROW TO WIDE ARCS. ITS EFFECT IS SIMILAR TO THE VOLTSTRIKER PISTOL ON A LARGER SCALE. MULTIPLE ROUNDS SPLATTER AND CAUSE A MINIATURE STORM OF ENERGY INCAPACITATING ORGANIC AND MECHANICAL TARGETS. IT IS A NON-LETHAL GROUP AND LARGE ASSAILANT MANAGEMENT TOOL. EACH AMMO DRUM HELD TWENTY-FIVE SHOTS. ITS MAIN CON IS THAT RELOADING CAN BE DIFFICULT ON THE RUN.

By the time the words scrolled away, her cheeks ached from smiling.

"Final lock bypassed." Boris' words were all she needed to grab it off the wall.

Hot pain flared in her chest and raced down to her gut as she supported the weapon's weight. Jolene gritted her teeth against it. The contoured, textured grip felt as right as her pistol. Finger off the trigger, she checked the drum. Fully loaded with shells of blue gel rounds. The weapon's programming synced with her H.U.D., instantly giving her crosshairs that she could line up with the barrel for easy bulls-eyes.

"It suits you." Boris said.

She turned towards his voice, keeping the gun barrel down, he'd scurried to two black steel doors with giant red letters.

Security Drone

Light shot from his eyes at an access panel to the left and a cool synthetic voice filled the room. "Access granted."

"Uh what's the plan?" Jolene asked, but Boris didn't answer as the doors slowly opened white light hit her eyes hiding what was inside.

"If we're going to survive I need a new ride." Boris said, as the white light faded Jolene groaned. It was a floating cube. Sleek black metal that almost looked liquid, but still a floating box!

"We have bigger and better boxes in our cargo bay." Jolene said, turning to the security camera panel, looking for any signs of trouble.

"This is not just a box!" Boris said, and before Jolene could think of an answer the sound of metal scrapes drew her attention back to the security drone.

"Override in progress." A synthetic voice announced. Boris had jumped on top of it tiny legs sinking into the liquid looking metal until he was flush with the top. "Let's see what this box can do!" Boris announced, wet sliding scrapes started as six familiar looking arms came out the side of his box chassis. He floated forward and gave Jolene six thumbs up, which was the perfect time for her to snap a picture and start laughing. In between gasps of pain, because laughing with possibly broken ribs hurt like a bitch, she sent the picture to Murph. They started laughing over the comms.

"Challenging the space roaches of the Milky Way, it's Boxy Boris!" They said while still laughing, Jolene could see them making multiple mouths to keep it going. Murph's words made laughing easier and standing through her flaring aches and pains impossible. She slid down the wall, leaning the Storm Cannon against it.

Boris looked from Jolene to the ceiling speakers. Jolene looked at the blood red borders and mirrored black metal and had to swallow more laughs. Someone in Spendicus' corporate R&D must have thought this was scary.

"Yes, yes, it is a box of doom. Hilarious. Now can you set your Bio-tech to healing, and you-" Boris' box body angled up to the ceiling. "Help us plot a path to communications."

"Aye-Aye Captain Cardboard." Murph answered the room's holographic projectors showed the station as a wireframe again.

Jolene entered the command through her H.U.D. and got a list of damages: bruised sternum, two cracked ribs, muscular hematoma. A graphic showed a black line across her belly. It ended with an "Estimated treatment time of two hours. Please refrain from increased physical activity, and repeated bouts of laughter."

"Looks like this might be the best bet." Different colored arrows for the main halls and maintenance tunnels traced paths to a large room two sectors in.

"Best bet?" Jolene asked the ceiling.

"Yea, why do you think nothin's labeled? Network on this place is insane. Every time Boris and I try to gain higher-level access, it kicks us out." Murph griped.

Boris floated past the wall of weapons, each arm grabbing a new gun. Each one grabbed a weapon off the wall, mounting them on the sides and top of his chassis.

"Your ammo drums are on the back." Boris said.

Jolene got up, ignoring the under skin itch of her Bio-tech healing her injuries.

"Maintenance tunnels are not an option for me." He followed up.

Jolene didn't hesitate.

"Yea, looks like a square frame round hatch situation." And looked back at the security hatch.

"Hilarious and unhelpful." Boris said, head swiveling

sending ripples through his liquid metal frame, as he focused on the station hologram.

"Not gonna grow legs?" Jolene asked, without laughing but couldn't help smiling.

"Gives Cthullians less to grab if I just float." Boris answered without missing a beat.

"How does the floating thing work?" Jolene asked, trying not to panic at the countless Cthullians swarming the halls.

"Anti-gravity generators in each panel." Boris answered as the gears behind his eyes cranked to make a plan. Jolene's trigger finger itched for them to move and shoot their way through the mess.

"You got enough ammo for the main halls?" Jolene set the Storm Cannon for widespread shots in her H.U.D.

"Not for all of them, but I have an idea." An artificial villain laugh left Boris' speakers. Jolene almost felt sorry for the Cthullians.

Purple Vacuum

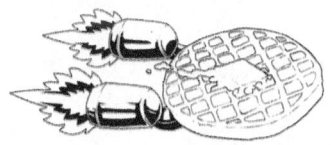

Boris floated over to the security panel. Two side panels opened and Jolene watched pale white cables plug in. "Initiating fire containment protocol." The cool automated voice did not match the reality on the security screens. Jolene sat next to him, grumbling at her Bio-tech, while fire-retardant foam filled corridor after corridor. Swiveling in her swivel chair let her watch the holographic wireframe turn the corresponding halls red.

"Countermeasures Deployed. Oxygen Depletion in progress."

One by one, the shielding between space and the outpost shut off.

"Depressurization and gravity shutdown in progress. We apologize for any discomfort this may cause in 5. 4. 3. 2-"

Jolene activated her suit's mag-boots before the countdown ended. The gravity shutoff made her stomach rise and drop. Burning acid hit the back of her throat. She never looked away from the screen.

The sudden temp drop created a fine mist. Air pressure plus disabled gravity flushed the Cthullians. Their bodies created vapor trails into space. Abominations bowled over each other. Spawns shot into the darkness. Their beaks biting into metal ripped away. Tentacles suckered to the floor tore free. Docking bay debris turned into shotgun shrapnel. Spinning and slicing through metal and flesh alike. Manic survival glee sent delightfully cold shivers across her skin.

"You better save that footage for Murph."

Boris' head swiveled.

"Already uploading it to the ship." Jolene's smile shrank as she watched Boris' handiwork. Across the outpost, a splatter art horror show was in progress.

Gray mist saturated into purple fog. Ripped wriggling tentacles. Flattened Cthullians smashed on corners. Jolene swallowed the urge to vomit.

"That should buy us enough time." Boris said and turned all the screens off.

A bead of cold sweat raced down her spine. Jolene's brain frantically spammed the words: *"MECHANICAL MASS MURDER."* Boris unhooked from the panel and floated towards the door without a word. Her finger twitched toward the Storm Cannon's trigger. She forced the impulse away. If Boris could handle a Cthullian madness like this, she derailed and destroyed that logic train before it picked up speed. Boris stopped in front of the door. Jolene forced her finger to stay away from the trigger.

"I'm sorry." His head turned. He only had four eyes open. "If you wish to return to the ship, it should be safe, and I can assume full risk for the rest of the mission."

Galaxy Waffles

Jolene hated the survival reflex trying to jump out of her throat to scream. *"YES! You freak me the fuck out and holy shit, I wanna live and not die because of a code glitch."*

Instead, she closed her eyes and exhaled. "Boris…-" she opened them to see him tipping forward. Eyes fixed on the floor. The tension and silence made her skin itch. She stepped forward and said what needed to be said. "Shut up and open the damn door. We've got shit to do."

Boris righted himself. His four eyes blinked on and off. Then his black cube body shook up and down as that familiar belly laugh rolled out of his speakers.

"Da Captain." His head swiveled back, and they stepped into the oxygenated corridor. Jolene had never subscribed to any religion surviving or dead. Instead, she thanked the forces of Astro-Physics, that she couldn't smell the dead Cthullians.

She could still hear.

"Warning: your current actions are inadvisable." Boris continued to float forward, each of his guns scanning every shadow. Jolene swept every vent, grumbling at the giant green backwards arrows the outpost was looping on every screen. The automated emergency system continued to announce with a smooth synthetic calm only a computer could generate.

"Please return to a secure area until fire containment is complete."

Jolene rolled her eyes, glancing around Boris' edges. "Continuing will be documented as insubordination and will absolve Spendicus Unlimited of all obligations. This will include, but is not limited to, life insurance, medical treatment, employee pensions, and should you survive, loss of employment."

"Hey Captain Cardboard, you know where to find the mute button?" Murph interrupted the system, and Jolene sent multiple thumbs up emojis in the group chat.

"Working on it." Boris said.

"Spendicus Unlimited officially-" The words died in a fast series of crackles.

"All in favor of adding an asshole tax for this entire job?" Murph asked.

"Da!" Boris shouted.

"Absolutely," Jolene joined in.

"I knew there was a reason I liked you two. Soon as we get comms back up, I'm messaging Calico. Gonna give the engines a break. Call me when you need me." Murph said and closed the comm connection.

Jolene checked her map, Communications was close. She fought to keep breathing and not just run. Every passing second, the Cthullians could swarm back in.

"Deep breath, hold, release, and repeat." Boris said, head swiveling back at her. "Good for focus, and maybe your system will stop spamming me with medical alerts."

Jolene stuck out her tongue at Boris and decided it was worth a shot.

Deep breath in and out. Nervous sweating slowed to a trickle. It didn't stop her heart from drumming. Failed to fill the pit in her stomach. With a thought, she pulled up a playlist of her favorite SUCK MY VOLTAGE songs. First up was *NEURON OVERLOAD*.

FLASH THOSE LIGHTS!
SELL THAT VICE!
BURN MY NEURONS BLACK!

In moments, the singer's battle-cry and guitar solo helped her find her smile. The break in hyper manic panic allowed a detail to jump out at her. She stopped, and Boris halted.

"Hey guys?" Jolene asked.

"Yea?" they both answered.

She loaded the wireframe map into their chat, zooming in on multiple rooms across the outpost.

"Anything look off to you about this?" She asked over comms.

Boris answered with a red question mark. Murph answered with a blue one. She mentally ordered the map to display all the room labels. "Mines need miners. Check it. No bots. No bunks." Jolene answered her own question.

Murph groaned over the speakers. Boris sighed.

"Better triple that tax, Murph, cause what kind of mine doesn't have miners?" Jolene grumbled, and started streaming a connection from her Bio-tech back to the ship for Murph and O.D. to keep tabs on everything. If they died at least it would be documented.

Mining Outpost?

O.D.'s maple syrup brown message popped in the group chat.

O.D. (CHAT MESSAGE)

"The outpost systems show ten personnel assigned to this site. This supports your suspicion that this is not a mining outpost."

"How the hell did you get that kind of info!" Murph's question popped in blue, with an animated head scratching pixel person.

O.D. (CHAT MESSAGE)

"I connected with the outpost systems and explained our contract with Spendicus Unlimited."

O.D. typed out, sounding smug without a single emoji.

MURPH (CHAT MESSAGE)

"You asked nicely and it let you have full access?"

Murph responded ending their question with the mind blown emoji.

"I provided documentation. It gave me entry level access. It also explained higher-level access requires DNA registration, Bio-Tech

implants, and-" O.D. pontificated.

JOLENE (CHAT MESSAGE)

"WE GET IT! Big scary security. Nothing we can do. Can you at least get me camera access?"

Jolene typed in green letters. She and Boris picked up the pace. Rounding a corner, she got an eyeful of brown text.

O.D. (CHAT MESSAGE)

"ACCESS DENIED."

Jolene blinked it away and wondered how much a replacement A.I. would cost. At the end of the hall, her H.U.D. outlined the communication door in bright yellow. At least it tried to. Fresh Cthullian remains mixed with older carcasses. Dripping purple blood splatters alongside paler coagulated streaks. Salty methane gore assaulted Jolene's nose before she could slam the suit's helmet shut.

"FIL-RAHH-FILTER,"

Retching through the word, her suit hissed with air venting and sucking in clean oxygen.

"Heads up goombahs! The Cthullians are coming back!" Murph announced over the comms. Boris and Jolene booked it towards the door. Even as four black turret barrels that deployed from the ceiling to aim at them.

"HALT! State your name und affiliations!" A voice snapped through the hallway speakers.

Physics is funny about momentum. Jolene and Boris were the objects in motion. The unbalanced force started with the whine of the barrels spinning up and ended with a barrage of red lasers! There were no bulkheads. No crates. Nothing but smooth hallway walls. A red aura grew larger and hotter around Boris. The sides of his cube rippled. For a moment she saw her reflection, then red faded. She looked around him and whistled. The mirrored surface had bounced the lasers back up the barrels they came. Metal heated. Lenses cracked. The barrels drooped, drops of molten metal fell to the floor.

"Scheisse!"

Jolene's H.U.D. translated the word and told her the language was German. She set her suit's speaker to max and used it.

"Calico Jack sent us!" Silent seconds ticked. Screeching metal ripped apart. Jolene turned in time to see a swarm of Spawns running towards them. Snapping beaks and popping suckers easily the size of dinner plates. She took a stance and aimed for the horde's center.

"Hold fire!" One of Boris' black steel hands grabbed her suit's shoulder. "Tight spread. Shoot when I say." Boris ordered.

Jolene's finger itched to squeeze. She eased it away. Two of Boris' guns hissed behind her. Streaks of white flew towards the swarming horde. They painted down the walls of the hall. Sheets of white ice locked countless Spawns in place. The remaining horde bunched together, pushing and shoving towards them.

"FIRE!" Boris ordered.

Jolene squeezed. The suit absorbed the recoil,

allowing Jolene to watch a tight sphere of blue gel rounds charged towards the Spawns. Electric current combined with kick ass kinetics. It carried them, fried them on its surface. One by one the rounds burst, showering them in super charged conductive fluid. Not even one survived.

Jolene gave Boris a thumbs up. He was looking past her at clustered Abominations! Too many to count. All those eyes, blood vessels inflamed with rage fixed on them and charged.

"Let us in or we're dead!" She shouted through her speaker, glancing at the door.

"You mooks better not die on me!" Murph demanded.

The doors split down the middle. Magnetic locks powered down. Deadbolts slid back. A process of tedious top security level bullshit!

She and Boris backed up to it, firing at will. Streaks of purple flew alongside the white beams. She watched them sink into tentacles. Slowly bringing down Cthullians.

Flipping to the Storm Cannon's widest possible spread, Jolene fired. Gel rounds spiraled into a web of interconnected lightning arcs. Landing on and bursting on every leading Abomination.

They clogged the hallway for precious seconds; that ended when the ones in the back stomped over the injured. Beaks snapped every sucker step of the way.

"Our odds of survival diminish without you. Please come back soon," O.D. pleaded.

"We're coming back." Jolene whispered.

Lights hit the Abominations! Jolene popped an

ammo drum and loaded a new one. Boris' black arms wrapped around Jolene and yanked her inside. Lying in Boris' shadow, she watched his barrage of white beams and purple projectiles. The room boomed and snapped, howling protests and tentacles beat on metal. She let out a desperate laugh. They'd made it!

"Und now, please begin zhe rescue!"

Jolene groaned at the manic, demanding voice.

"We have a ship in the docking bay." Boris answered the demand. He offered a hand that Jolene took and held on as it pulled her to her feet.

"Yes, und what else?"

Jolene turned to the speaker, a woman with black curly hair streaked with silver. She was wearing a lab coat with circuitry and woven plating. The air surrounding her pulsed with energy. The white lab coat was knee-length, with more pockets than made sense. She stood in front of a holographic wall of screens. Each one showing cameras, numbering Cthullians, and sensor readings. She glanced at all of them before turning towards them. A segmented visor hid her eyes.

Her thin lipped expression turned into a deep frown as she took them in head to toe. The battering sounds behind them intensified into frenzied random chaos.

"Ach such noise! One moment." She turned back to her console. The screen above her showed outside the door. A tangle of tentacles and beaks that only scratched the door.

"Zhat's right, stay right zhere!" She cackled and

tapped a few buttons.

The floor beneath the Cthullians dropped into a large hold. The walls slammed in right as she shut off the screen.

"Now zhat's done, please tell me your plan is not simpler than two plus two." She lifted the visor, showing black eyes with red pupils. She crossed her arms, staring down her nose at them.

Jolene decided diplomacy be damned, they needed answers.

"How about who the hell are you?" Jolene racked gel rounds into the chamber, electricity crackled alongside grinding metal. One eye focused on her, the other on Boris.

"What did Calico tell you?" the woman countered.

"About you? Nothing. Job said you were a mining outpost and had missed your check ins." Jolene answered, watching the woman's synthetic eyes narrow.

"Zhen zhat is all you need to know." She took something out of her many pockets and drank.

Boris floated up and forward until he stared down at her. "If you could have escaped, you would have. Now talk or we will leave you here. Who are you and what is this place?" Boris demanded.

Jolene swore the woman's pupils flashed and watched as her shoulders slumped, and she leaned back on the console.

"Ach, fine, I don't have patience for zhe Cat and Max's paranoia." She clicked a few keys on the panel.

Jolene felt her mouth drop as the words. "Dr. Wilda. Renowned Exobiologist," typed out on the screen, along with her employee ID number.

"Satisfactory?" she sniped.

"And you shot at us because?" Jolene pointed the barrel to the door and then to Wilda's feet.

"We've had issues with pirates und corporate espionage." She explained without remorse.

"All this for a mining outpost?" Boris asked, floating down to eye level, closing in to grappling distance. Jolene moved to the side, giving herself a clear shot for the Doctor. While her synthetic eyes followed them both.

"Mining outpost, feh! Nothing so pedestrian. We are a research station!" She answered.

MURPH (CHAT MESSAGE)

"And now the network security makes more sense."

Murph messaged the group chat.

O.D. (CHAT MESSAGE)

"Indeed. Spendicus Unlimited is notorious for secrecy."

O.D. added.

BORIS (CHAT MESSAGE)

"Which apparently includes us!"

Boris finished.

Jolene's brain clicked on the last question she wanted answered. "What the hell are you researching in an asteroid field?"

GARGANTUAN DINNER BELL

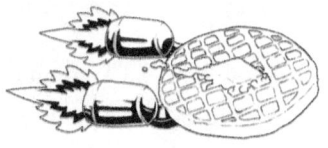

Dr. Wilda grinned, showing teeth as white as her lab coat. "One of zhe galaxy's apex predators!"

"Cthullians are-" Boris began and didn't get to finish.

"NEIN! Not zhose bottom feeders." She turned and typed furiously on the console. Every screen on the wall went dark.

On the far left, pale light shone on crater dented asteroids. Jolene watched Dr. Wilda dance in place, tapping her knuckles together. Until she noticed Jolene looking at her.

"Eyes on zhe screen!" She shouted, pointing at the far left.

Jolene watched three shadows wrap around the crest of an asteroid. As one, they cracked ice. Buried into stone. Splintered raw metal ore into the void of space. Her mouth went dry. Dim starlight illuminated dark purple skin at the base of the claws. It pushed off the enormous asteroid, filling the end screens with a face full of teeth and pale eyes. Jolene's every muscle tensed. Survival instinct fled as it spread its wings and filled multiple screens.

"VACUI DRACO VORAX." Dr. Wilda said with a rapturous smile. She placed a hand on the screen.

Boris floated back over to Jolene. He whispered the same words over and over. "Asteroid Wyrm."

'We are so fucked.' Were the words Jolene wanted to say.

Then the wyrm's light blue tongue shot forward, sticking to the asteroid surface and pulling it into its waiting jaw. Sandwiched between skyscraper teeth, the stone held for a second before the beast crunched through it like a fried snack. At some point, she'd started streaming the video to Murph. Surprisingly, they had nothing to say.

Boris' arms extended and pressed a few buttons. The reality shattering video ended.

"We do not have time to gawk and shit our pants. Doctor, gather your research. I'll escort you and Jolene to the security office. Then we'll set this security cube to distract the Cthullians on station."

Dr. Wilda patted two enormous pockets on her left and right. "Zriple backups und top level encryption. Zhis data is-"

"Won't matter." Jolene said, mechanically walking over to the nearest table to lean and make peace with reality.

"What is she talking about?" Dr. Wilda demanded.

Jolene flipped open her helmet, not caring about the stench rubbing at her leaking eyes. "We can't out-fly the Cthullians. We don't have enough weapons to kill an entire Madness. With the massive light show those mining charges put on," Jolene rubbed her forehead hating the next words. "We might as well roll around in salt and pepper so we get eaten faster!" She slid down, ass hitting the floor hard. "We're on the menu either way. All that's left is who gets the bill."

She let out a manic 'I can't believe this is how it ends laugh', stopping long enough to suck in a breath and started counting metal seams in the lab's ceiling.

Boris floated over beside her, landing with an inch between them. "You're not wrong, but giving up isn't who you are. Isn't who we are."

Jolene couldn't face him. She rested her forehead on her knees. "Starblood. Terrablood. Doesn't matter what or who I am. We're holding off the Madness by luck and strategy. Both mean nothing to the Wyrm." She didn't, couldn't deny the tears as the truth hit her. The diner ship would never be theirs. Boris and Murph were going to die. Their ship, family, and future were dying. She wanted to repress that thought, to grab and strangle it into silence. Instead, she let herself fall to the floor. Cool steel comforting on her cheek and temple.

Black steel hands laid on her hand and cradled her shoulder.

"Maybe not, but our plan is worth fighting for." He pulled her up, head detaching, to walk down the side of the cube. His red four eyes fixed on hers. "We are worth fighting for." She let her eyes drop to the floor. One of his hands pushed her chin up. "You are worth fighting for."

New tears fell for different reasons now. She leaned her head on Boris, his cool metal frame giving her a moment of calm.

"Initiating   GARGANTUAN   DINNER   BELL

PROTOCOL. Please evacuate the station. Spendicus Unlimited does not guarantee your survival." The station's system announced.

"Uh, what the hell is that?" Murph shouted through their comms. Jolene turned, staring at Dr. Wilda who scratched the back of her head.

"Zhat was motivation." She crossed her arms.

Jolene's brain made a context guess. "You're baiting that thing? We still don't know if anyone else is on the station!"

"Yes, I refuse to wait for death. Either you rescue me, or I die collecting data for my life's work. Win-win. As for the others-" she tapped away on her console until nine images showed up. All of their pulse monitors showed flat-lines. She pulled another tube from her lab coat, "For zhe fallen." and swigged something neon and shimmering. She smacked her lips making satisfied sounds. "So, zhen, what will you do?"

Jolene looked at Boris and nodded. He climbed back to the top of his cube. "The rescue will continue. Do something like that again. I will incapacitate you."

"Noted! Now less chatting, more running." She pulled two pistols from inside her lab coat, black as her eyes, both ending in narrow nozzles. Each one had blue glowing lines connected to the bottom of their grips. Jolene's H.U.D. scanned them and popped their name.

ATOMIZERS

BEAM TYPE WEAPON. !ILLEGALL! REPORT TO THE GALACTIC GOVERNMENT ON SIGHT.

The doors to the lab started opening. Boris floated forward. Jolene took the right. Cthullian tentacles blacked the first rays of light out. From the floor to the ceiling, beaks snapped. Tentacles pushed in.

"Zhey don't know when to quit." Dr. Wilda said as she marched towards the opening. She aimed one pistol at the ceiling, one at the floor and fired. Dark blue energy struck multiple Cthullians. Tentacles bubbled. Beaks cracked. Cthullians screamed before melting into purple-black puddles. Dr. Wilda blew away non-existent smoke at the barrel tips. Boris didn't have a jaw to drop. Jolene's mouth opened and closed like a flapping door.

"Disrupts cell structure." She explained and walked through the Cthullian puddles.

MURPH (CHAT MESSAGE)

"Did you mooks just witness a war crime?"

Murph messaged.

BORIS (CHAT MESSAGE)

"The GG suspended the rules of war for Cthullians."

Boris typed and started floating forward. Jolene took up a position behind him.

MURPH (CHAT MESSAGE)

"One of these days, you two are gonna bring home someone nice!"

Murph messaged ending with a facepalm emoji.

They caught up with Dr. Wilda at the end of the hall. Boris checked left while she and Jolene went right.

"Clear." They all confirmed and ran for the security office. Their boot steps meshed with Boris' low hum into an echo that traveled ahead. Until the entire station shook. Jolene and the Doctor stumbled; Boris caught both with his arms.

"The Wyrm?" Jolene looked at the Doctor who rubbed her black eyes, red pupils expanded as she smiled that manic smile.

"Phase 1 of the protocol." Dr. Wilda said and flicked a finger at a wall monitor. A livestream showed what Jolene would one day describe as a corporate LSD ad attack. Every single structure projected images of food. Everything from fried noodles to beef wellingtons. One projection looked like crystals carved into drumsticks. Flashing taglines showed above and below each one in multiple languages.

SPICY SPICY SPICY

.... --- -- . / -.-. --- --- -.- .. -.

434f4d4520414e4420474554204954

65 108 108 32 121 111 117 32 99 97 110 32 101 97 116

Jolene's H.U.D. flooded with translations until she

shut her eyes and ordered it clear.

"Holograms don't cause vibrations," she said.

"Zhis is true." Dr. Wilda confirmed as another tremor shook the station.

"Mag boots," Jolene ordered, and messaged Murph on the comms. "Can you see what's doing this?"

"Yea, sorry. That was me." Cold fear goose-bumped Jolene from head to toe.

"Murph, what the-" Boris started and didn't finish before Cthullians rounded the corner ahead of them.

"I'm getting the ship ready to launch, and we kinda buried the front crust into the hangar floor."

Boris' guns aimed and fired. Jolene set her shots to narrow. Dr. Wilda steadily marched, picking off the ones Boris froze. Sacrificing distance was suicidal, but so was standing still. Jolene aimed, fired, and pumped. Shells ejected. Ozone burned. She and Boris screamed at the Madness.

"For the Motherboard!"

"Chew on this!"

Dr. Wilda only stopped to eject empty tubes and connect new lines of energy.

The sounds tore at Jolene's ears and brain. Grunting through the last of her bio-tech's healing process. She started a new mantra. "We're coming back."

"Zhey're behind us!" Dr. Wilda screeched, wheeling and beaming. Blue energy hit the walls first, fracturing spidery patterns into the metal. Spawns and Abominations did not stop. Some leaping over. Others pushed the dead forward. They were stuck! She saw the Atomizer beams hit more walls, spreading more cracks. "Sorry!" Dr. Wilda shouted, but Jolene was too busy remembering that not too long ago robbery. She aimed and fired her last shell. Scrambled behind Boris and shouted at the Doctor.

"Is that a spacesuit?"

She cocked a salt and pepper eyebrow. "It can be. Why?"

Jolene racked an ammo drum, smiled, and pointed at the wall across from them.

"Make a hole!"

Dr. Wilda turned and fired. Jolene set her shot to the widest spread and covered her. Sucked out into space or smashed to jelly on the walls. Both options seemed better than being eaten.

Dr. Wilda's lab coat lit up, coating her body from head to toe in a green energy field. "Built in atmosphere" She said and held the Atomizers inches apart. Out of the corner of her eye, Jolene hoped she wasn't imagining layers of metal flaking away, with the cracks were growing wider and deeper.

She couldn't flinch from the shrill, hissing Spawn or baritone roaring Abominations. The sizzle and cracks of Boris' ice beams. The whistling of his dart weapon. She didn't let it bring her down; she breathed. Bit her cheek. Thought about coffee. Aiming and firing at the monsters closing in. They swarmed the walls and ceilings. The Storm Cannon's barrel tip glowed from the shots. She reached for another drum and touched only smooth steel.

"I'm out!" She screamed, tossing the Storm Cannon into the oncoming Madness. She pulled her Voltstriker. An ice beam stopped firing long enough to swivel and backed her up. Jolene kept her shots to center mass.

"Breaching!" Dr. Wilda screamed. Jolene mentally ordered her suit to seal. The walls peeled away like rotten fruit. The void ripped them from the station into the silence of space. Spinning them head over heels.

"Murph we-"

Spin

"Are out-"

Spin

"Side the station" Boris' arms wrapped around both of them. While the remaining four swatted at grasping tentacles.

She'd seen slow motion in Murph's old movies. Floating in a frictionless vacuum, Jolene was living it!

Dr. Wilda's Atomizers blasted for brief seconds. Boris' shots glided at their targets. Their missed shots flowed into the distance.

The Cthullians pushed off of station debris. Off each other.

Jolene kept one arm wrapped around Boris' arm, hyperventilating through her oxygen supply. Eyes on the move, she saved her shots for point blank. She didn't notice the creeping arms of the Abomination below until they squeezed her legs.

She pulled the trigger as fast as physics allowed. Three crackling gel rounds gently floated towards the

Abomination's open beak. Its tentacles broke one, then two, and missed the last one. She watched it recoil and almost wished she could hear it. Instead, she shouted over the comms.

"SUCK MY VOLTAGE BITCH!" Jolene crowed and wriggled out of its loosened grip.

"Someone order a rescue?" Murph asked. The diner ship, in all its neon yellow waffle glory, flew around the station. Cthullians from the surrounding asteroids jumped, only for the dynamic shielding to bounce them back.

"Better late than never!" Boris answered, extending his arm into and through a descending Abomination's tentacles until he jabbed two fingers into its eye.

"Tractor beams gonna be tricky with you three so close." Murph said, and the sound of human knuckles cracking came over the line. "Boss, I'm gonna have to get creative!"

Surrounded by Cthullians, an Asteroid Wyrm closing in, and hyperventilating through her limited oxygen supply. None of that sent Jolene into a panic more than those words.

One thruster dimmed while the other brightened. The ship wheeled around missing some asteroids bouncing off others.

"Shot looks good. I'm taking it."

"Murph, you crazy-" was all Jolene said before the cargo bay doors opened and it started racing at them! The ship's reverse thrust was less than half when going forward. Murph was flying at them at top speed.

Galaxy Waffles

"Break! Break! BREAK!" Boris shouted into the comms. Less than one thousand feet away, the ship started slowing. They floated past the door, some Spawns grabbed onto it as it started closing.

"Hold on to your butts!" Murph announced as decompression and artificial gravity hit simultaneously. Air punched out of Jolene and the Doctor, then slammed them to the floor. Boris only dipped slightly.

Jolene shut off her H.U.D. before it started flashing with warnings of things she was already feeling. Gasping lungs. Aches from face to toes. Sharp fiery pain surged from her pistol hand. The suit's helmet showed three broken fingers around the Voltstriker's stock. It would have been easy to pass out. She'd earned it, and darkness was filling her vision. Then Dr. Wilda flipped open her helmet.

"Keep your tongue away from teeth, please." She said and injected something into Jolene's neck. Energy hit her entire body. She flipped over and jumped to her feet.

"What was-" she started asking and stopped as she noticed fresh purple streaks on the cargo bay floors.

"Murph, what did you do?" The comms stayed silent for a grand total of five seconds.

"You two familiar with salvage laws?" They asked.

"No," Boris and Jolene answered.

"Well, I am now!" They laughed through the comms.

"We literally don't have time. Just fly!" Jolene ordered, hoping she could yell at them later.

"Eh, boss, we got company, Looks ready to shoot

something!" Murph answered, and all three of them rushed to the bridge.

DON'T GET EATEN!

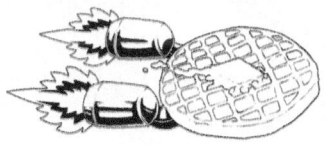

"Details, Murph!" Jolene shouted, loving the suit's artificial muscles and hating its weight. The dull burn of her Bio-Tech repairing her body added more adrenaline to everything.

"Big mouth. Bright light. Lots of tentacles." Murph shouted back. The ship turned on its side, spinning their stomachs, allowing Jolene and Dr. Wilda to run on the wall. Boris just kept floating. Jolene's stomach gurgled as the ship went right-side up.

O.D. started taking shape in the hallway. No one bothered to stop. His colors and shape went erratic. A staticky voice called after them.

"Rude!"

"What's the light?" Jolene asked the exobiologist, whose thin-lipped smile stayed fixed on Boris.

"Vacui Draco Vorax can emit a beam of concentrated light or plasma. Zhe phenomenon is so rare zhat we haven't been able to confirm which." Racing up the stairs to the bridge, they pushed in, stumbling into a dead stop.

The bridge's view had one hundred eighty degrees of energy field reinforced glass. Giving Jolene the perfect view on why Murph was short on words.

The Wyrm's finned tail wrapped around a moon-sized asteroid. Stone cracked into dust beneath its crushing coils while pools of bioluminescent teal flashed along its dark purple hide. Jolene held up a hand against flaring light stabbing her eyes. Squinting through her fingers let her watch wyrm's mouth drop, and the void of space burned! Blue-white light cut across the darkness. The Cthullians in its path broke into charred pieces. It burned into and through an asteroid, leaving a glowing molten hole. Cthullians swarmed out of its every nook and cranny. Jolene's vision cleared in time to see the Wyrm's tongue shoot forward. Cthullians, dead and living, stuck to it.

"Zhat is incredible!" Dr. Wilda shouted, a holographic pad filling up with scratchy notes. The beast's tongue pulled the asteroid it had cut through into its maw. Razor fangs slammed down and through everything. Purple ichor gushed into space.

"We are so underpaid." Murph said. Everyone on the bridge nodded, except for Dr. Wilda, who'd run up to the glass.

"VDV hunting pattern uses light based breath and Chameleon tongue in tandem." Dr. Wilda typed and recorded.

"Sorry to bring more bad news." O.D.'s voice entered the room above their heads. The waffle's marshmallow smile turned upside down, bacon eyebrows lowered, even his pompadour drooped.

"Suspense will literally kill us. Spit it out." Boris said in a dangerous 'I'm about to start shouting' tone.

Galaxy Waffles

O.D. didn't react; he looked at each of them. "The rest of the Madness is closing in."

Jolene and Murph turned to Boris.

"You think I'd fight a Madness head on?" A manic nervous laugh left his speakers. "Last time it cost me my body and an emergency upload. I'm not gambling that again!" The room silently agreed.

Boris twiddled his thumbs. Murph shifted a full beard and mustache to scratch and stroke. While Jolene rubbed at her temples.

"For the record, I'm sorry." O.D. muttered. They all looked at the rule worshiping waffle. "You were right, Jolene, I wasn't myself. Erabella uploaded code into my system."

"That violates-" Jolene started counting in her head.

"131 Galaxy Waffles Regulations" O.D. finished.

"What kind?" Boris said gently, with all eight of his eyes open.

"I don't know if it has a name, but it gave her on demand overrides." O.D. said it all with his chocolate chip eyes dripping yellow butter. "I'm supposed to make sure things are working. I'm not supposed to-" He stopped as Boris floated over and gave him a hug. O.D.'s force-fields distorted but didn't break. He hugged Boris back, all the while repeating.

"I'm sorry."

Jolene's tired frustration with Erabella evaporated in the wake of a new rage that wanted to ask Murph if they actually could throw her into a black hole idea after all.

"Ok little guy didn't deserve all that, but gang we still got problems!" Murph pointed at the window before the world went blue-white again.

"VDV breath confirmed to scorch und smelt. This suggests breath composition is plasma! Apply my signature on all data." Dr. Wilda's words were the sort of loud hyper Jolene heard when children had their birthday dinners on the ship. She rubbed her eyes and wished reality was different.

The research station was in two pieces!

"By all motherboards in the Milky Way." Boris whispered. Murph took off their fedora, and it shifted into a white flag as they waved passively. Everyone looked at them.

"What? You got any better ideas?"

"Fly at und past the VDV! Is it possible to have less chatter?" Dr. Wilda shouted, tsking in disgust before resuming animated mutterings.

"That's not a better idea-" Jolene began, but Murph's white flag was gone, and they were wearing their fedora again.

"Nope, but I'm not wasting the chance to do it! Better strap, buckle, and magnetize cause it's time to fly!"

"Suicide is not a valid flight plan!" Jolene screeched moving towards the pilot seat.

"Nobody's dyin' when I'm flyin'!" Murph crooned back at her as they shifted shiny reflective lenses over their eyes. Blink by blink of her eyes Jolene watched their hands shift into a mass of fingers that charted a course. Jolene groaned in resignation, ran for the co-pilot seat, strapped in and magnetized her boots.

All six of Boris' black arms and additional wiring looped into the floor grates.

O.D. hid under Boris' arms.

"Dr. Wilda, get secure or get a concussion!" Jolene lectured. The aged scientist waved a hand at them.

"Lab coat is enough." She said before pulling up a wall of hologram screens to her left and right. "Time to analyze!"

Murph aimed the ship at the Wyrm and slammed on the thrusters. G-forces hit all of them as they closed the distance. The Wyrm's tongue shot over them, catching many Cthullians. Jolene realized what it wanted.

JOLENE (CHAT MESSAGE)

"PULL UP PULL UP PULL UP PULL UP PULL UP PULL UP"

She spammed the chat even as Murph complied. The ship climbed towards the stars above them. The sight was as breathtaking as the physics pushing down on her lungs. Jolene carried little hope on the best of days. This was a terrible day. When the shadow of the bisected station fell over the ship, it got worse.

O.D. (CHAT MESSAGE)

"FTL!"

O.D.'s brown text bubble popped. Jolene watched Murph grow extra fingers to follow through, swiping and smacking away all the emergency notifications on the console.

The first absolute rule for flying FTL and keeping your DNA intact: ONLY USE IN OPEN SPACE! Staring at the molten interior of the station flying right at them. None of them cared about the damn rule.

MURPH (CHAT MESSAGE)

"Love you guys!"

Murph messaged. No one answered before the G-forces went up by several Gs. The station, Wyrm, Cthullians, and asteroids blurred for precious moments. Nanoseconds later, everything unblurred. As the ship smacked shields first into an asteroid!

The dynamic shielding absorbed the impact. Every light on the bridge flickered. Murph shifted into a metal cube before physics came knocking. The ship's weight plus speed multiplied by several thousands of newtons equaled out to them bouncing back. Spinning uncontrollably.

Jolene gasped. Boris grumbled. Murph toppled over, clanging every time.

"Permission to pilot for a second attempt?" O.D. asked over comms.

"YES!" Everyone except Dr. Wilda answered. The spinning slowed. Jolene looked away from the station eating Wyrm. Someone groaned behind her. Turning, she saw Dr. Wilda was spreadeagled on the wall, somehow still smiling.

"Zhis footage will get me a G.G.N.!" she screeched, looking at the room expectantly. She stopped smiling when silent confusion answered her. "Galactic Government Nobel!" Everyone groaned. Her priorities killing all concern for her. She pried herself free from the human sized dent she'd made in the wall. Rolling her eyes, Jolene braced herself as the wyrm filled out every inch of glass.

"O.D., please tell me you charted a new course?" Murph asked slowly, turning back to their default shape.

"New and better." The waffle answered flashing Murph a full marshmallow grin. Murph's glowing narrowed but they said nothing. Boris floated up and twiddled his thumbs. Jolene sat back and played a favorite song in her H.U.D.

All while, O.D. navigated through floating Cthullian bodies. Dipping below the Wyrm's eye level. They raced over the pale ocean with no idea if it cared for their existence. Then it jerked back and forth as its launched its sticky tongue.

The ship barrel rolled away. As the slimy shadows extended, the ship's rear cameras showed it pulling the other half of the station into its waiting jaws. Dr. Wilda stepped in front of Jolene leaned in, giving a magnified view of her crow's feet.

"Tell me zhat footage is being saved!"

"Yes, it is, Doctor. For the right price, we can provide it." O.D. said over the ship's speakers before Jolene could answer.

"Wunderbar!" She smiled and ran over to watch the live feed.

"Since when do you haggle?" Murph asked. O.D. didn't have time to answer.

From tail tip to belly, thousands of Cthullians scurried

along the Wyrm. Their beaks constantly ripping. Tentacles pulling the wounds open. The Wyrm reared, its wingtips pushing into the ship's shielding, swatting them further away. Alarms blared overhead. Multiple consoles lit up with warnings.

None of the crew paid attention to them. They watched the Wyrm's wing slam into the asteroid. Millions of shrapnel shards shredding through everything they hit.

"O.D. shields can't take much more!" Murph's voice climbed higher and higher.

"Voiding engine warranty." O.D. said with disturbing certainty. Jolene's co-pilot console showed the engine's temp rising. Right before a wave of gravity pinned her to her chair.

"Stabilizing G-force at 7gs. Higher forces will cause irreparable damage to human anatomy." Jolene closed her eyes. She refused to stare death in the face... for the umpteenth time... today!

Time didn't stretch the same way at Sub-FTL speeds, but in the darkness of her eyelids, SUCK MY VOLTAGE playing on her bio-tech, G-force pressure on her skin. Jolene couldn't tell minutes from hours.

"Employee Jolene?" O.D.'s voice said in the more familiar sugary dictator tone. "Your approval is required."

Jolene gripped her toes and wiggled her fingers successfully. The only pressure was the artificial gravity. She crossed her arms and looked toward O.D.'s voice.

"Empl- Jolene, please help." She smiled at O.D.'s voice without the higher peppy pitch, and opened her eyes,

Galaxy Waffles

"Move slowly, or risk injury." Boris followed up by resting his black steel hand feather light on her shoulder.

"We're alive." Murph said without an accent and shifted into their tiny army of mini-Murphs doing cartwheels all over the bridge. Jolene's empath blocker dose had expired. Murph's joy filled her with warmth.

"You will all be part of exobiological history books!" Dr. Wilda pumped her arms and kicked her feet in a pattern that barely qualified as dancing. Electric ambition surged from her, adding to Jolene's euphoria. The whole time O.D. floated nearby, their marshmallow smile on full display.

"What's up O.D.?"

"I need your approval on this message to Spendicus Unlimited." A holographic pad floated over to Jolene's waiting hands.

Mr. Jack,

We have successfully rescued Dr. Wilda from the mining outpost, and are en route to Horsehead station at Sub-FTL speeds. Navigation says we will arrive in 1,170 years. Please send the necessary resources for repairs. We can attribute all damages to undisclosed hazards. We look forward to re-negotiating compensation.

Sincerely,

Jolene

She looked at him straight in the chocolate chips,

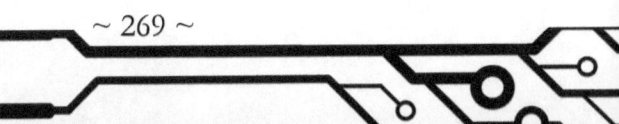

his smile replaced by a curvy line of waffle squares. He'd made her sound professionally snarky, and she loved it. "Looks great. Send it, and then we are all gonna make a plan for Erabella."

Everyone but Dr. Wilda turned towards her. Boris rubbed his six hands together.

"What is the mission?" He growled.

"We are going to bury her!" Jolene returned with a bloodthirsty smile.

O.D.

Species: A.I.
Pronouns: He/him
Abilities: Anything Corporate Approves
Likes: Rule Enforcement
Dislikes: Rule Breaking and Loopholes
Role: Mascot and Watchdog

CHROME KARMA

Two weeks later.

"I still say we should actually bury her." Murph grumbled for the thousandth time. Checking their cards. "I'll hold at 200 sq. ft. After this job Spendicus can spare the shovels." They spat the words and then spat at the defunct Erabella android in the corner.

Jolene bit her lips through a smile. "I'll match the 200. I'd rather take the credits, forget about Spendicus, and let Erabella rot in a corporate jail." She said, rubbing at her tired eyes. The ERS, emergency rescue ship, had top of the line FTL, but it would tear the diner ship apart going those speeds. Looking through the back window of the dining room she smiled as the waffle ship floated behind them in a tractor beam.

"I'll hold at 200 as well. Your ideas are enjoyable fantasies Murph, but we've fought too hard to get this far only to end up in prison." Boris said his baritone sounded as tired as Jolene felt. Every eye at the table turned to O.D.

"I'm matching the 200. Also, Boris is right murder is illegal." O.D. said both statements in the same peppy tone, but finished staring at Murph. They didn't have credits to spare. Instead, each bet represented a square foot of ship that needed cleaning or repair. The winner got the day off from cleaning. "Continued threats are grounds for harassment and civil lawsuits. Please don't give her ammunition to shoot us with. I raise with grease trap cleaning." O.D.'s bottomless chocolate chip eyes stared at each of them. Everyone matched, but no one joked. "No more bets." O.D. announced and looked at his cards.

Murph looked at all of them and literally zipped their mouth shut.

MURPH (CHAT MESSAGE)

"Could ask the Union to handle it."

Murph messaged in the private chat O.D. still wasn't in.

Jolene answered with an eyeroll emoji.

Boris followed up with a mute emoji.

MURPH (CHAT MESSAGE)

"Fine fine, we wreck her career and let the courts ruin her."

Murph sent.

"19," O.D. flipped his cards over.

"17" Boris flipped and pushed the cards to the center.

"18," Jolene showed and shoved hers towards Boris' pile.

Murph smiled, stretching the gray zipper teeth.

Jolene leaned away, bringing up her one-on-one chat with Boris. "Are you sure O.D. is safe to be around?" She scratched her head and stretched her arms, grateful their rescue ship came fully stocked on Empath blockers. Boris shuffled and didn't look her way.

"When he was transferring over from the diner, he practically begged me to scrub his code down to the binary. He's clean." Boris messaged back. Jolene answered with two thumbs up in the chat and looked at her cards. She threw them to the center. The current bet was for cleaning the grease trap. Everyone hated cleaning it, and you didn't bet when you had nothing.

Meanwhile Murph raised an arm that shifted into a blinking neon sign that blinked the in pale green letters: Read 'em and Weep

They flipped over two aces.

"21. Murph takes the pot!" O.D. said, the tips of his marshmallow teeth turning burnt black. Murph's mouth zipper unzipped.

"Pleasure doin' business. Now how's about you handle cleaning the grease trap and the rest of the ship. Seeing as how you helped make the mess." Murph said, putting their feet up on the table staring at O.D. through the brim of their hat.

"Impossible. I can't be outside the ship." O.D. said their marshmallow teeth, still burnt black.

"Oh, well. In that case you can hire cleaning services with your share of the job." Murph flicked their hat up and gave a full needle toothed smile.

O.D.'s pale golden squares started turning black as well.

"That is a valid solution." His voice sounded like he wanted to boil Murph. Jolene was spared from being the referee by an announcement.

"Arriving at Horsehead Station."

Jolene stretched her arms. Boris got up and headed to the cargo bay door.

"I'll send you some numbers to call." Murph said and tipped their hat at O.D.

"Whatever she says, we have your back." Boris looked at Jolene while the rest of the table nodded. He passed her a black coffee and multiple Empath blockers. The bittersweet blackness washed them down. Caffeine always helped her smile but looking around the table helped make it stick.

As they walked to the cargo bay, she started breathing faster. "Dr. Wilda, are you coming?" She asked on the comms channel they'd finally set up. A black text bubble popped on the white background.

"Yes! Yes! I'll be zhere for zhe witch." Dr. Wilda answered. Every step closer without one of their star witnesses supercharged her anxiety. Thoughts of things going wrong started forming knots in her stomach. Those knots tightened into steel lumps as the ship's cargo bay door lowered.

Erabella was flanked by two Galactic Government Peacekeepers. Their firepower and her snow white power suit with gold trim, drawing a small crowd. She tried to snap her fingers, instead her arm spasmed. She glared at it, then at them. Her other hand flicked, sending a flurry of holographic headlines at them. The multi-colored boxes had animated accusations like:

"STARBLOOD ASSAULTS TERRABLOOD."

"RECKLESSLY ENDANGERS A.I. WAR HERO."

"SUSPECTED XENOPHOBE."

"KYANESE UNIONER THREATENS EXECUTIVE,"

"ROGUE EMPATH."

The noises of the docking bay cut off the watching crowd's murmurs, but Jolene could see heads turning, lips flapping, and multiple sets of eyes growing wide. Rage melted the lumps in her guts. She balled her fists at the words. Boris and Murph's hands grabbed the back of her brown jumpsuit. "Since you like headlines so much." She smiled, platinum teeth reflecting the docking bay lights. "I thought you'd like to see the ones coming out tonight."

Boris successfully snapped all six of his hands, and holograms fizzled into nothing.

"You are standing on thinner ice than you believe." Boris rumbled, each of his hands balling into fists. Erabella's eyes narrowed, but her smile stayed in place.

Murph let go of Jolene and swept their hat off their head, shifting it into a rolled up paper with large letters. Jolene's H.U.D. popped with the word NEWSPAPER. Murph meanwhile was busy pointing it at every random passerby while their other hand shifted into a megaphone.

Galaxy Waffles

"Extra! Extra! Read all about the privileged corpo suit violating A.I. sentience, sexually harassing staff, emotionally abusing loyal Starbloods, and threatening to fire a Union Kyanese. All while we fought for our lives! Yes, folks, we've got all the juicy details. Corruption, lust, and vengeance are all wrapped up in a shiny little package called Erabella!" Murph's voice blared into the docking bay, stopping multiple species in their tracks.

Eyes of all kinds fixed on them as Murph's single newspaper turned into a bundle ready to be tossed to them. Erabella turned on them, "Galaxy Waffles internal matter move along or get a call from our lawyers." There were people who scurried at the mention of a corporation. Everyone scattered at the word lawyer. She turned back, smile gone now, a nose wrinkled chrome scrunched sneer.

"Do you really think anyone is going to care after they hear you caused me permanent injury?" Her eye and cheek twitched. "That you damaged corporate assets. Potentially cost Galaxy Waffles a relationship with Spendicus Unlimited? All of that!" She drew a circle with her hands. "Matters, more than your clown!" She stepped closer.

Boris and Murph stepped up shoulder to shoulder with Jolene.

"I will bury you!" She hissed in Jolene's face, shooting venomous glares at Boris and Murph.

"You're right." Jolene hated the cutting hurt inside as she said the words. Erabella's wide-eyed gaze and raised trembling finger were minor comforts. "Anyone who matters will write me off."

Jolene stepped in, and Erabella didn't move.

"That's why I have witnesses who matter." She whispered and stepped back. Dr. Wilda, wearing her visor, salt streaked black curls bouncing with every step. Her pristine white lab coat floated on circulating air. O.D. trailed her, rubbing his gloved hands over each other.

"Zhis is her?" She pointed at Erabella. All three nodded. The doctor's black and red eyes dissected her from head to toe. "With all zhose modifications, it is unfortunate you did not invest in any intelligence."

Erabella's jaw dropped as her arm spasmed, throwing her off balance. "Your zhreats are as dull as your wits. I've reviewed und endorsed all zhe evidence zhey have."

Erabella's glowing eyes fixed on O.D.

"Access and override attempt recorded." O.D. announced. He floated just behind Boris' shoulder.

Erabella's eyes turned blood red. "One whack job hermit and malfunctioning A.I. won't be enough."

Everyone smiled and pointed behind her. She rolled her eyes and turned to find an upright feline in white silks trimmed in gold and a royal purple neckerchief. Two Pricklebeards flanked him, all their facial hair trimmed to sharp points, bespoke black suits with gray button-down shirts and extra wide security visors cover all three eyes. Scarred hands balled into fists at their sides. Between the flamboyant centerpiece and intimidating entourage, the smart thing would have been to stay quiet.

However, Jolene was busy fighting off sniggers. Their badges, shaped exactly like the flamboyant horsehead, announced they were station security were shaped like the station, in all its gaudy glory.

MURPH (CHAT MESSAGE)

"You think they try going undercover with those?"

Murph messaged.

BORIS (CHAT MESSAGE)

"More like under spotlight."

Boris sent with a laughing emoji at his own joke.

Calico marched across the docking bay. Everyone stopped to let him pass. His furry cheeks swelled with a smile at the crew and flicked his tail when he faced Erabella.

"Sector Supervisor Erabella." Calico Jack purred, "How unfortunate to see you again."

"Mr. Jack, I was just-"

"Abusing your authority. Being recorded by our security system. Insulted a corporate officer? Oh my, I believe you've done all three." The cat's smooth purring voice dropped into a feline rumble as they spoke.

Jolene mouthed the words *"officer"* at Dr. Wilda.

"V.P. of Exploration and Exobiological Research." She answered, walking down the ramp with a bounce in her step. Calico pushed past Erabella, throwing his arms open. "Darling!"

"Sweetie!" Dr. Wilda exclaimed with girlish glee.

They embraced. She lifted Calico in a spin. Nuzzling noses before separating. "Wait till you see zhe data, your whiskers will dance!"

Jolene scratched the back of her head until Erabella's eyes resumed their blue glow, as she plastered a smile on her face.

"Galaxy Waffles is proud to have satisfied the terms and conditions of your mission." Calico Jack's ears flattened his eyes narrowed. Erabella continued. "I would also like to offer a personal apology to Dr. Wilda and promise to exercise better judgment in the future." Erabella bowed her head. Calico's whiskers stiffened. His lips curled, showing all four canines before hissing. Erabella raised her head, lip wobbling, eyes wide.

"Your judgments always serve biased, greedy verdicts!" Jack hissed as the hackles on their neck rose.

Dr. Wilda placed a hand on Calico's arm, even as the Felinoid's claws came out. "Now, who's insulting a corporate officer?" Erabella bit back with a haughty smile.

The Pricklebeard's bristled as they stepped up. Erabella held her ground as two Galactic Government Peacekeepers joined her. Their crackling energy shields, black faceplates, and weapons adding to the verbal standoff.

Jolene didn't need her Empath senses to feel the tension escalating.

JOLENE (CHAT MESSAGE)

"Uh, Boris is it-"

Jolene started.

BORIS (CHAT MESSAGE)

"Use me as cover or I will put you both through basic boot camp!"

Boris finished.

MURPH (CHAT MESSAGE)

"Thanks Tin Can."

Murph said in the chat with two thumbs up.

A man in mechanic's overalls stepped into the middle of everything. He was rubbing grease from his hands on a rag. Everyone shut up as his cool gray eyes passed over them. He placed his index finger over his lips. In moments small drones surrounded them. Soon they stood in silence. "Now that we can all hear ourselves think." He turned to Calico, whose claws retracted.

"What's going on?" His soft voice matched the politeness of the words, but Jolene's H.U.D. showed zero results, no matter how many times she refreshed the search.

"I'm managing a legal dispute." Calico glared at Erabella, then smiled at the man.

"Mr. Spendicus, I'm sorry to-" Erabella started until the richest man in the Milky Way raised his hand to stop her.

"You will get your turn when Calico is done." With the same hand, he waved at the two Peacekeepers. "You're dismissed."

"Yes, sir!" They answered simultaneously through voice scramblers and marched away. Erabella struggled to stay silent, metal fingers grinding on each other as her limbs took turns spasming and fidgeting. "Now then, Judge Jack, why are you litigating in my docking bay?"

Dr. Wilda locked arms with Calico and with zero

change in voice and tone, barked at Maximus. "Because zhat one has no manners!" She pointed, while her red pupils widened into solid circles.

Running his hands through neck length black hair, Maximus sighed. "Thank you, Dr. Wilda. Now let him answer."

Erabella stepped up, adjusting her cuffs. "I was exercising my authority over Galaxy Waffles property." She growled the words through a smile.

Maximus sighed and faced her with his jaw set and brow furrowed. "You're fired and banned from this station. You have one hour to vacate or be removed."

The words chilled Jolene's blood. Murph had the jiggle shivers. Boris never stopped watching Max.

"I-" Erabella's entire face twitched. "You-"

An email popped on Jolene's H.U.D. marked urgent and mandatory reading.

"HELLO VALUED EMPLOYEE,

SPENDICUS UNLIMITED HAS SECURED A CONTROLLING STAKE IN GALAXY WAFFLES. PLEASE CHECK YOUR INBOXES FOR ALL UPDATES INCLUDING BUT NOT LIMITED TO: SALARIES, EMPLOYMENT STATUS, BRANDING, UNIFORMS, AND BENEFITS.

WE ARE EXCITED TO BEGIN THIS NEW CHAPTER IN OUR COMPANY'S HISTORY, AND EAGER TO HAVE YOU ALONG FOR THE JOURNEY.

SINCERELY,
GALAXY WAFFLES CORPORATE."

In less than ten minutes, Maximus had rearranged her reality. Every rational brain cell and animal instinct agreed. Stay away! Erabella spluttered, rubbing her fingernails on her suit's lapel faster and faster until she grabbed and tore it off.

"You can't- I'm not-"

She started and stopped grabbing fistfuls of her hair, her mouth dropped open and she screamed. An ear-splitting explosion of sound and emotion that tore through Jolene. Then the world went sideways. Boris caught her. His words drowned in a high-pitched whine, filling her ears. Every muscle in Jolene's body clenched and released, robbing her of all balance and stability. Her H.U.D. flashed the messages:

"EMPATHIC OVERLOAD!"
"DEPLOYING EMERGENCY BLOCKERS!"

Twinges spread across her body. Sounds and emotions slowly quieted. Everything in Jolene wanted to smash life's nonexistent mute button. She breathed through that impulse. Murph's cool, smooth hand wiped sweat from her forehead. Boris tried to hum a SUCK MY VOLTAGE song. All of it let her open her eyes to see something all Empaths feared. Mental Collapse.

Erabella was on her knees. Tears falling to the steel

floors. Fists full of her snow white hair. Torn pieces of her power suit surrounded her.

"Ruined again."

"Nowhere to go."

"Shamed."

"Nothing left."

"Can't be me."

"Wake up."

Were the words Jolene understood. The rest were half-formed syllables and grieving groans. Every Empath knew the dangers of Empathic Overload. They trained their minds, kept their meds on hand, and developed coping strategies. Mental Collapse was an emotional earthquake shattering all of that.

Maximus walked over, pulled up her chin. One of his summoned drones floated over and scanned Erabella.

"Calico, add full psychiatric care to her severance package. Last thing we need is a lawsuit."

"Consider it done!" He licked his chops, a predator's grin on his face, glee in both blue and green eyes as he looked down at Erabella. Ten percent of Jolene wanted to know their story, the other ninety wanted to go back to her bed and curl up in a ball. The two Pricklebeards hoisted Erabella over their heads and marched out of the docking bay. Calico and Dr. Wilda followed.

"Shall we continue this inside?" Max asked, while walking up the ship's ramp.

Jolene half-walked, half leaned on Boris all the way back to the dining room. She plopped into the booth without ceremony. Murph slid in next to her while Boris and O.D. floated nearby. Max sat across from her and smiled as he interlaced his fingers.

"I'd like to thank you. When Calico hired you, I was skeptical." He stopped and lightly clapped his callused hands. "You've exceeded expectations across the board."

The soft-spoken praise filled Jolene with a fire that she couldn't stop herself from spitting.

"Oh, yay, thank you. That makes it all better-" She poured on the sickly sweet tone she knew egomaniacs adored. Max raised an eyebrow and then she hit him with, "Also, go fuck yourself!" She flipped him both fingers as she finished. He looked at each one and then met her gaze. Every other eye turned towards her, and she muted the chat before any of them could start.

"We were understaffed, under-equipped, and ignorant. We should be dead. So, let's start with why the fuck did you hire us?" She demanded.

All the eyes fixed on her now turned to him. "Plausible Deniability."

"What?" Everyone asked with different levels of outrage and confusion.

"The Untamed Sector offers a lot of legal liberties for people like me, but that doesn't mean I'm not being watched. The G.G., rival Corps, and believe it or not, internal factions within Spendicus Unlimited." He stretched his arms over his head. "If I tried to get enough of them in my corner, Dr. Wilda would still be there."

Jolene and Murph shivered at those words. Boris let

out a low growl. O.D. shrank till he was palm sized. Jolene pushed her hair off her forehead and pushed again. "And that gives you Plausible Deniability because?"

"Who would believe us?" Boris answered.

She turned towards him, waiting for more.

"Exactly." Max smiled at Boris, giving him two thumbs up. "Love it when someone gets with the program."

Jolene looked at each of them, her brain working overtime.

"No one who mattered." Murph added to the conversation, giving Max their own needle toothed grin.

"Bullseye." Max cocked and shot a finger gun at Murph, whose glowing eyes narrowed.

She groaned at the picture all this painted. Alive, they returned a valuable asset, reported findings, provided groundbreaking research. Dead, he could send a proper search and rescue, discover everything, and ride the PR sympathy wave to get everything he wanted.

"Doesn't matter if we win or lose. You still win." Jolene finished. Max nodded, leaning back on the booth cushions, arms resting on top. He looked out to the docking bay. Jolene's fire was gone, replaced by cold slimy anxiety at the incoming consequences.

"Please breathe, I'm not gonna smite you." He said with a lopsided grin as if he hadn't just done that to Erabella minutes ago. Jolene complied and stayed silent, unwilling to risk more. "I can't stand rude people, but I despise wasting useful ones more. Let's move past that outburst and talk business." His smile belonged on billboards and commercials.

She still didn't trust herself to speak and just nodded.

"Great!" He clapped once and a hologram bar chart projected onto the table. "So good news first is your pay." A green bar rose through numbers that seemed unreal. "Bad news is the rescue and insurance fees for the research station." A red bar rose next to the shrinking green.

"A rescue was only necessary because-" O.D. started until Max held up a hand.

"Emergency supplies need to be restocked." He said and in the same soft tone with zero compromise.

"Dr. Wilda was the one who baited the Wyrm. Why are we-" Boris shot back, floating closer.

"From what I can tell, she did what was necessary for your rescue to continue. Is that inaccurate?" He stared into Boris' unblinking eyes, tapping his thumbs together as the silence continued. Boris sighed and backed off.

"Glad I could clear up the confusion. Looks like your final pay is going to be... thirty thousand credits."

Jolene felt tears building. Even with all their savings that put them thirty thousand short of buying the ship. Max frowned at her.

"Is this about your quota problem? I'll get that taken care of. Call it a goodwill gesture from the new boss." He winked and dismissed the holographic bar chart with another clap. "Pleasure doing business." He was halfway out of the booth when Murph leaned forward.

"How about some new business, then?"

Maximus Spendicus froze and turned to face Murph.

The sly perfect teeth smile was back as he rested an elbow on the table. "Is this a Union deal?"

"Nah, just me and the crew." Murph gestured at all of them.

Jolene wanted to know more but didn't want to kill the hope Murph's words created. They sent a message to everyone in the open chat:

JOLENE (CHAT MESSAGE)
"Trust me."

"What's the market rate for Cthullian meat?" Murph asked.

"Criminal," Max answered.

"And if I said we had half a ton? What would that be worth to you?"

Maximus Spendicus' smile vanished. He fixed a pensive stare that bore into Murph as he scratched his chin.

"After a thorough inspection… let's say five hundred thousand." Jolene had to bite her tongue from shouting the word SOLD.

"I'll need time to discuss your offer with my associates." They said.

Max nodded. "Contact Calico for details and payment."

Murph tipped their hat at him, and without another word, the richest man in the galaxy left the room. Murph shifted three heads to face each of them, turning their original face towards a ghostly pale fit to bursting Jolene.

"So, what do you think?" They asked.

Galaxy Waffles

Silent seconds answered them until Jolene couldn't hold it in anymore.

"You beautiful bastard!" She shouted and jumped in to hug Murph.

Boris followed up with a bearish hug around them. O.D. floated to sit on Murph's hat. They stayed like that longer than any had planned for but that was ok, it wouldn't be the first or last time.

Favorite Kind of Boring

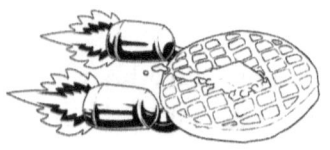

With a few clicks of Calico's furry fingers, a chrono-stasis crate hissed closed. Colors and shapes spread across the shiny lid, spelling out.

Certified Grade-A

100 Lb

Cthullian Meat

He dabbed away lines of drool with his silver edged black handkerchief. After several hours, he'd saturated the poor cloth. He turned to Murph, chuffing to clear his throat.

"How much for the stock you've kept back?"

He pinned Murph with his green and blue eyes. Each one with paper thin slit pupils. Muscles tensed with predatory anticipation.

Murph's needle tooth smile stayed in place as they twirled their hat on a finger. "Afraid that's all we have for sale to Spendicus Unlimited."

Calico's feline grin matched Murph's energy as he slipped a holographic puck from his sleeve and slid it to Murph across the container lid. "And for private individuals?" He asked as the puck projected 3D neon gold numbers, twenty thousand.

Jolene half expected Murph's eyes to shift into literal dollar signs. Instead, they turned to Boris, who was currently just a head again, after he gladly returned the security cube to Spendicus. Since then, his perch of choice was the top of Jolene's head, like a talking helmet. "Hey Tin Can, what's the split on selling your ingredients?"

"Ninety ten for salt and pepper!" He growled, sending vibrations down Jolene's spine. "And for something rare, no split." He followed up, still growling. Jolene nearly snorted her coffee. Murph blanched from shocked white to furious red in the blink of an eye. She petted Boris and sent a message in their private chat.

JOLENE (CHAT MESSAGE)

"Any word from corporate HR on a replacement chassis?"

She asked.

O.D. (CHAT MESSAGE)

"Last conversation they tried to pressure me into a shitty, obsolete model. I threatened to message Max directly. They are ordering what I asked for- "

Murph rolled their hat up their arm, landing it on their head before turning back to Calico. "Is Dr. Wilda still interested in our footage?"

The Felinoid crossed his arms, creasing his poet shirt's amethyst puffy sleeves, and flexed his whiskers. "Trying to sell something, not yours again?"

O.D. took shape over the container. "They are now

my authorized negotiator."

Calico nodded at O.D. "Clever. Mr. Spendicus also wanted me to convey that we are still considering the petition you organized."

O.D. pompadour bounced with approval.

JOLENE (CHAT MESSAGE)

"Petition?"

Jolene sent to O.D. as the question formed in her head.

O.D. (CHAT MESSAGE)

"Allowing us access to Spendicus Unlimited networks."

He answered. A.I. restricted access was part corporate policy, part legal paranoia from the G.G. Jolene had no doubts that Max could change both.

Murph's palm shifted into a manual calculator.

"Let's itemize. Length of footage." Jolene had to spit back some coffee into her cup as plastic clacking filled the cargo bay. "Resolution quality. Rarity. Demand." Murph's face shifted into a human mouth with blood red lipstick and let out a long whistle. "Darlin this is gonna be- " Calico Jack stepped forward and his furred paw engulfed Murph's hand, palm calculator and all.

"I am a great lover of theatrics." He swept his free paw over his shirt and sapphire blue pantaloons. "But I loathe every syllable in the word patience. Throw in five pounds of Grade-A cuts, and I'll let you name your price."

Murph's eyes still didn't shift to dollar signs; instead, they turned green as an old earth dollar when they heard those words.

JOLENE (CHAT MESSAGE)

"Stay frosty, Murph. You don't rob Max or his people and end up kissing the fishes."

Jolene messaged in the group chat.

MURPH (CHAT MESSAGE)

"You FTLd so close to good and still crashed and burned into the sun."

They answered dollar bill green, fading to their usual blue.

JOLENE (CHAT MESSAGE)

"Wait, what do you mean?"

She asked.

BORIS (CHAT MESSAGE)

"It's sleep. Not kiss. Sleep with the fishes."

Boris answered in the chat. Jolene couldn't see how red she was turning and didn't want to.

"Fair is fair. Your boss got the bulk rate. You're doing a small batch, so let's say five thousand a pound."

Calico released Murph's hand and waved his hand over the puck. Its numbers changed to fifty thousand.

Everyone in the cargo bay gasped and looked at him.

"That covers the footage and I want first pick if you end up hunting again."

Murph ran without shame like a marathon runner getting and returning with a five-pound chrono-stasis bag of Cthullian meat.

"Pleasure doing business."

They swiped the puck, and Calico snapped his fingers. A team of human and non-humans rushed in and started pushing floating flatbeds out to the docking bay. A fully armed squad of Galactic Peacekeepers waited to escort them.

Calico stretched and yawned as he laid down on the last set of crates, and waved them farewell as he floated away.

"So, I'll just be taking my forty percent." Murph said while knuckle dancing the puck.

O.D. crossed his arms, marshmallow smile never moving as they spoke. "Interesting choice of words for the system who handles your paycheck."

Murph's eyes narrowed.

MURPH (CHAT MESSAGE)

"You guys wanna help me take his waffleness down a level?"

They typed and were answered simultaneously.

BORIS/JOLENE (CHAT MESSAGE)

"NO."

In red and green.

MURPH (CHAT MESSAGE)

"Oh, come on, what's he gonna do with-"

JOLENE (CHAT MESSAGE)

"What's that old Kyanese saying? Never cross your own."

Jolene said and watched Murph's chinless jaw drop to

the floor.

"Damn boss, way to play dirty." A drawstring dropped out of the side of their face. When they pulled it, their jaw rolled back up into place.

"I'll consider twenty percent a fair share." They said, looking at O.D. again.

"Galactic Government Law says the standard is ten, but since he paid double the price. I'm willing to accept fifteen." O.D. finished the offer by holding out a hand. No one spoke or moved. Murph stepped in and shifted their hand to match O.D.'s oversized white gloves.

"Deal."

They shook on it, and forty thousand five hundred flashed over O.D.'s pompadour. Jolene smiled at the sweetened coffee, at O.D.'s growth, Murph being Murph, Boris sending her recipe ideas, and most importantly that they'd survived!

She looked at the plaque welded above the cargo bay door. Bright chrome letters reflected the rainbow L.E.D. lights tracing the letters.

<u>Ship Owners Crew 3371</u>
<u>Murphreezius Imital, Boris, Jolene Starblood.</u>
<u>Galaxy Waffles Licensed Franchisee</u>

"Ready to budget our future boss?" Murph smiled at the sign as much as Jolene. She finished her coffee.

"There's about a gallon ready for you in the kitchen." Boris said without a hint of sarcasm.

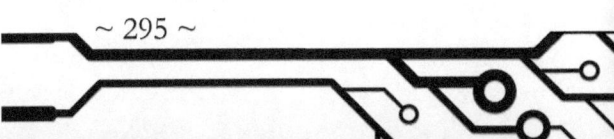

"May I be part of the meeting?" O.D. asked, waffle squares closed over his teeth, floating back and forth in a pacing pattern. He had been everything from annoying to directly malicious, and still saved their lives.

JOLENE (CHAT MESSAGE)

"We gotta start trusting somewhere. Thoughts?"

Her green text bubble popped in their private chat.

MURPH (CHAT MESSAGE)

"Little guy's got moxie and skill. Let him in, but watch him closely."

Murph's blue bubble came up as Boris' red bubbles floated.

BORIS (CHAT MESSAGE)

"If he allows me to monitor his code, I say yes."

Jolene fought down the urge to assume O.D.'s reactions and shared their thoughts. The hologram smiled and floated closer until she got to Boris' request.

"And if I say no?" O.D. asked, with no parts of him turning black.

"You can get reassigned to another ship with all your assets." Jolene said without hesitation.

"Is it permanent?" He looked up at Boris, still nested in Jolene's hair.

"Absolutely not!" He stepped gently down to her shoulder. "Go one year without sabotaging or spying and it stops. We can even talk about ways to protect you."

O.D. smiled again and floated over to sit on Jolene's

other shoulder.

"Deal."

They started walking through their ship. O.D. listed the mandatory repairs. Boris rattled off his menu ideas. Murph brought up mandatory repairs, insisting they inspect the quality of Horsehead's inspections. It was exactly the boring Jolene loved.

Hours later, she stopped in the kitchen to refill her coffee. She'd been smiling so much her cheeks ached. She picked a booth facing towards the docking bay doors, cushioned seats cradling her. She looked out into untamed space. Turning back to her dining room, she finally let herself say the words.

"I'm home."

And they flew off to the distant stars never to be troubled again!

NOT!

Galaxy Waffles Season 2 has lifted off on Kindle Vella!

Come read about the chaos they face in the absurd nightmare

the

Milky Way

has become.